ASCEND THE DAUGHTER

The Dawning of Heroes

Book 3

JEREMY FLAGG

Cover Art by

SEAN CARLSON

For the women who continue shattering expectations.

Children of Nostradamus Universe

The Synthetic Wars

Nighthawks

Night Shadows

Night Legions

Night Covenants

Morning Sun

The Dawning of Heroes

Awaken the Daughter

Anoint the Daughter

Ascend the Daughter

Wayward Orphans

Sentinel Rising

Seraph Falling

Chapter One

1943

The city needed saving.

In their bags, the robbers had a small fortune, a jeweler's finest collection. Without the mob guiding criminals, they took matters into their own hands. The heist had been planned, two men collecting the diamonds while two others pointed guns at the owner and his assistant. By the time I had the vision, they had already shot the guard hired to protect the store.

Through the eyes of a gunman, I had watched the scene unfold. The visions never provided a date or time. At best, a feeling in my gut estimated how soon or far away the event might be. The biggest mistake the robber made was glancing at the clock hanging above a calendar on the wall. Keeping the heist on schedule had been their biggest mistake.

Blocking their escape in the alley, Frank sank his knuckles into a man's face hard enough teeth launched across the room. When he shifted his weight, leading into the uppercut, the man tried to block. Tried, but failed. What teeth remained ground together and shattered. We no longer played. There was no pretending to be heroes, we were a line of defense the city didn't know existed.

While it appeared only me and Frank stood between the robbers and a clean get away, I brought more friends. Ghosts filled the alley, seconds, minutes and even hours into the future. Once they had been the bane of my existence, a curse from Satan himself. They revealed inevitable futures, unchangeable destinies and I lived every atrocity twice.

That was then.

Now, the ghosts came at my call and I pushed against fate, demanding she loosen the reins.

"Shoot 'em," said the remaining robber, holding a heavy brown bag.

The closest gunman raised his weapon.

For three months I had been trapped, trapped in bed as I recovered from Olivia's near-killing blow. The stitches had done the job. Now I sported a lengthy scar running up the right side of my stomach. Three months I spent recounting every word Gregory had ever uttered. I couldn't train my body, but while staring at the ceiling of my teenage bedroom, I uncovered new abilities.

I discovered ghosts existed in objects without souls. Phantom bullets exploded from the gun. In slow motion, two tiny pieces of lead crawled toward me. Time resumed, and the gun exploded and I leaned far enough to the side that the vibration rippled across my cheek as the bullets passed. Time slowed again.

The first few weeks of being bed ridden were shrouded in half memories. I recalled the sight of Susan Lee and Claudette standing over my bed, patting my head and changing my bandages. Frank camped in the corner of the room, head hanging as he slept in his favorite chair. Susan Lee admitted later I had nearly died. She believed God answered her prayers and spared my soul. Having seen Poppa and Benjie the night of the stabbing, I couldn't argue with a higher power intervening.

The robber attempted to shoot me in the head. Cute. Adorable, even. This hooligan believed with the squeeze of a trigger he'd put a round between my eyes, then he'd escape down the alley. It was the first outing in six months. Frank only conceded if he could join me in my crusade.

I ducked as the gun fired. It sped harmlessly overhead. By now, the man probably thought I moved with lightning speed. Truth, my muscles ached. I hadn't done any stretching before we ventured out, and it was already catching up to me. The stiffness in my side was more of a challenge than these goons.

"Damn bitch," yelled the man.

I sprung forward just before time slowed. Sitting in bed, I had nothing to do but practice. For a woman capable of seeing the future, the tempo of time worked differently. Seconds dragged out as the ghosts emerged, stepping from their owners. My ghost tackled the closest man, but with my back exposed his buddy would point the gun at my head before he pulled the trigger.

Perfect.

I barreled into the man. I managed a weak jab. It didn't matter as two knuckles connected with his throat. He wouldn't be alive long enough to get in my way. As we fell to the ground, I rolled right. Falling off the man, another bang echoed in the alley. The bullet meant for me penetrated the fallen man's forehead. I closed my eyes as blood splashed across my face and neck.

Even with my eyes closed, the ghosts were visible, another new trick added to my growing arsenal. He'd cock and fire his gun again. If I let him. For a moment I caught a glimpse of multiple ghosts. I struggled, letting the flame grow. I could continue rolling, but find myself trapped by a trio of trashcans, or I kick at his knee, breaking the bone. I tried to force more ghosts to appear, more options, variables in the timelines. The supernatural power resisted, refusing to unlock.

Three months in bed meant three more months of training. Every veteran at the gym recognized a wounded fighter the moment I threw the first punch. For the last week, they gathered around me like an extended family. Michael worked with my endurance. Vince insisted I relearn my balance and foot work. Even Tony watched his mouth as he pushed me to pick up the pace. Seven days a week, I showed up despite my body screaming at me to slow and take it easy. New York City needed me now more than ever.

I kicked his knee. The bone snapped. He cried out, buckling over. I snapped the toe of my boot into his nose. Frank charged in, grabbing the back of his head. With one knee raised, he smashed the man's face against the joint. Frank let go and the man slumped. I should care if he was alive, but I had admitted, my moral compass wasn't aligned as of late.

"Who the hell are you?"

Paralyzed by fear, the robber's scanned the carnage before raising his hands. Frank offered me a hand, helping me off the ground. Sirens grew louder as police cars converged on the jeweler's location. I thought about jabbing him in the throat, knocking him to the ground and walking away. I restrained myself, a personal victory if I do say so myself.

"Tell the police what you saw. Tell everybody."

Frank walked back into the alley, preparing to sink into the shadows and vanish before the police arrived. We had planned our escape, an agreement Frank required from now on. No more rushing into a fight without an exit. That had cost me dearly in the past. My adopted father still had things to teach.

"A hero watches over New York City."

I turned and watched as Frank almost vanished from sight. The smile spread across my lips. No longer did I prowl the streets alone. While they might not always be seen, a team supported me. This was a test run, and eventually I'd return to the streets to stop the Society before they secured their hold on Bertolucci's shattered empire.

"No," I corrected, "*heroes* watch over New York City."

It was a good start, but if I was going to stand against that bitch, Olivia, I'd need more than a retired soldier at my side. The

Society thought themselves safe, protected by the arrogance of their abilities. Humans couldn't resist their intrusions, and without another mentalist to stand against them, they'd infiltrate the city more than Bertolucci could have ever imagined.

Eleanor Bouvier held the moral high ground, determined to make the city a better place. She died that night on Claudette's operating table. Reborn with a grudge and a singular mission, I embraced the darkness creeping into my heart. Eleanor Bouvier wouldn't win a war against the Society.

Eleanor Valentine, however…

Chapter Two

1943

New York City no longer slept as the darkness rolled in. I climbed through the window to the fire escape. Frank followed up the stairs leading to the roof. He insisted on seeing me home. I worried him plenty, so I entertained his sense of duty. I wanted him to come with me, to partake in the conversation I had been dreading for months.

Each step resulted in a loud clacking. The places where the fire escape was attached to the building held secure, but by the noise, it sounded dangerous. With each stair, it wasn't the plummet to the alley I feared. Waiting on the roof, a young woman, arguably my best friend, puffed on a cigarette, washing away the stress of the day. Best friend. I feared neither of those words applied anymore.

Susan Lee no longer hid the cigarettes. Anxiety caused her to chain smoke as worry dug its fingers into her brain. At least she took her habit to the roof as she waited for me to return. We had talked at length about what had happened that night, and every day leading to it. Unlike Frank, she asked a thousand questions.

Not convinced of my abilities, she wrote a string of numbers asking me to prove it. We repeated the trick, each time successfully predicting what she wrote. I still didn't know if she quite understood. I couldn't blame her, not after the manner in which I dropped the entire situation in her lap. There had been plenty of apologies for that night and for making her a pawn in this game of chess.

"What happened?" She'd been holding onto that question since Frank and I left earlier that night.

"Jewel thieves. We stopped them."

"By stop, you mean…"

Both Frank and I leaned over the wall, resting on our elbows. He answered for me. "We handled it. That's all you need to know. No point in getting graphic, Susan Lee."

"I see." She took a long drag of the cigarette before replying. "Tell me. I can't do this if there are going to be secrets."

"Frank shattered the teeth of one man. One man shot the other by accident. Then I broke his leg before Frank crushed his nose. We let the last one go as a messenger."

Susan Lee sucked on the filter of the cigarette. I tried to imagine myself in her shoes. Here was this woman who became a nurse to help injured people. Despite saving lives every day, she rose above the role of sainthood. Rolling bandages on her off days and knitting socks when listening to the radio at home had not been enough for the woman. Everything about Susan Lee revolved around her persistence and desire to make the world a better place. I commended her hope, we just had a different path to the same destination.

"Did you know it would happen?"

"I did," I said. I had made peace with the fact I lied to my closest friend. But my heart broke every time dissatisfaction crossed her face. She no longer considered me a friend, or at least not the same one before that day. To her, I was a stranger, and she had yet to decide if I was to be trusted.

"Susan Lee," Frank started, "this isn't easy to understand.

Eleanor's father had told me about her gifts. He believed her with every ounce of his being. But when she came to live with me, I thought something might be wrong with her. I've had nearly a decade to come to terms with this."

"Do you know why I became a nurse?"

In all our time together, I had never asked the question. I believed we were close, almost like sisters. We cohabitated, but the more I thought about it, did we really know each other? I had been a miserable friend, self-centered, and consumed with my own problems. Worse than being a terrible friend, I had treated Susan Lee as a disposable human. Those awkward looks from the woman were well earned. If I dug deep enough, I wasn't sure I quite knew who I was either.

"People think I am this champion of the sick. But I'm not. I'm not that innocent girl the doctors say I am. I became a nurse because my next-door neighbor…" Susan Lee paused. Neither Frank nor I interjected. We waited for her to light another cigarette, take a drag and let the smoke roll from her lips.

"We were walking along the tracks. Our parents swore we going to get run over one day. When the train came, we were safely out of the way. The train hit a bit of metal that swirled through the air. It hit him in the stomach. He died on the ground while I held his hand. I couldn't save him. I didn't know what to do. He died because I didn't know how to save a life, *his* life."

She didn't hide the trauma in her voice. It trembled as she spoke. The cigarette shook as she tried to take another puff. Aggravated, she threw it over the side.

For years I considered Susan Lee a delicate woman. Consumed with mundane tasks like work, church, and finding a husband; I understood I had lumped her into a category that left a sick feeling in my stomach. She wrapped her arms about her shoulders, struggling to withhold a sob. Tears streamed down her face, but not once did she flinch.

"I'm so sorry." Typically, we'd share in an awkward hug.

However, I stood a few feet away as the woman relived the horrific memory. No, neither of us was the person we were six months ago. "I guess I'm not sorry. It's terrible, but look at who you are now. You save people. You're helping the war effort."

"To what end, Eleanor?" She turned to face me. "If what you say is true. Then all those lives and the war effort are putting a band-aid on a bigger problem. This group of, whatever you are..." —That stung. — "They're using people like me."

"That doesn't negate your work. The world isn't perfect, it never will be. But each person you save has the potential to make a difference."

"No, Eleanor." She stomped her foot down on the ground. "You don't get to brush aside my feelings. I'm angry. I'm hurt, and honestly, I think it was better when I didn't know about the monsters hiding in the shadows."

She brushed by me, climbing onto the fire escape and descending to the apartment. In all the years I lived with the woman, I had never witnessed her in a sour mood. We had cried on more than one occasion. When one of us fell, the other lifted them back to their feet. I wanted nothing more than to repair the damage I created. But I couldn't fix it. It bothered me almost as much as the real threat to the city.

"Give her time," Frank said.

"Susan Lee shouldn't be part of this. I should never have gotten her involved."

Frank had never been on the roof before. He stared at the city, the lights turned off to hide from enemy planes. It was beautiful to see, even in the dark of night. Buildings stood like massive black voids in the dark purple of the night's sky.

"I can't rely on Susan Lee to fight this battle."

"You might see the future," Frank stood straight, resting his hand on my shoulder, "but you're none too bright, 'Nore."

"Thanks, this is quite the pep talk."

He pushed my shoulder until we were standing face-to-face.

He lifted my chin, making sure our eyes locked in the diminishing light. "None of us want to be part of this. That woman brought you back from the dead. I just beat a man within an inch of his life. We're standing beside you. This is your fight, Eleanor. We're supporting *you*. She's rebuilding the image of a person she once called a friend. But make no mistake, she'd die to save you."

He didn't need to say it. Much like Susan Lee, Frank would lie down his life if it meant saving me. The burden of their loyalty pulled at my limbs as if I had been lifting weights. I didn't want that type of loyalty, but there would be no undoing what had been done. I was their commander.

"There is no way I can stop the Society with a soldier and a nurse, Frank. I need allies, powerful ones." The admission startled Frank. Life had been cruel, and since landing in the hospital, I had only counted on one person. Even Frank, my savior, I tried to keep him away from danger. Yes, it was time to admit I could not win again the Society alone.

"I suspect they will have enlisted the help of Bertolucci's former clients."

I shook my head. "No, Frank, I don't mean *normal* humans."

"I thought they killed all the mentalists."

"That was their plan," I said, "but I got in the way. Maybe there are more out there. With them on my side, we could stop them."

"I know you don't want to hear this." Frank walked with me toward the fire escape. "But what if you let it go? Let them get their fingers into politics so they can bore themselves to death. Why must you intervene?"

I thought of Edward, a young gentleman who literally stole my heart. Somewhere in the city, I imagined him staring out the window, appreciating the same sky as myself. Thinking of that quirky smile that created the perfect blend of arrogant and sultry tightened my stomach. The vision had shown him on the floor bleeding out, and so help me God, I was going to do everything in my power to make sure he survived.

"Oh," Frank said with a bit of annoyance creeping into his voice. "You think you can save him."

Edward. And yes, there was still room to save the man I loved.

Spring bloomed silently in the city. The air in my room was just warm enough that my winter blanket was too hot. I still slept with a pillow on either side, forcing me to stay on my back. It was the only position preventing the injuries from flaring up overnight. The nights were the same, I couldn't sleep until exhaustion claimed me. Until then, I ran my fingers along the scar, feeling the raised and jagged skin.

Olivia branded me with an awful reminder. Try as I might to be the best person in a fight, she had proven a masterful opponent. Without my ability to see the future, I would have died. It punched at my ego, leaving it bruised and battered. She could have a thousand more tricks up her sleeve. I also developed new skills.

My eyes grew heavy. I gladly shut them and welcomed sleep.

"'Nore."

My eyes shot open. At the foot of my bed, Edward waited for me to react. I expected him to sit on the edge of the bed. Instead, he waited quietly while I collected myself.

"You're not really here?"

"Is that a statement or a question?"

"But you brought your arrogance." I struggled to remember the man who spent nights admiring me. The playful nature, the madly in love boy who pushed me on the swings, he wasn't standing at the end of the bed. The tailored suit bore elements of Olivia, and her incessant need to impress those around her. Once you got past her flashy nature, it became obvious she overcompensated.

Vile hag.

"It only took six months. I'm glad to see you care, Edward."

He flinched at the comment, his armor easily broken. It gave me hope that somewhere away from Olivia's machinations, my Edward struggled to tread water. He had shaved his head, leaving just enough hair to know he wasn't bald. He stepped through the bed, his legs vanishing in the blankets.

"I needed some time to think."

"About how Olivia tried to kill me?"

He frowned. "About how my fiancé lied to me. It seems we have more in common than you'd like to believe."

"What are you—"

"Not a telepath? If it was just about your abilities, I might not be wounded. But you kept it from me, why? Because you didn't trust me?"

"No. And can you blame me? They tried to kill me. And you knew all along." While I trained with Gregory, Edward had been joining a cabal of mentalists hell-bent on ruling the world. Gregory went to the grave keeping my secrets, so I had to believe he only harbored good intentions.

"We both carry our sins, Eleanor. Neither of us is without blame."

"Your sin tried to kill me, and nearly—"

"I'm not here to argue with you." He walked forward, his body passing through mine. I had grown accustomed to joining him in the white room, where the laws of physics didn't matter. His ghosts invaded my dream, perhaps the only way he could communicate with me since I shut him out.

"Why are you here, Edward? What the hell could you possibly have to say?"

As the sadness creeped into his eyes, his head dipping low, I could see the boy I loved. Somewhere, deep beneath the surface,

I had faith he remained. I didn't know how, but I could save him.

"I have brokered a deal."

I sat up in bed. "A deal? Just be out with it so I can get a restful sleep."

"Olivia wanted to hunt you down. Not only that, she wanted to erase your existence, starting with those closest to you."

"If she—"

"She won't. I have seen to it you and yours are safe. As long as you make no move against the Society, Olivia will behave."

"I'm going to—"

"No." We fought plenty while together, but he had never put his foot down. He understood he had fallen for a strong-willed woman. To say no would drive a wedge between us, especially since he knew I'd do it anyway.

"You will honor this, Eleanor. I put myself between the two of you. The next time I try, I can assure you, they will deal with us accordingly."

"What happened to you, Edward?" I reached up, my hand grazing the edge of his face. Even in a dream, my body remembered the sensation of his skin. He held my hand, pressing it against his face. Leaning into my palm, for a moment we were nothing more than Eleanor and Edward.

"You saw a path toward saving the world. I saw one as well." He kissed my hand and my entire body shivered at the gesture. "We want the same thing."

"But this isn't the way." I refused to cry in a dream.

"Please, Eleanor. We will never see eye-to-eye, but let me do this. Promise me."

The words sounded dangerously close to a farewell. This wasn't how it was supposed to end. I would bend fate and we'd discover our happily ever after. There was only one thing I couldn't save Edward from—himself.

"I promise."

The sadness didn't clear as he stepped back. As he faded from my dream, we both knew I lied. Edward struggled, trying to balance his love for me with his misbegotten sense of duty to the Society. He put himself at risk to protect my family. My love, my husband, he was in there, somewhere.

My eyes opened. There was no point in sleeping. I lied. I would stop the Society, and part of me hoped that meant killing Olivia. Light had barely cleared the horizon. It was time to begin my day.

Chapter Three

1931

The city played a song filled with discord. The bedroom was no bigger than my room at the farm, but the rest of the apartment paled in comparison. Frank had walked me into the cramped space and presented it like I had won a prize. Quickly, he tripped over himself, unsure of how to communicate with a teenager.

Frank saved me.

Carrying me out of the hospital, we started a journey east until we reached New York City. From the train, the lights were unlike anything I had ever seen. Where there should be darkness rising from the horizon, tiny specs of light pierced the darkness. The buildings rose into the sky like monoliths, stretching until they were close to the heavens. When we pulled into the station, the number of people surprised me. So many men and women waiting to come or go. Even at the market, I had never seen this many people gathered in one place.

The taxi through the streets displayed how mankind sacrificed the land for homes, storefronts, and roadways. Their definition of nature came in the form of small saplings spaced evenly along the sides of the street. When we came to a halt, Frank paid the man, and we ventured into the building. Each time he put his hand on the center of my back to usher me along, I tensed.

"Sorry," he'd say. He might have carried me from the hospital, but I still wasn't sure if I had exchanged one hell for another.

Staring out the bedroom window, I couldn't fathom the number of souls littering such a small island. Living on top of one another, the walls of the room seemed hardly enough to keep them at bay. While they might keep the people at bay, the demons found every crack. The room only had two ghosts, myself and Frank.

I watched as they moved about the room, neither in time with the other. The man came in and changed the sheets, fluffed the pillow and went about his business. Even our ghosts were two strangers passing in the night. While they insisted on stalking me, I breathed a sigh of relief that Frank remained cordial.

"Eleanor." Several light taps on the door followed. I made no move to answer. I expected him to barge in and make demands. Like the orderlies, he'd force me to eat, drink, and take pills.

"I cooked a steak." The smell was less steak and more charred meat, but I commended his efforts. "There's a potato and some corn." I waited for the door to open, but as seconds turned to minutes, no ghost of Frank entered my room.

"I'm going to leave it by the door. The shower is across the hall. I left a towel out. Help yourself to anything."

With my father's dying breath, he begged Frank to take care of his family. I was the only member alive. Frank's sense of duty, his loyalty to my father, forced him to save me from the hospital. But other than a quick glance as a child, we had never exchanged words. We remained strangers, bound together by a dead man.

Whatever his reasons, Frank displayed a kindness I hadn't seen in years. Even my own mother considered me cursed. But this stranger, this former soldier, he found it in his heart to inter-vene. Somewhere in the coldness consuming my heart, I found a moment of warmth. With a single action, he halted the darkness and provided me with something I hadn't experienced in years. Hope.

One emotion led to the next. For years I held them at bay, convinced the only way to survive was to cut myself off. Waves of emotion washed over the darkness and wiped it away, leaving me defenseless. I crawled onto the bed and buried my face in the pillow. The barriers I erected to protect myself vanished all at once. Confused, tears filled my eyes. They came with such ferocity, the pillow turned wet in seconds.

In the midst of unloading my soul, I found myself asleep. I woke, frozen in place, determined to not let the orderlies know. It took a moment before the smell of burned steak brought me back to the present. On the nightstand, a wind-up clock had nearly reached nine. For hours I slept without a single dream. At the hospital, without the medication, I had been unable to sleep.

I reached for the night stand lamp. Pulling the chain, light filled the room. The noise outside my window continued, lighter than before, but still a dull roar. Rolling over, I inspected the room. I wanted to learn something about the man who rescued me. Watching the ghosts only showed me the room and his insistence on changing the sheets and taking away the dishes on the night stand while I was out of the room. They told me, eventually, I dared to leave the room.

I couldn't imagine what awaited me on the other side of that door. Would Frank expect me to talk, to have discussions and explain my past. How much did Frank know about me and the demons that followed? Had my father confessed, describing the relentless manner in which ghosts tormented me? Had he explained I could only see the inevitable? Would he distrust me and turn me away when I had another episode?

I slid off the bed, tiptoeing through the room. At the end of the bed sat a footlocker. Lifting the latch, I eased it open, curious to what mementos the man held dear. There were badges, pins, and even an old uniform. Unwashed, I could still smell the sweat and earth. Others might wrinkle their noses, but I lifted it, inhaling deeply. The clothes smelled of my father. For a moment, I could feel the memory of his arms around me.

I neatly folded the jacket, putting it back into the green box before shutting it. The only other furniture in the room was a short bookshelf reaching my waist. There were a couple books with titles I had never heard. On the top shelf, however, a single picture frame claimed the space. I let out a gasp.

Lifting the frame, it showed two soldiers with their arms around each other. One held a fag between his lips while the other gave a thumbs up. Even underneath the dirt and grime, I could see my father's smile. Frank clung to my father as if they were brothers. My fingers touched the photograph, running over a crease that showed it had been folded time after time.

I turned it around, pulling off the back of the frame. I carried the photograph to the bed and crawled under the covers. In the light, I could see buildings in the background had been blown apart, destroyed by war. But the expression on both men's faces held a bit of levity, a hope that things would be okay. I couldn't help but wonder how long after they had taken it had he died?

My head rested on the pillow, staring at the only man who ever tried to understand me.

I startled as something big hit the wall outside the door. Pulling the blankets up high like a small child, I slid the photo under the pillow, worried Frank would be mad I had gone through his belongings. There was movement outside the door and a groan as something bumped against the floor. I peeked over the blankets, waiting for the moment the door cracked.

"The room ain't much," said Frank through the closed door, "but I thought you could make it your own."

Frank didn't own many things. I couldn't recall seeing any photos in the living room. Even the furniture he had was sparse, a chair, a couch, a radio on a stand by the window. It was obvious a woman didn't live in this apartment.

"I forgot to put this in there." He let out a slight laugh. "I won't pretend to understand what you went through or what you're going through now. But I've been told I'm good at listening. When you're ready that is."

Was I going to live with Frank from now on? Would he try to be my father? There was nobody in my life caring that a man stole me from the hospital. I felt alone, and even the nice man outside my door was a stranger. He was trying to do right by my father, but nobody stopped to ask what I wanted.

"Your dad talked about you and your brother. It made me happy to hear a man talk about his kids like he did. I don't have any family. The closest thing I ever had to a brother was your father. I guess that makes you like my niece or some shit." He paused for a moment and I could hear him curse again. "I mean my niece."

There was a long pause. I wondered if he had moved back to the living room. "I don't know what I'm doing, Eleanor. But I figure we're both alone. So maybe we can do this together." I sobbed quietly into the pillow.

"I thought I might read a little before going to bed. Your dad said you and he liked to read together."

I thought Frank meant he was going to the living room to read, but he cleared his throat. Then he started reading aloud through the wall.

"Dorothy lived in the midst of the great Kansas prairies..."

Chapter Four

1943

It would be at least another hour before the gym opened. Veterans stuck with a regimented schedule, the aftermath of serving in the military. Before long, there'd be twenty men and even a woman or two joining. Word of Susan Lee's involvement had transformed the gym from a veteran rehab to a more inclusive environment.

That inclusive environment had brought the only occupant who would be inside. The moment I walked through the doors, I found him kneeling on the mats. Frank had surprised even me with his ability to put aside his prejudices. Basking in the morning light pouring through the tall windows, the petite Asian man meditated.

My nose scrunched up as the smell of men and sweat swept over me. I enjoyed a vigorous workout and a glistening man didn't hurt either. This permeated every exposed wooden beam and into the cement itself. Stale. Between the boxing ring and the free weights, I'd have to ask Frank to include something that smelled pleasant. I'm sure he'd be thrilled when I suggested he include potted plants by the jump ropes.

Koji had come to the gym late one night when Susan Lee produced meals for struggling New Yorkers. I never asked how desperate he must have been, but it was obvious. For a Japanese man to scurry into a room with veterans, the situation must be dire. Grabbing just enough food to survive, he tried to exit, only to find the less scrupulous trainees blocking his path.

Frank corrected the situation immediately. He remained my hero. Not safe for Koji on the streets, Frank offered him the cot in his office. Koji had refused, not willing to take a handout. The price of a cot, a shower, and food in his belly paid by sweeping the floors. It took a few weeks, but nearly all the vets overcame their grudges. Those who didn't, they were shown the door.

I dropped my gym bag on the floor and kicked off my shoes. I knew little about the man, but we found comfort in our differences. He hid his shock at a woman in the gym, and I ignored his ethnicity. Eventually we would discuss our origin stories, but for the moment, I relished in our respectful and simple relationship.

I quietly lowered myself to my knees. I bowed down, my forehead touching the mat. Sitting upright, I started the breathing exercises. Similar to Gregory's teachings, I wondered if the Scot had adapted eastern philosophy to train mentalists?

I mastered the flame in our meditations. Erecting stone barriers about my mind, I nurtured the tiny fire. Quieting my mind, I found it easy to summon the ghosts. One by one, I let my mind graze the most emotional memories, Frank carrying me from the hospital, Momma hiding her face as the orderlies took me away, nights spent writhing under Edward. Each memory provided fuel. My heart developed a direct line to the palm of my hand. Every feeling contributed until even the dim spark contained enough power to burn down a building.

"You're early."

Koji's English was immaculate. The child of Japanese immigrants, he defied the stereotypes shown on the television. If anybody let the secret slip that we harbored a Japanese man, police would take him away. American concentration camps showed that even the righteous make poor choices during times of war. The similarities between him and my turbulent relationship with Edward was not lost on me.

"I couldn't sleep."

Koji continued looking forward, raising his head with eyes closed. He drank in the light, his skin almost glowing. I envied the man's ability to savor these moments.

"You have much on your mind?"

"I do."

"And your heart?"

Ten years my senior, he spoke with more wisdom than I expected. When life returned to normal, I promised myself I'd learn more about his heritage and culture. Perhaps when the war ended, we would call one another friends.

"Heavier."

"You understand that mastering the body isn't enough for a fulfilling existence."

"I do."

We sat in silence for minutes. This had become our relationship since I returned to the gym. I boxed with Frank, lifted weights with Michael, but it was Koji who taught me to connect the pieces. He moved with the grace of a ballet dancer, but underneath, a ferocity of the most skilled fighter. Even Frank, though he wouldn't admit it, had taken to sparring with Koji.

I worked through my muscles. Starting with my feet, I wiggled my toes, bent my ankles and moved along my legs until I reached my torso. Tensing and relaxing, I awakened each, alerting them to a day of hard work. Last night had been a breeze, a test run. Koji was often more brutal than any mugger I encountered.

For a man, he might be short, but for me, we saw eye-to-eye. His hair fell from his short ponytail, framing his face almost beautifully. If we met on the streets, I wouldn't have believed him a threat. The unsuspecting package reminded me to never underestimate an opponent.

We bowed. Boxing required holding your hands up and being light on your feet to maneuver. Jujutsu was unlike anything I learned in the ring. Instead of absorbing punches, and seeking openings to land a blow, this required redirecting the force of your sparring partner, creating a window. Strikes were delivered with accuracy. It felt counterintuitive to what I learned while wearing gloves.

"Half speed."

At any moment I could summon the ghosts and predict his every move. Before we moved to full speed, I allowed my body to learn the techniques and moves. Then I worked to incorporate the ghosts, blending the ability to see into the future with the graceful movements. Despite that, more often than not, Koji pinned me to the mat.

I narrowed my gait, turning my hips so my left foot rested forward of my right. I held my hands up in tight fists.

"Loosen your hands."

Old habits crept their way into my form. I followed his instructions. Even at half speed, Koji moved quickly. He pivoted his weight, moving forward with his rear foot, preparing for a palm strike to my sternum. He hesitated, giving me the chance to respond before he knocked me on my butt. I used my left hand, pressing against his forearm, pushing him out wide.

"You are thinking about your reactions."

Right, less thinking. He tried the maneuver again, and this time I pushed his wrist in so it crossed his chest. He followed with the other and I repeated the tactic, stepping in close to trap his arms against his body. I felt my mistake as his foot slid behind my leg. With a slight thrust of his shoulder, I tumbled backward onto my butt.

"You treat your fists as a weapon."

"Usually they are."

"Boxers are talentless brutes." He reached out, helping me to my feet. "Do not tell Frank I said that." I laughed. Koji repeated those words to Frank every time the brute fell on the mats. Father like daughter, I guess.

"Eleanor," he raised my hands. I hissed as he slapped them. "Your body is a tool. Your little finger is as powerful as a fist. You are more distracted than I anticipated."

"Sorry, it's just—"

"Did I ask for an excuse?"

Okay, new game plan. Instead of mastering my powers, relearning to fight, and waging a war, I was going to send Koji in my place. If he couldn't beat the stuffing out of Olivia, his mastery at silencing a person would destroy her. I'd pay a dollar to watch him shush her.

"You fight with your heart. But why at one moment, your Ki is in alignment, and the next," he gestured up and down my body, "this."

"I'll focus more."

"No," he walked to the mat and grabbed one of the sweat rags that littered the gym. Tearing with his teeth, he ripped off a strip. "Blindfold yourself."

"Then how will—"

"More excuses?" Yes. Koji's refusal to be swayed could single-handedly backhand Olivia. He'd mop the floor with her attempts at talking down at him. I'd pay far more than a dollar at this point.

Praying the rag was clean. I tied it around my eyes, shifting it so it blocked my sight. I could see the shadow of Koji, but not enough to know if he was moving. Just as I was about to speak he slapped me across the face. Before I recovered, he did it again with the other hand.

Slap me once and I might let it slide. But after the second, there was no point in playing fair. I inhaled through the nose, drawing in the musty smell of the gym. I expelled it through my mouth. My left forearm shot up, stopping the next slap.

There was no warning, no moving at half speed, no restraint from Koji. I closed my eyes as I exhaled. Koji's ghost stirred, punching for my sternum. I leaned forward, blocking his hand with one arm and thrusting my palm toward his chest. He moved quickly enough I didn't see his ghost block the blow before it happened.

"Better."

He stepped back. Now, we both assumed the proper stance. Koji favored a sweep, and I wasn't shocked to see his ghost move into position. As he spun about, dropping low, I jumped. I allowed time to slow, to watch his ghost continue to spin about again. A sidekick at chest height. I ducked.

In Jujutsu, it's about blocking when necessary, but more about using the momentum of an opponent to do the work. Attacks are necessary, but if timed right, they need only be few and far between. I redirected a punch, countered a kick, and even attempted a sweep. While low, he attempted to drive his knee into my face, a move that would have shattered my nose. I moved with inches to spare.

Koji knew. He might not know the specifics, but he knew I'd predict a potentially lethal blow. He didn't predict me wedging my shoulder under his leg and standing upright. Improvise. I slid a hand up his torso, resting on his chest. I launched him into the air and then drove him down to the mat.

"Ooof."

"You shouldn't slap a lady."

Koji insisted on standing watch at the entrance of the locker room. I found it charming to know that even after trying to break my nose, chivalry persevered. I stripped and threw my clothes into a locker. Tucked on the inside of the door, I had a photograph of Frank and me from when the gym first opened. It had faded with time, but it served as a reminder.

"Simpler times," I mumbled.

In the shower, I rinsed off, savoring the scalding water. I took a moment to inspect the scar. Despite having healed, the skin remained red and raised. Both Susan Lee and Claudette assured me it would diminish. There was no doubt anybody who saw the eight-inch gash would know I had nearly lost my life.

My skin reddened from the temperature of the water. For a moment the scar looked at home on my body. Would the next scar be worse? Confidence might run deep, but I also knew my opponent was more than capable of defending herself.

"Eleanor," the echo of Frank's voice made me gasp. I shut off the water quickly. "We need to talk." For Frank to enter the locker room, even the area by the benches, with me inside meant his news was urgent.

"Be out in a minute."

"My office."

I toweled off, squeezing the excess water from my hair. Another morning workout ruining my hair and leaving me on the outs of the latest hairdos. How women could spend the time to spin their hair around soda cans and curlers was beyond me. Thankfully, light curls were natural in my family. I could lie and say I attempted the next trendy style.

I needed a vision that told me how long before women partook in sensible shoes, lazy hair, and comfortable clothes. Protecting New York might be important, but I needed to know how much suffering I must endure before dresses came with pockets.

I patted Koji on the back as I rushed past. He might suspect something, but there was no way he knew about mentalists or my ability to see the future. In honor of Susan Lee, I would tell him when the opportunity presented itself. No more secrets. I wouldn't broadcast my abilities, but with the Society already aware, what was the point in hiding?

In the rear corner of the wide-open gym stood a small single square room. It stood out like a sore thumb and must have been added after they had erected the original building. In the middle of the wall stood a door with a frosted window that once held the name of Frank's father.

I barreled through the door. "What is it?"

"We have a problem."

I hadn't been in here since Koji started sleeping at the gym. The office was the neatest I had ever seen it. The surfaces were clear of dust. Even the newspaper articles hanging on the wall had been straightened. When Frank inherited the building from his father, he had done little to clean the space. Either out of a sense of obligation or nostalgia, it had gone untouched for years.

"Did you clean?"

"Koji."

"Should have known."

Frank walked behind me, shutting the door. This signaled that it either had to do with my abilities or the Society.

"They used you to remove Bertolucci."

"I know that now."

Frank shook his head. The man ran his hands over his face. He grew more agitated by the moment. "Frank, what's wrong?"

"Eleanor, they've already done it. They got to them." He stopped fidgeting and sat down behind his desk. Glimpsing my face, my confusion must have been obvious. "I was at Mary's Deli, and in walks a police officer. I give him the normal nod and smile. He goes to raise his cap for me and there, on his wrist, three wavy lines."

The brand of the Society. "Are you certain?"

"I didn't know what to do. I offered to pay for his sandwich. He gave me a handshake, and I saw it again. Then he went about his business as if it were no big deal. The police work for them, but it looks like they don't know who I am. Maybe we're safe."

"We are." He wouldn't like what came next. "Edward visited me last night."

"Visited? Or like *visited*."

I ignored the insinuation from my father. "He came to me in a dream. He bartered with Olivia. As long as I stay out of her way, the Society will leave me and mine alone."

"Are you sure it's real?"

I raised an eyebrow and cocked my head to the side. I knew it wasn't easy to understand the world according to mentalists. Frank however knew more about our world than any other human I encountered. He asked because he refused to believe Edward capable of honor.

"Fine." His pouting bordered on comical. "Do you think you can honor those terms?"

I laughed. Frank asked questions all the time. The man wasn't scared of being wrong or showing his lack of knowledge in a subject. Even if we weren't related by blood, he knew me well enough that he should have expected the response to a foolish question.

"That's exactly what I thought."

I thought about it for a moment. I could easily tackle the problem of their henchmen. Night after night, I'd clear the streets of those tattoo wearing minions. However, the first time I struck, the treaty would break, and I'd be putting Frank and Susan Lee in danger. I would only have one opportunity to take care of the Society. One chance and no room for errors.

"I—" For a woman who always had a plan of action, I didn't know what to do. Save Edward? Protect Frank and Susan Lee? End the corruption of New York? Prevent a secret organization from rising to power? I could beat up people all night long, but that wouldn't achieve one goal, let alone all of them.

"Frank," I sat down across the desk from him, "I don't know what to do."

"You're not alone."

"Let's say you get involved, hell, arm Koji and Susan Lee. They have a city of people working for them. We can't do anything without bringing that down on us."

"When we'd infiltrate enemy territory, a scout would always look ahead. They'd scour the area looking for intel we could use to our advantage. When they returned, we'd share everything we knew. Then we'd formulate a plan."

"We have almost no intel. Olivia told me about the uprising. She bragged about freeing herself from the Society. They're not even the Society by her account, not after fleeing. I don't know how much of that is true. Her lies are almost as convincing as the truth."

"So we find out." Frank leaned back in the chair. The man reached for a pencil, spinning it around in his fingers. I didn't know what he might be thinking, but I hoped something turned on the proverbial lightbulb. Right now, I grasped at straws, weak ones at best.

"Who knows about the Society?"

"The only members I know of are the doctor and his wife. Dead. Everybody's dead."

"Perhaps a historian? Maybe there's somebody at the university?"

My back straightened and eyes widened. New York University might know something about a bunch of dusty old men studying weird paranormal experiences. Maybe. But there was a man at Harvard who knew everything.

"I need to go to Boston."

"Boston? Why?"

Dr. Butler was in part the reason for serial killers running amok in New York, but perhaps he provided a clue. A collection of photographs occupied the dead man's shelf, and one had showed a chum, another doctor from Harvard. It was a long shot, but perhaps he knew something about Dr. Butler's involvement in the Society. Right now, long-shots were all we had.

"A dead man's former colleague might hold the answer."

Chapter Five

1943

I didn't think I'd experience this much anxiety as the train rocked back and forth. The clacking underfoot should have been soothing, even sleep-inducing. For many, the travel between New York City and Boston offered the chance to indulge in the daily newspaper. But this trip seemed similar to the one where Frank rescued me. Instead of wearing a man's long coat, I wore my most civilized garb, but it was hard to not feel like the young girl in that hospital gown.

It had only taken a phone call to the registrar before identifying the man in the photograph. To my surprise, Dr. Butler was well known, but even more was his college roommate, Dr. Stewart. I shouldn't be surprised that he was now a tenured professor at the same institution he had attended.

"Ticket please." The words startled me.

I jumped as the short, stout man held out his hand. I reached into my purse, fishing for the paper ticket. Beneath the knives, I found it. I forced a smile as I handed the slender paper to him.

"I haven't seen you before. Pleasure or business?"

He handed the ticket back. "A bit of both, I suppose."

Bowing slightly, he tipped his hat. "I hope it's a prosperous trip."

I inspected his wrists, checking for the wavy lines. Did they only mark themselves in one spot? If I tossed him to the floor, would I find it scribed across his neck or under his clothes? Every person on the train could be a member. The woman in the wide brim hat, or the man reading the morning paper, any of them could follow me out of the city. It was the first time I wished I could see backwards in time, or know their emotions like Gregory. I bet he could identify an individual with malice in their hearts.

It was after the rush of businessmen traveling to destinations unknown. These were leisurely folks, sitting scattered throughout the train. I lacked discretion as I eyed each of them, letting their ghosts run loose. None of them moved more than a glance out the window. The travelers all held fast, enduring the journey. All except one. A woman in a lovely dress tried to hide her wandering eyes, but the ghost frequently stopped to stare in my direction. As my ghost walked down the train, crossing between cars she followed.

"Let's do this," I mumbled.

Edward might believe a ceasefire existed between us, but I didn't trust Olivia or her minions to uphold the truce. For all I knew, the woman staring at me could function as Olivia's eyes and ears. She had proven herself more powerful than Edward, but I hoped as the train rocked through upstate New York, we left the range of her influence.

This particular car had seats in groups of four facing one another with a small table separating the passengers. Two cars down held the sleeper cars, private rooms for those wanting to nap or meet in private. I hadn't thought of prying eyes when I purchased my ticket. Frank promised to watch over Susan Lee and check in with Claudette. I purchased the first ticket I could, wanting to be done with the experience in a jiffy.

I made a show of standing, smoothing out my dress. Who knew how much walking I'd need to do, so I wore flat shoes. With the rocking of the train back and forth, I believed I had made the right decision. A dress might not be the best outfit to fight crime, fashion had yet to incorporate practicality. They didn't care if I could kick above my head, they couldn't even bother to include pockets.

I over dramatized the teetering back and forth, clutching the bar above my head. I felt as much the klutz as I tried to display. Stumbling along, I reached the back of the car and lifted the handle, opening the door into the next. The slight space between the cars gave away how fast we were moving. My hair swirled about my face as I shouldered the next door open.

In the glass I could see her standing, waiting patiently for me to move forward. She wasn't dumb, but it was obvious Olivia hadn't given her the full dossier on my abilities. Was there a general order to avoid me? Did she think she might score brownie points with her puppeteers by tackling me? Or perhaps my paranoia bested me and the woman only needed to use the lavatory?

I hurried through the next car, careful to inspect the reflection at the end. She followed. I slowed, struggling with the handle on the door. If I were her, I'd use the sleeper car to attack. Narrow hall, with only one potential exit, it'd be perfect. If this was the type of thing the future held, I'd grow increasingly annoyed with their lackluster and predictable attempts.

At the end of the sleeper car, I paused and turned. The woman, an ordinary housewife who I might find at the local market, held a meat cleaver in her hand.

"Honestly? A cleaver? Could you not find the butter knife?"

She raised it at shoulder height, believing she wielded the upper hand. "They'll have to let me into the inner circle." It was good to know she operated on her own. That solved at least one problem.

She growled, then charged. How was she selected? Did they go to the hairdresser and recruit women with nothing occupying their free time? Because this almost seemed ridiculous.

I dropped my purse and lunged forward with my palm. Striking her chest hard, she staggered back. I might have cracked her ribs, but she convinced herself the knife provided all the security she needed. She swung it downward like an ax as I rocked back. Before she could change direction, I kicked, slamming her arm against the sleeper car. She dropped the cleaver.

"How did they recruit you?"

The woman reached out with her other hand, clawing at empty air. It wasn't even worth the effort. I pushed her hand to the side and chopped her neck with the side of my hand. She choked, struggling to breathe. I reached for the handle of the nearest sleeper. Opening the door, I shoved her inside.

"How did they recruit you?" It was pointless asking. The woman could hardly breathe, answering questions was outside her abilities.

I spun her about, wrapping my arm around her neck. Koji had shown me how easily a person would pass out with the right amount of pressure. With a light squeeze, she tried pulling my arm off, but this poor woman had already admitted she lost our fight. Limp, I eased her to one of the seats. I scanned her pockets, pulling the few loose bills she hid. As I left, I kicked the cleaver into the room and shut the door.

"These are not the problems," I wipe my hands before dipping to pick up my purse, "I expected to have as an adult."

Boston. The train station didn't have the grandeur of Grand Central, nor did it have as many people. The train eased to a stop before a gentleman on the platform opened the door. I stepped out and inhaled deeply. It smelled older, as if there were a bit of dust in the air. It wasn't until the breeze wormed its way inside the doors that I could see the sea. Unlike New York, the water smelled fresh. When this was over, I promised myself I'd begin traveling.

"May I help you?" The ticket taker helped me take the final step from the train. I stood in awe of the building. New York was a spectacular testament to the determination of mankind. This, however, this spoke more about the longevity of our creations. This building held a rich story, and I'm sure if I looked long enough, I'd be able to unravel it.

I walked through the station, no longer concerned with potential killers. Spending so long in New York, I had forgotten the sense of awe the first time Frank walked with me along the streets of Manhattan. I felt small, almost insignificant. In the newness, I wanted to explore and reach out into the city and bask in this feeling.

I held my purse close, walking toward the exit. The people were like any other, each of them looking as if they could be my neighbor. I don't know what I expected, but I imagined they'd be different, unique, or at least have some element that screamed, "Boston."

Stepping outside, the buildings surrounding the train station were as quaint as I expected. I approached a taxi and slid into the back. Unlike the ones in New York, this one almost had a pleasant smell. The driver must take care of the interior, keeping it clean despite the passengers coming and going.

"Where to, miss?" In three words, his accent gave away the change in location. The burly man straightened in the seat and adjusted his mirror.

"The Museum of Fine Arts," I said.

"You're not from around here," he said.

"No, New York. I'm here to visit a friend."

The man pulled out onto the street. The buildings were beautiful, and each one seemed older than the last. New York prided itself on being modern while Boston clung to its old charm. I understood why Bostonians were quick to celebrate their heritage.

"Can you tell me about Boston? It's my first time here."

"The Irish run the city. Don't let any Italian tell you differently," he said with a wink in the mirror. "The winters are fierce. So are the summers. Folks are a bit standoffish, but they're good people. It's a working city, and the people work hard."

"It's beautiful." I stared out the window, inspecting the buildings as he zigged and zagged through the streets. There might have been a slight squeal as I watched a horse-drawn carriage working down one of the streets. The lack of familiarity transformed me into a teenager again. Yes, when this ordeal had passed, I'd travel the world.

"Appreciate art? The museum, I mean."

I had never thought of it before. Other than the art gallery, I had never stopped to appreciate art. "Not really. But perhaps that will change."

"I'm sure you're aware, being from New York, but be careful at night. It's not as rough as New York, or so I'm told, but it can get lively when the bars close. I'd hate to see Boston treat you wrong."

The man's warm disposition contrasted the frosty welcome I expected. I had heard about the pubs late at night and the drinking stamina of the Irish. "Thank you, good sir." I believe Susan Lee would be delighted at my attempts at civility.

"Of course, Miss…" the word hung in the air as he subtly tried to uncover my marital status.

"Mrs. Valentine." I didn't want to say I distrusted the man, but being leery, I wanted to keep my presence undercover. I wore Edward's family name like a crest, part of this identity emerging from the ashes of Eleanor Bouvier. There was no good dwelling on it, but if I died that night on the street, this might be an opportunity to reinvent myself.

"Here we are, Mrs. Valentine." I leaned forward, handing the man far more money than necessary for the fare. "I can't accept that."

"Good people deserve good things." He reluctantly accepted the money. I opened the door and stepped out.

He rolled down the window as I faced the stairs leading into the museum. "I don't know much about art, but the big hall with all the large paintings, they're my favorite."

The car had pulled into a circular courtyard in front of the building. There were sculptures in the circle in the middle, but nothing compared to the grandeur at the end of the sidewalk. The building's large stones struck me as old, perhaps as old as the city itself. When life returned to normal, I'd make a point to spend more time admiring the architecture and visiting the museums.

I almost chuckled at the idea of normal.

The stairs led to a row of doors, but it was the massive columns spanning the second floor that made it impressive. The stonework and enormous windows were a spectacle of their own. I knew nothing about architecture, but it struck me as a building that housed artwork. On each side of the stairs, large metal pans rested, and I wondered if they ever held fire at night. I almost forgot the reason for my visit as I absorbed the beauty.

While the outside might be impressive, the inside was an overwhelming artistic spectacle. A large staircase climbed to the second floor, while large vases sat to the sides of each of the three landings. I approached a man in a uniform behind a small desk.

"Excuse me, but I am looking for the European Masters?"

"You'll want to climb the stairs, you'll see it across the rotunda. It's the largest room on the second floor."

"Why thank you." Yes, I even curtsied.

I was grateful for the flat shoes as I climbed the stairs. I could manage in heels, but a woman's feet weren't designed for such an act of barbarism. The vases were massive, almost large enough for me to fit. Around the outsides were drawings of ancient civilizations. I felt out-of-place looking at worlds long gone. I always focused on the future. Looking backward might be something I had to focus on more, or even living in the present. I'd worry about self-improvement once people stopped trying to kill me.

The rotunda was magnificent. Greek statues stood in tiny alcoves. A trio of men held spears in one, while a woman held a sword and scales in another. Beneath each statue rested a small gold placard with the artist's name.

"Cassandra," I whispered. I stepped back and eyed the woman. Boldly, she held out the scales, perfectly balanced while she gripped the sword, preparing for battle. Claudette claimed signs appeared to us in a time of need. Her eyes lacked definition. Certainly, she was beautiful, but she lacked the conviction of a woman brandishing a weapon.

"I need a sword."

The circle room had exits in each of the cardinal directions, but only one with a wide entrance. Even before I stepped through, I knew I found the room of masters. The gallery in the salon had artwork evenly spaced out, allowing each painting room to breathe. But in here, frames nearly touched, and they climbed the thirty-foot walls.

"Breathtaking," I whispered.

If I felt small when I first arrived, now it was more like being invisible. Some paintings were twice my height and three times as long. Men hunting with dogs chasing foxes, while others held images of Mary with her golden halo.

The ghosts walked along in the room, stopping and admiring a particular work of art. The only person not taking in the art was a stocky man who hovered near a bench against the far wall. I walked to the seats lining the middle of the room and made my perch. From a distance, the wall appeared to be a montage of dreamlike scenes. The chiseled torsos of men surrounded by women covered in red cloth were like seeing into an artist's fantasy. Someday, I'd travel to Europe and see the origins of these creations.

"Eleanor Valentine," the voice matched the man's stocky appearance. He stood behind me, attempting to be discreet. "We need to talk."

I watched as the ghosts, each and every one of them, glanced in my direction. I hadn't seen it at first, too caught up in the artwork. The man behind me had not come alone. Perhaps every patron, from the docent to the taxi driver was part of their network.

"There's no need for your companions. I come in peace."

"You called me inquiring about the Society. Consider my organization startled at being discovered by a woman from New York."

I turned around on the bench, holding my purse on my lap. The stocky man was older than I guessed from his ghost. He wore nice clothes, but nothing as prim and proper as the doctor. The years had worn on him, leaving deeply chiseled grooves on his face. I tried to recall the photo on the doctor's mantle, but I couldn't be certain this was the same man.

"Who are you, Mrs. Valentine?"

Yes, the taxi driver had been in on it. I commended them on their subtlety. We could easily continue this dance, prying bits of information from one another, but I had a city to save. I stood slowly, and the gentleman took a step back.

"Dr. Stewart," I held out my hand, "I'm Eleanor Valentine."

He glanced over my shoulder and with a slight shake of the head, he stopped his cadre from approaching. He hesitated, eying my hand.

"I know you shake my hand," I stretched it out further, "Because I'm a precog."

Chapter Six

1943

It was the tenth correct guess. Turning around the card to show the square, he slid them back into his pocket. We had wandered from the European Masters into a room holding white marble statues. He had sent away his colleagues. Did he find me not worth the protection, or did he understand the futility involved?

"You could be demonstrating telepathy and reading my mind before I read the card." It was the first time someone had called me out for being a potential liar. But it made sense, I had lied to Edward much in the same way.

"You're carrying thirteen cents in your right pocket. You'll reach in and run your fingers along the edges of the change before you pull it out. When you open your hand…"

He did just as I suggested. When he pulled out his hand he held his fist shut for a moment. When he opened, we stared at the dime and three pennies.

"Impressive," we said in unison.

"We have never discovered a person with precognition. At this point, it's spoken of as a myth. The claim of Michel de Nostredame knowing the future has come into question more than once. But I believed. I just never thought I'd meet somebody with foresight like yours. It's simply amazing."

"It's been less than amazing at times."

"Does it come to you in visions? Or a dreamlike trance?"

I found it fascinating to speak with somebody who knew the background of my abilities. Had I met this man as a child, things might have turned out significantly different. I had to remember to keep my desire to converse in check. This man belonged to an organization that created the Barren and held mentalists hostage. I might need his help, but it was a case of an enemy of my enemy.

"They come as ghosts, transparent apparitions. Every room, every space, ghosts give me clues to what the future might hold."

"Much like the way a telepath or an empath is constantly receiving projections from those around them. I wondered if it might be more like a telekinetic and come with an on and off switch."

"I have learned to temper them. But there are times they demand my attention."

"I see." Dr. Stewart held his hands behind his back as we walked. I don't know what I expected, but he embodied the image of a university professor. His jacket was well worn and his glasses frequently slid down his nose, requiring him to push them up again. Once he believed I told the truth, he moved onto academic discussions about abilities.

"Do you believe in determinism?"

I tried to place the word, but in all honesty, I don't think I had ever heard of it. "You have me at a disadvantage, Mr. Stewart."

He stopped meandering and pulled out a penny. With a well-rehearsed hand, he flipped it into the air. Spinning quickly, he snatched it and slapped it down on the back of his other hand. He kept it covered, not letting me see the result of the coin flip.

"Currently, there are two possibilities. It is either heads or tails. We know this. The Copenhagen Interpretation states that there is one outcome. However, Everett believed that at this very moment there are many outcomes and the future will diverge. One will have it be heads, and the other will be tails. However, at this moment, we do not know any outcome, so it is in fact both."

It only required a nudge for the ghost to appear, holding the coin up to my face revealing it was indeed heads.

"You just looked," he said with a slight grin.

"I did."

"Were there many versions, or only one?"

"One. Heads."

"Interesting," he uncovered the penny to verify the truth. He held it up for me to see. "So, let's believe the Copenhagen model is correct. This particular coin flip was destined to be heads. Are you prepared for your head to hurt?"

"This is more science than I ever considered. Go for it, make it hurt."

"Was the coin heads because it was destined to be heads? Or is it heads because you saw it in the future?"

"You're asking which came first, the chicken or the egg?"

He clapped his hands, almost skipping a step. "Fascinating to consider, is it not? Do you create the future or did the future create you?"

"But what about the other theory? What if that was correct?"

"You're a curious person," he said. Had my past not been riddled with so many gaps in education, perhaps I would have gone on to study at a university like Harvard. I would like to think, even in a time when female academics were rare, I might find a way to excel and help pave the way for women's liberation.

"Dr. Stewart, a woman with my gifts spends time dwelling on the possibilities."

"This is why I helped found the Boston Society for Psychical Research. There are many things that exist that our definition of science has yet to understand. I can understand the agitation of particles until an object bursts into flame, but how does a pyrokinetic agitate them? I want to know."

"This is not the welcome I expected. To be quite honest," I decided I might as well confess my intentions. "I was prepared to beat you within an inch of your life to get the information I needed."

He scrunched his nose face up, taken aback by my honesty. "I suppose you could manage with your skillset. But I would appreciate it if you left me without bruises."

"I counted seven associates with you. You didn't come here thinking this would go as it had."

"Let's say that we have been quite guarded since—"

"Olivia." I didn't hide the disdain from my voice. I wanted the man to know how much I disliked the woman. If we weren't in a public place, I'd raise my dress until he saw the scar running down my abdomen. If I discovered a man who loathed her as much as me, then I might have the foundation for an alliance.

"Yes. The news of Ms. Sincerbeaux has reached us in America."

"You don't know," I turned to face him. The raised eyebrow gave away his confusion. "She's not in London. The Society has come to New York City."

"Olivia, Robert, Gregory, and Catherine are in New York City?" He pushed up his glasses and started rubbing his chin. The news alarmed him. Compared to the hostility from Olivia, I would gladly side with this man and his organization if they could help me.

"They claimed they fled Europe because of the power struggle within the Society. She didn't paint a very positive picture of your organization."

"Of course, she didn't. I've never had the chance to collaborate with any of the mentalists. The UK branch of the organization was," he searched the air for the next few words, "insistent, let's say. We had a philosophical difference of opinion. We maintain the lines of communication, but we're far more focused on the ideology behind the paranormal. They preferred a more hands-on approach."

Behind the doctor, was a white marble statue of a young man holding a severed head in his hands. His sword arm had broken off, but the arm with the head remained intact. It took a moment before I realized her hair was made of snakes. I might not know much about mythology, but even I recognized Medusa. It seemed fitting as we talked about Olivia. Perhaps I'd hold her head much the same way when I killed her.

"So what she said wasn't entirely lies?"

"There is a bit of truth in every lie."

He dodged the question with an expertly mustered counter. There must be a requirement to lead a secret organization. They were all capable of answering with half-truths. I would have to work on my skills after this was done.

"I must meet with the others. Can you speak with us this evening?"

"Is this going to involve me getting stabbed?"

Dr. Stewart shook his head, perplexed by the statement. "Is this something you deal with often?"

"The world is a dangerous place these days," I said, holding out my hand to shake.

"I feel attacking a precog would not end well for me."

He reached out to shake my hand, and I pulled back slightly. "No, Dr. Stewart, it wouldn't." The threat was laid bare, and he continued holding his hand out. We shook vigorously.

"Feel free to wander about. I'll send a driver to pick you up."

"How will you—"

The man smiled. Checking the many exits, I could see one or two people milling in each doorway. They weren't attempting to hide their prying eyes. They might not know me, but they knew him. Dr. Stewart might be far more charismatic than Olivia and her brood. The man was not without resources.

"I look forward to it."

He let go of my hand and walked toward an exit to the right of a massive bust of a man in armor. He paused for a moment and turned around. "If it helps, Mrs. Valentine, I have never believed in the Copenhagen school of thought."

He believed there were many possibilities. If there wasn't a set future, that would mean with each decision, there would be choices, versions, multiple ghosts. It wasn't by chance that I developed the ability to see variations seconds into the future. This meant I might have the ability to see thousands of possibilities throughout time.

Dr. Stewart exited with several disciples following him. The exits were empty, and they left me standing alone in a room full of ancient sculptures. In a single conversation, the man had spoken to the one thing I truly wanted. If what he said was true, if Everett's idea of multiple outcomes and divergent futures were possible, I had only to find a way to expand my abilities.

The cuffs secured by fate suddenly didn't feel so tight.

Chapter Seven

1943

Boston attempted to freeze time. Where New York insisted on advancing, pushing forward, and being the beacon of a new age, Boston resisted change. The buildings were old, historic. Large windows and expert masonry came across as charming. The people here appeared no different from New York, almost luring me into a sense of familiarity.

Bostonians might be familiar, but I eyed each of them cautiously. It was impossible to tell who might be part of the Society. Either, Society. My pursuit of allies required me to share my most intimate secret. I had no idea if Olivia had distorted the truth or if the Society had been tamer than she described. Caution. I observed each individual, letting their ghosts step in front of them, ensuring nobody brandished a knife or revolver. I might be paranoid, but the scar throbbing on my torso served as a warning.

There were many ways to know the heart of a person. You could observe them from a distance, eavesdropping on conversations. In the parks, watching them play with children would give away the mothers who gossiped while watching kids run through the grass. There were many ways, but with a brief stay, I needed to cut through the shroud and get to Boston's soul.

I needed whiskey.

The bar reminded me of Harry's. The wooden sign above the doorway proudly displayed O'Connors, a strong Irish name. Unlike my local pub, this one had large windows letting in light from the street. Through the glass, I could see a handful of patrons. We were only a few blocks from the school, and the men inside wore similar jackets to Dr. Stewart. If I was going to trust this man with my secret, I would do my version of intelligence gathering. The alcohol wouldn't hurt either.

I walked through the door and headed straight to the counter. I pulled a stool out with my foot and took a seat. The men at a long table held the same expression as the one in Harry's. A woman violated their private sanctum. I had become so wrapped up in secret society power struggles and evil mentalists I forgot the satisfaction in planting myself where women should not go. But just like Harry's, money spoke and the bartender hardly cared who sat at his counter as long as they paid.

"Whiskey, please."

He paused. "Are you sure, ma'am?"

I ignored the ma'am, I wasn't there yet. I set money on the counter, ensuring I received his attention. The moment I did, a smile spread across his lips.

"Whiskey. Straight."

He flipped the glass in his hand and set it in front of me. Grabbing a bottle from the shelf, he poured slightly more than was customary. I appreciated the attention.

His eyes widened when I slammed the drink. I put my glass down and tapped the rim. The man knew how to earn a tip. He poured another drink. This time I swirled it about, taking in the aroma. It wasn't the finest whiskey, but it had a mossy quality I enjoyed. Now I sipped.

"You're not from around here." He made it a statement. He

grabbed a rag from below the counter. If he had a wooden leg, I could imagine he and Harry were the same person. He started cleaning the counter, polishing it as if there were hundreds of patrons spilling their spirits.

"No. I'm from New York."

"Business or pleasure?"

"Are they exclusive?" I teased. Susan Lee might even ask if I attempted to flirt. I found men were more than willing to do business if there was a hint of sex on the table.

"Business," he laughed. "And you're a woman who knows how to get what she wants."

Bartenders by nature had their own superhuman abilities. The best of them bordered on telepathic. Reading their patrons, they knew how to direct conversation. They played confidant, lending a listening ear for the price of alcohol. He might be younger than Harry, but he had learned his trade well.

"Observant," I said, taking another sip. "I could use your observation right now."

"I suspect I don't have a say in the matter."

Was he flirting, or was this the charisma Harry lacked? Perhaps when I got back to the city, I'd make sure Harry developed some new business skills. I leaned over the bar with a slight glance over my shoulder.

"Do they work at Harvard?"

He nodded. "They come in after work on most days for their afternoon spirits. They're academic types, always talking some nonsense I can't follow."

"Do you know what departments?"

"Math and science, I think. They talk a lot about theories. I can never follow them."

"Drink of choice?"

"Bourbon. Cheap. You're going to need to bribe them."

I smiled. The man knew exactly where my questioning led. I

took another sip from my glass. With one last swirl, I finished the whiskey. Dr. Stewart might have a secret organization supporting his efforts, but I had the people. Susan Lee would be proud of me connecting, but she'd be none too thrilled to know why. I put this in the win column.

"A bottle of your finest. I need a few academics to sing."

The bartender might be in his mid-thirties, and if I had enough time, I might consider seeing if his torso was as muscular as his arms. I had to stop undressing him with my eyes. While I paraded around as Eleanor Valentine, I didn't know if Edward and I were still an item. Did almost dying from his associate nullify our relationship? I didn't quite understand where we stood as far as he and I were concerned. Thankfully, I didn't have the time to question my choices.

"Any woman willing to barge in here and buy her way into a conversation with those professors is somebody I'd like to know."

I blushed as he slid the bottle across the table to me. Setting down five glasses, he made my face turn a darker shade of red as our eyes met. A man's smirk reveals as much as a woman's hides. If I had the time, I had no doubt, he'd let me see his naked torso.

"Keep the change." I set the money on the table and grabbed the bottle and glasses.

I accentuated my hips as I walked toward the long table. They quieted as I approached, but their eyes couldn't decide if they should stare at my breasts or the bottle of bourbon in my hand. I sat at the end of the long table, getting comfortable as I pulled out the cork.

"Can I help you, miss?" asked a gentleman with white hair.

"Harvard's elite? Why yes, I'm sure there is plenty you could teach me." Yes, tease them with sex and booze. Just because I didn't like being treated as an object didn't mean I wouldn't weaponize my sex when necessary.

"Elite?" The man with mutton chops laughed. "This young lady has given me more recognition in a greeting than my department has in six years."

I poured the alcohol. Sliding a glass to each of the four men, I poured a drink for myself. "If I'm going to interrupt this meeting of minds, the least I can do is provide a hearty drink."

The men picked up their glasses. I gave a wink to the bartender who watched the scene unfold. He winked back and returned to cleaning. The men swirled their drinks, sipping carefully.

"Bold, a hint of citrus, quite a spectacular blend," said the white-haired professor.

All four men froze as I gulped down the liquid. There were those who appreciated alcohol for its complexity. Then there were drinkers who appreciated its effects. I made it well known which side of the fence I preferred.

I poured another. "You teach at Harvard?"

"Yes," said a man with a thick mustache. "We're in the math department," he pointed to white hair, "physics, and then there's poor Malcolm."

The man was younger than the other three. While the others sported intricate facial hair, it appeared puberty hadn't been so kind to Malcolm. He joined in the ribbing and waved the man off.

"Philosophy," he said.

I decided to try my hand in the conversation. "Is science and math not the execution of philosophical matters?" I was not an academic. I hadn't finished secondary school. If we discussed the particulars, then I'd promptly be lost. But I could pretend to understand their fields.

"That sounds like the hogwash Malcolm is always spouting," said the mustache man.

"Earlier today, I had a riveting conversation about the idea of determinism and the differences between the Copenhagen Interpretation and Everett's theory. Isn't this just the theory behind math or science?"

All four men took a moment to stare while Malcolm finished his drink. "I like this woman already," he said, raising his glass in the air. I shoved the bottle in his direction and let him refill his glass.

"Quantum mechanics," white hair said, "is not so easily explained."

"I agree. But I believe while you're looking at the specifics, our dear friend Malcolm is giving you theories to test. Am I right?"

The white-haired man gave a slight nod. "Not quite elegant, but I see your point of view."

The man with the mustache raised his glass. "To the mysteries of the universe."

"Cheers," I raised my glass to salute.

They asked questions. "Where did you come from? What brings you to Boston? How long are you staying?" We jested back and forth. While a war waged overseas, these men preferred to discuss the world of academics. I wondered if they were courageous men, or if they hid behind degrees hanging on their walls?

"I must admit, I didn't come over here to talk academics." The truth always seemed to be a shocking item that halted conversation. "I am interested in learning about one of your colleagues."

"A scorned lover?" asked Malcolm.

"An aspiring academic with an air of suspicion," I added

His words slurred. "Get to it, miss. Who?" The mustache man had drunk more than his share of the alcohol.

"Dr. Stewart, what can you tell me about the man?"

Three of the men shook their heads and rolled their eyes. It was Malcolm who maintained his composure, sipping from the glass. If I didn't know better, I'd believe the philosopher grew nervous at the mention of the doctor's name.

"He's a hack," white hair said with conviction, "pseudo-science at best."

"A hack? That's being polite. The man only has a position because of nepotism. I heard his grandfather is a legacy."

"A legacy? I heard he and the dean …" mustache man let his mumblings fade as he sipped.

"Malcolm?" I knew in my gut, this man knew Dr. Stewart.

"He talks about …" Malcolm searched for the word, "theories. It's not science, but he has wild ideas about things science can't explain."

"Do you believe him?"

Malcolm nodded. "There are more things in heaven and earth, Horatio, than are dreamt in your philosophy."

White hair laughed loudly. "Did you just quote Shakespeare to justify a man's mad ramblings?"

"To be honest, I'm more surprised that you knew it was Shakespeare." Malcolm shot the man a stern glance. The gentle ribbing between the men was admirable, but I still didn't have my answer.

"Is he a good man?"

"Are you fishing for a husband?" asked mutton chops.

"A man should be so lucky," I gave him a grin, joining in their levity. "I've read his research, and I have to admit I'm intrigued."

"He's harmless," white hair said.

Malcolm eyed me intently, giving a slight nod toward the door. He finished his glass and stood, gathering his things. "Gentleman, as always, it's been a pleasure, but I must be on my way."

Malcolm made his way to the door, giving me one last glance as he left. I'd wait a few minutes before I departed. Whatever he wanted to say, he didn't believe he could speak in the presence of his peers. I finished my glass. I might be a veteran drinker, but loosening these men's lips had left me wobbly.

"Gentlemen," I gave a slight bow, "I thank you for your company."

Raised glasses saluted me as I headed for the door.

The lack of facial hair made it hard to determine his age. Malcolm's baby-face hid the growing crow's feet at the corner of his eyes. At first glance, he might be in his mid-twenties, but the way he carried himself, I suspected he had reached forty.

"I wasn't sure if you'd come," he said.

I followed as he crossed the street. Discretion wasn't a worry as we walked within view of the bar window. I paused, staring at the building. An uneasy feeling set in my stomach as I caught sight of the man behind the bar restocking the shelves. A shiver worked its way up my spine until my shoulders shook. I couldn't put my finger on it, but the bar burned its way into my mind. When I could call the visions freely, I'd be sure to see into its future.

"Are you okay?"

"I'm fighting a sense of déjà vu," I said.

I walked away from the bar, following Malcolm along the streets of Boston. The man didn't hide the paranoia as he glanced back and forth. He knew. It was the same feeling I had on the train.

"You know more about Dr. Stewart than you're letting on."

"I know plenty about the man," he said, "he's the topic of many whispered conversations."

Truth? Sure, why not. "You know he's the head of a secret organization in Boston?"

Malcolm stopped walking. I caught up to him, shoulder to shoulder. We continued along the sidewalk. "I didn't come here without doing my homework."

"Then you know they are everywhere," he whispered.

"I am certain of it," I said. "I wouldn't be surprised if they followed me now. Dr. Stewart and I met earlier. He struck me as…" I couldn't quite sort out the word, "good? Yes. Good."

"Good?" he repeated. "I guess I could say good, but I have only met with him a few times. I harbor no ill will toward the man. But they say his academic pursuits into the pseudo-sciences get somewhat extreme."

"How extreme?"

He stopped again. "Miss, are you sure you want to associate with a man who believes in ghosts?"

I let out a slight laugh. His choice of words couldn't have been more ironic. "I believe his sciences are more accurate than you may believe."

He raised an eyebrow. "I do not want to know."

I shrugged. Malcolm held onto his beliefs, refusing to let Dr. Stewart shake them. Something about the man struck me as weird. I couldn't quite put my finger on it, but his willingness to divulge information away from his peers made me nervous. I wouldn't turn my back on Malcolm as I walked away.

It was good, however, to know there was a certain amount of openness about Dr. Stewart's pursuits. Where the Society had remained clandestine, a secret cabal, it appeared Dr. Stewart preferred a route of legitimacy.

"And what of this organization? What do you know?"

The buildings seemed to spread out as we walked. The road split and we arrived at a common area, brick laid out in a vast island. Flat space only made the church at the other end more spectacular. The tips of the building reached the heavens, towering over all the other buildings. I found myself fixated in the same uneasy feeling from the bar.

"I hear they meet in the dead of night," Malcolm said, "trying to summon spirits. Devil worshippers, I say. He might be a cordial man, but you do not want to associate with them. Their very souls are corrupt."

Would Malcolm feel the same about me if I revealed I knew

his fate? I had once believed that the Devil himself taunted me with images of the future. As this educated man spoke of the damnation of men, I understood the Society's need for secrecy. Just as Susan Lee found it difficult to digest my abilities, perhaps mankind was not ready to know we walked among them.

"Be careful," he said.

"Do not worry about me. I have seen the face of the Devil, and Dr. Stewart is not she."

Malcolm raised an eyebrow and quickly dismissed his curiosities. "I must be on my way. I hope you find what you are looking for."

"As do I," we shook hands, and he started in the direction of the bar.

I wandered across the plaza, admiring the monolith of a church. The spires were intricate, not quite gothic, but similar. In a city that prided itself on the preservation of history, the church had modern touches to it. The balcony high above the doors allowed its occupants to see into Boston, a beautiful view in every direction.

I squinted, staring at the balcony. A lone figure stood outside, perched, watching the expanse of Boston. At this distance, I couldn't make out the occupant, but it wore robes, making it impossible to tell if it was a male or female.

The hair on my arms stood on end, surprising considering the lack of wind. I waved my hand in the air and found there was no breeze, not even by my own making. While there might have been a scattering of people about the plaza, now it stood empty. I spun about, hunting for Malcolm, but even he had vanished.

"I'm not here," I whispered. These were the commons signs of a vision. Whatever power allowed me to see the future sent me a message. All I could do in response was observe.

The figure on the church balcony remained. I gasped aloud as wings spread—I had seen the woman before. She climbed onto the wall surrounding the balcony and I imagined to any other onlooker, they'd believe God had sent an angel to watch over them. But I knew there were no angels, this woman, she was something the world had yet to see.

The buildings decayed, entire sections of walls were blown away, crumbling. Even the pavement of the plaza looked worn, grass growing through the cracks. The scene shifted, and I was no longer standing in the Boston I knew. It appeared as war-torn as Europe, and I imagined this must be what it looked like after the Nazis attacked.

Giant metal things crashed into buildings. Men made of steel were strewn about the street. My heart quickened. I had seen the future a thousand times, but none felt as bleak as this. I worried. Did mankind do this? Was our destiny for a world on the brink of destruction?

The woman with the wings came running toward me. Where I expected feathers and a halo, I could only call her a serpent with legs and wings. I braced for impact as she charged. Eyes clenched shut, I felt a cold rush along my skin.

I spun around to see her running away. The ground shook under my feet. I nearly tumbled. The woman with wings slowed until she came to a stop. Turning around, she looked at me. Not near me, not through me, but me. She locked eyes, walking closer.

"Eleanor?"

I gasped at the mention of my name. Never had a vision acknowledged my existence. Always the observer, I found myself part of my own vision.

"How do you know me?" I asked. If this desolate future were to come to pass, I needed to know what role I played. This was the reason I continued trying to shake the restrictions of fate.

The woman was green, not sickly, but a bold deep forest green. Her eyes were almost as alien as the rest of her. Despite the yellow, they held a sense of compassion. Whoever this woman might be, she had a story to tell, and somehow, I was now part of it.

"You do something that changes the world, Eleanor Valentine."

As she mentioned Edward's name, I nearly cried out in joy. If she knew me as Eleanor Valentine, perhaps there was hope to save him. There were so many questions I wanted to ask this phantom from the future. How did she have wings? What shook her? What did I do to change the world? My head swam with the possibilities.

"Did I do this?" I waved to Boston's destruction.

The woman shook her head. She didn't quite smile, but her lip turned upward enough to signal she understood my question. I wanted to reach out, to touch her skin, to make her real. Her clothes were fitting, almost as tattered as this world. The ground shook again. I ignored it, fixated on her eyes. I imagined if I stared hard enough, I might see more—discover her identity.

"You prevented this from being so much worse." The words were cryptic but sympathetic.

"I can do better."

I believed my words. If this was a future yet to come, I could find a way to rectify it. There would be no desolation in Boston. If I could choose the right actions, I might prevent it. Dr. Stewart held answers, I needed him to help unlock an ability I had tucked away.

"Thank you for saving me, Eleanor."

The woman gave a slight bow and turned to run. I listened as the world exploded behind me. Falling to my knees, I covered my head, fearful debris would strike me dead. A war had reached Boston, and somehow, I found myself in the middle of the battlefield.

Then nothing.

I peeked, worried I might have died. My hands touched the pavement, and I found myself joyful as I returned to my own time. The sun continued to shine and the splendor of Boston had yet to whither. I whispered a thanks, glad to have returned unscathed. I stood, brushing the gravel from my knees and hands. Turning to the church, I set aside my doubts and forced my determination to the surface.

"I will do better," I whispered.

Chapter Eight

1931

Frank did not know how to cook. Despite that, I finished the bologna sandwich, saving the potato chips for last. It wasn't until the third day I dared to crack open the door and slide the plate into my room. I sat on the foot of the bed, careful not to get crumbs on the blanket.

One by one, the chips vanished. I washed it down with a glass of warm milk. It wasn't the most memorable meal, but it hit the spot. My stomach grumbled, thankful I finally braved the open space. It wouldn't be long before biology required me to brave my way to the bathroom.

The orderlies required daily showers, threatening to hose us down if we didn't comply. They'd watch, staring with uncomfortable expressions plastered on their faces. The hospital left no room for modesty. I raised my arm, scrunching my nose at the smells my body insisted on making.

I set the plate on the nightstand. The ghosts had made it clear I'd leave the room and while I was out, Frank would see to the dishes and make my bed. They were as persistent here as they had been within the walls of the hospital. I didn't resist.

Standing at the door, I reached for the handle. I paused to consider what lay on the other side of the door. Not Frank, him, the ghosts had already shown me. But in New York City there were tens of thousands of souls, ghosts I had yet to see. Opening the door meant inviting them in, expanding my world. Over the past few years, that world had been restricted until I stood alone in a room, in an apartment, somewhere in New York.

Whether bravery or stupidity, I opened the door and decided to face the world.

Across the hall, I darted into the bathroom. I shut the door, trading a small room for an even smaller one. Inside, on a hamper next to the sink, Frank had neatly folded clothes. A small note rested on the top, "I didn't know your size." A t-shirt and sweatpants with a change of socks waited for a cleaner me.

The circular mirror over the sink revealed a disheveled girl, hair matted and knotted on one side. I touched my face, to ensure I was looking at myself. In my mind, I still thought of myself as the little girl on the farm, but that girl had vanished long ago. I pulled off my shirt and removed the blue pants supplied by the hospital. At one point, I might have been a young girl, but she had grown into a teenager. I gave a slight nod, introducing myself to a new version of me.

Turning on the shower, the hot water surprised me. It had become a luxury in the hospital. As I stepped in, I never wanted it to end. I doused my hair in shampoo and took the bar of soap and lathered it on a washcloth until foam appeared. I covered every inch of my body, washing away the last remnants of the hospital.

As I stepped out, I toweled off. The fabric was soft, almost fluffy. It was hardly new, but it beat the towels I had grown used to. I wrapped it around my body, satisfied that a new Eleanor emerged from the shower. My fingers ran over a brush. I was certain it hadn't been used on Frank's bald head.

The morning my mother took me to the hospital had been the

last time I'd brushed my hair. She pulled at the knots, tugging harder than normal. In the mirror, I could see her crying softly, focused on the task at hand.

I held no ill will toward Momma. In her situation, I might have done the same. Cursed with a daughter who refused to talk, a husband buried in the cemetery with a smaller adjacent plot for her son, I understood her decision. Despite my empathy, I had no desire to seek her out and learn what became of her. Perhaps she remained at the farm. Or maybe she had started a new life. I wished her the best. *My* mother only lived in memories.

I tugged at my hair, brushing it until the rat's nest straightened. It hadn't been cut in years and nearly reached my waist. I searched a basket by the sink and found a pair of scissors. I collected my hair by my neck and cut. The scissors trimmed bit by bit until I held a handful of blonde hair. I continued until I stood with uneven shoulder-length locks. It'd dry and be shorter and perhaps it'd look a mess, but this new Eleanor didn't have long hair.

I gathered the severed locks and tossed them in a tiny wastebasket. Now, staring in the mirror, I almost didn't recognize the woman gazing back. Her hair might be lopsided, but the new Eleanor didn't care. I touched my face again, and for a moment, I almost spotted a smile. Fleeting, yes, but it was the start.

"Hello." Raspy, the voice was almost as different as my face. While I had grown, in my head my voice remained that of a child. But I was surprised to find it had changed as much as my body.

"My name is Eleanor," I whispered.

I touched the glass, wiping away the thin layer of fog. I glanced at the change of clothes, and imagined the world beyond this room, beyond this apartment. Scary as it might be, I wanted to explore.

"Nice to meet you, Eleanor."

Chapter Nine

1943

The arboretum did not disappoint. As the car pulled to a stop, I waited for the driver, the same man from the taxi, to step out. Peering through the window, I found myself amazed at the archaic architecture of the building. It reminded me of something from Europe, like the pictures of Grecian Temples. The driver had said they filled the interior with exotic flowers from around the world. As he opened the door, their fragrant scent wrapped about me.

"Good day, Mrs. Valentine. When you are ready, I will take you to the train station."

I gave a quick curtsey and proceeded from the driveway up a long and wide path. The tiny pebbles forced me to stop and collect myself, pushing away the effects of the alcohol. Drinking with scholars wasn't much different from drinking with former military. They put away the booze and as quickly as you allowed them, they told their stories.

The interior of the arboretum defied all expectations. The lobby was a small rectangular room, the corners occupied by marble pillars. While it didn't make an impression, the expansive doorway into a large domed room made up for it. The pillars grew, towering high above my head to hold the dome above a large tree. I expected potted plants, but what I found was a small jungle filled with flowers along the wall. The ceiling was composed of windows, letting in the setting sun. Striking the glass, the light fractured into rainbows dancing along the upper walls of the room.

"It might be one of the few locations in Boston that leaves you as humbled as the museum."

I didn't look to Dr. Stewart. I craned my neck, watching how the light hit tiny prisms and dispersed into the tree below. It appeared a feat of science that they kept such a majestic tree in pristine condition inside the room.

"It's beautiful." I couldn't find a word to encompass the immensity of the space.

"I wasn't sure if you would come," he admitted.

"You had me trailed. You know I spoke with your colleagues. Malcolm was a plant." I wasn't sure, but I would take the gamble. "The other three men, they truly think you're a quack. Malcolm, however, you put him there to feed me the information about your powerful organization."

"Observant."

"The question is why? Did you do it because you wanted to hold a bit of fear over my head?" I hadn't made eye contact with the man. I hated to admit it, but I tried to see this problem through Olivia's eyes. How would she play the man and what might she do to gain the upper hand?

"Let me begin—"

"Your organization is falling apart."

Now I eyed the professor. Dr. Stewart held a stern face. Had this been poker, he might have won the hand. But his refusal to speak confirmed my hunch. I suspected that Malcolm might have an ulterior motive. He had been a good operative, but I had been dating a telepath for long enough to know when words and actions did not align.

Time froze as I summoned the ghosts. I needed to confirm that there were none of his men and women hovering over us. If we were going to have an honest conversation, I didn't want him grandstanding for his disciples. There were only a handful of ghosts roaming through the massive room, all of them belonging to one of us. If there were people in the wings, they weren't close enough to hear our words. This time I checked over my shoulder. Clear.

"Let's be honest with one another." I circled the man, watching his face. While I might have seen through his facade, it didn't diminish his posture. Back straight and shoulders broad, the man didn't find me intimidating.

"Did you just look to the future?" he asked.

I nodded. The man's eyes went wide, surprised. I wonder if he watched me as a scientific curiosity or if he was more shocked at how easily I went in and out of my abilities. Or perhaps he knew more about my abilities than he let on.

"We left the Society, that much is true. Once it divided, we spread to the United States. We had particular areas of interest, and our research fed back into the Society."

"Until it didn't." I saw where the divide took place.

"I haven't lied to you."

"What is it with secret societies and their ability to lie through omission? Is it something they teach you? Or do you bring that nifty ability to the table?"

He didn't find my candor nearly as endearing as I did. The alcohol hadn't left my system and holding my tongue in check wouldn't happen during this conversation.

"They have systematically eradicated us. While we pursue knowledge, they find power more endearing. We study mentalists, hoping to bring in a new era where your abilities can benefit all of mankind. They want to hold people with abilities hostage and only use them for their personal gain."

"The men in bomber jackets."

"The Barren," he snarled as he spoke the name. It seemed we held a similar distaste for the sadistic men carving into our people. "At one time, they were a necessity when the church waged a war against enlightenment. But even then, they were men robbed of their souls, payment for the wealthy to enter the organization."

I found it even more unsettling to hear the thought aloud. "I've had experience with those damned creations."

Dr. Stewart nodded. "I suspected they were the culprits behind the killings. But whatever happened to Dr. Roberts?"

"Killed by his wife. Olivia had them use the Barren. They cleared out the mentalists once Olivia and her entourage arrived."

"Figures."

We were talking in circles. The man had something sitting on the edge of his tongue, a piece of information he withheld. I could see the way he paused, staring down at his shoes, giving himself time to formulate a plan. There was no way I could maintain this dance long enough for him to muster the gumption to speak.

"What is it you want, Dr. Stewart? Be frank." I walked up to the man, only a foot between us. I wanted to study his face as he spoke.

The ghosts abandoned me as he reached out, his hand gripping the side of my face. He didn't strike, just rested his hand as if he might pull me into a kiss. I found it flattering, but for the moment, I held out hope—

The doctor froze, the sensation of his hand becoming distant. I stepped back, thinking I moved away from his physical self. The room turned black and a faint outline of Dr. Stewart faded into the nothingness. I touched my cheek, searching for the rough edges of his fingers. Even though I couldn't find his hand, there remained an echo. It reminded me of the night with Edward on the roof while I beat muggers miles away.

If Dr. Stewart sent my abilities into action, then perhaps this trip to Boston had been well worth the time. Even Gregory hadn't been able to elicit this talent. I came to Boston seeking allies, but I had all but lost hope in a legion of academics. I might have been wrong in thinking it was brute strength I needed to win this battle.

"Geez," I said, annoyed that yet another person knew more about my gifts than me.

The lamps in the room revealed the edges of a bedroom. The walls were decorative, fine wallpaper giving away the luxurious nature of the room. It took a few seconds, but the four-post bed faded into view. Did he have abilities? Or did he understand how to trigger my gifts? If he did, could he direct them? Was I seeing a random event or did he steer the vision?

Laughter. *My* laughter. Bodies moved underneath a heavy blanket on the bed. I didn't need to see the writhing to know what took place. The blanket pushed back as a figure sat upright, gyrating in an all too familiar motion. The hair made it clear I was on top of a man. Perhaps this might be a celebration from defeating Olivia, a romp to congratulate me for saving New York.

The grunts were not as familiar.

My visions were almost as frustrating as they were revealing. The man I straddled was not Edward, and now I had a moment to speculate before I reached the bed. I suddenly felt Dr. Stewart's hand on my cheek, a reminder of standing in the arboretum.

"No," I whispered. "Really? Really!"

I moved next to the bed to see I had been right. Holding my future self's hips, Dr. Stewart had his eyes closed, enjoying his, no our, carnal pleasures. By seeing this, the future had become written in stone.

The room vanished. I staggered backward as I stood in the

arboretum. Dr. Stewart held his hand out, a look of worry spreading across his face.

"Did you see the future? What happened?"

"How did you do that?" I didn't know if I should feel violated by him triggering a vision. I was more annoyed than angry.

"Touch," he said if it explained everything. When I didn't nod in agreement he lowered his hand, tucking it neatly into his pocket. "Physical contact can cause a flare in a mentalist's abilities."

I was about to argue, but I thought back to the visions. There were plenty of instances when they flared to life. The ones without human contact seemed to vary wildly, sometimes focused on the person I was thinking about at that moment. But all the visions involving human contact existed between myself and them. Consider me impressed with this new bit of knowledge.

"What did you see?"

"Nothing you should be concerned with. I'm going to repeat myself one last time," I stayed out of his reach as I collected myself. "What do you want with me?"

"The same thing you want."

"To take down the Society, to stop them from securing a hold on New York? Please tell me you want to destroy them."

He shook his head. I would not like whatever came out of his mouth next.

"Not destroy," he said calmly, "claim."

The arboretum was more than a delightful stop while exploring Boston. While it served the public, it was a privately-owned business. Owned by one of Dr. Stewart's flock, it allowed him the ability to come and go without disturbance. He clarified that while his organization didn't flaunt their goals; they did unfortunately have to take on some social elite to continue funding. He claimed it was no different from a professor funding their studies, except there would be no published papers once he concluded his research.

We descended into the basement, and I couldn't help but think it was a bit too obvious a choice that a secret organization hid underneath an arboretum in the center of Boston. I expected cobwebs, perhaps dark robes, maybe even some light chanting. However, it appeared more like a library with lanterns lining the walls and gas lamps placed in the middle of tables surrounded by books on three of the four sides.

There were two dozen men and women gathered in the space. The people in the room ranged from university students to a man hovering near sixty. They were a motley crew, and I would have never suspected all of them belonged to the same organization. Even the taxi driver and Malcolm seemed out-of-place standing next to one another.

They tried not to stare, but it was obvious that I was the center of every discussion in the subterranean room. As we passed Malcolm and the taxi driver, they gave slight nods. Unlike the taxi driver, Malcolm refused to meet my eyes. Curious.

I waited to see men in bomber jackets or a vixen flaunting her sexuality.

"Everybody," Dr. Stewart said, "there has been much discussion about our newest guest. But let me introduce Eleanor Valentine."

There were whispers. I noticed several took a step back. Even in the dim light, it was obvious they feared me. After learning about Olivia and her tyranny over the Society, I understood their reluctance.

"Hi." Did I wave? Did I confess to being a precog? This was more attention than I had in years. I didn't like being the focus of so many eyes. I had to wonder how many of them knew more about me and my abilities than I did? Had Gregory known this bunch? Or did they scurry away when the Society grew corrupt?

Dr. Stewart pointed to one of the younger women in the room. "Precognition."

"The ability to predict events in the future."

"Noted precogs?"

Her head turned to the side. "Nostradamus. He is the only documented person with precognitive abilities. We have never—"

"We have." Dr. Stewart turned to me, stepping back. "We have discovered one, or I should say, she discovered us."

The whispering stopped being discreet. There were gasps, but many of them started discussing me as if I wasn't in the room. It was one thing to feel as if I was different, but to be the center of educational dialogue, I might as well be a cadaver with medical students poking at my dead body.

One of the young men raised his hand. "Did you know I was going to do that?"

I rolled my eyes. I assumed they would be of the same scholarly level as Dr. Stewart. It made sense that there were newer members, or those without his gift for scholarly discussion. I nodded. "I will do this once, and then you'll never ask me to perform for you again."

They hushed. For a second, I understood Olivia's annoyance with them. The mundane people found our gifts a spectacle. They wanted to see us pull a rabbit out of a hat. They gathered slowly, waiting for the magic tricks to begin.

"You ten. Hands behind your back. Hold up however many fingers."

Before they had even moved their hands, I summoned the ghosts. The room froze as I inspected the upheld hands of their future selves. Each of them had several digits hovering in the air. I ran through the numbers twice, making sure I didn't misspeak.

They put their hands behind their backs. "Two. Seven. Three.

One. Two. Four. Two. None. Three. One." Each of their eyes widened. "Come on now, show them."

They held up their hands. I performed for them. Now they whispered again, discussing the probability of me being able to guess accurately. They spit out math I couldn't fathom following. I would have done something more exceptional, but I didn't have time to be their magician.

"Come with me," Dr. Stewart said, "I have somebody who would like to meet you."

Underneath the arboretum there was the large main room where the majority of his disciples congregated, but there were more alcoves I hadn't noticed before. I wondered if they slept here, or if this was just where they gathered during the evening hours. How many were dedicated to this idea of a world beyond science? I had never given it a second thought, and *I* was somebody who defied logic.

Dr. Stewart led me to a small side room with a single table. At the far end of the table, a young girl hardly out of her twenties read an enormous book. It was almost comical, the size of the tomb compared to the wispy thinness of the girl. Lanterns hung about the room, but a small table light shone over the book.

"Veronica," Dr. Stewart whispered, "I thought you might want to meet Eleanor."

The girl moved a cloth bookmark into the middle of the book and heaved it shut. Her face confirmed that she must be a teenager. She smiled. The smile faded, replaced with a quizzical look. She stood, walking toward me, stepping around Dr. Stewart.

"She's one of them," Veronica said. Her voice held a sense of amazement, and I tried not to be startled by the way she violated my personal space. Dr. Stewart had done the same. I didn't like people who spoke too closely, and this was even more intimate.

"What is she—"

"She's not a telepath." Veronica eyed me from head to toe and back up again. She held out her hands, waiting patiently for me to take them.

"Be warned," Dr. Stewart said, "She'll take you for a ride."

Ominous. The man intentionally remained cryptic. Looking for the ghosts in the room, they all remained stationary. I checked over my shoulder again. I was learning.

Reaching out, I touched her hands. The moment we made contact, she gripped my fingers tightly. The room vanished, and we were thrust into the black. For a moment I thought she might be a telepath, and she thrust me into her version of the white room. Dr. Stewart was nowhere to be found, but Veronica remained in contact, her grip cutting off the blood to my fingertips.

"This isn't a white room, is it?"

I turned and found hundreds of Olivias, and hundreds of myself. We fought, hand to hand, beating the snot out of one another. In some she brandished a weapon, and in others I held a gun. As fast as I moved to inspect the scene, more appeared. Hundreds turned into thousands, and then it became impossible to count.

"You can see the future," whispered Veronica.

Veronica held onto one of my hands, letting go of the other. She pulled me along, watching the future play itself out. "You're fighting Olivia. Good. I hope you win. She's not a pleasant person."

I turned to look at my charge. "What are you?"

"I'm not like you, a mentalist that is. They call me a sensitive. I have no abilities of my own. But I can sense others. I'm the bridge between Dr. Stewart's world and yours."

"You made this vision happen? How?" I needed to know how she tapped into the visions. If I was going to defeat Olivia, I needed to master my abilities. All of them.

"I can interact with your abilities. They're there," she gave me a weak smile, "I just pushed them along."

"The visions never come when I want them. I've been trying for months…"

"They're there. The only thing stopping them from coming is you."

"I'm not—"

"You're scared. Knowing the future can be scary. Changing it is scary too."

The words were far beyond her years. The wisdom in those simple statements left me curious. What caused her to grow up before her time? Her face still held a fullness to her cheeks, as if puberty hadn't finished with her.

"I wish I could change the future. I'd finally be able to do good."

"Or perhaps you'd do bad."

I was about to laugh at the girl, but I held my tongue. Gregory had alluded to the same fact. I scoffed at the silly notion that I was too scared to summon my abilities. From the mouth of babes…

"How do you mean?" I was asking for advice from a child. Gregory, a knowledgeable empath hadn't been able to unlock my abilities. Edward, a gifted telepath in his own right, didn't hold the key. Could it be that this girl, this bridge, would hold the key?

"If you can change the future," her eyes reminded me of Claudette, wise in a way that defied her age. "Then all those moments you wished to change the future and didn't, they'd rest on your shoulders. For me, that's terrifying."

Benjie. Poppa. Olivia. Edward. The moments in my life where I stood idly by, cursing fate and swearing to destroy destiny, were too many to count. If I could change the future, then Benjie and Poppa might still be alive. Olivia would be dead. I squeezed her hand, suddenly aware of the guilt resting on my shoulders.

"You're wise, child."

"Will you tell me your story?" Much like Dr. Stewart, she held a curiosity. But unlike him, her youthful voice made the request sound benign. Did she come to this place because of her gifts, or had Dr. Stewart scooped her up as part of his research.

We were standing in the room again. She let go of my hand, taking a step back. Dr. Stewart had yet to lower his eyebrows.

"Was I right?"

Veronica nodded. "We saw thousands of futures. Her abilities are immense. I bet she rivals even Nostradamus."

Dr. Stewart pulled a chair from under the desk, taking a seat. "I assume Veronica asked for your story. She thinks of herself as a historian. She has heard my tale many times."

I shuffled across the room, sitting opposite Dr. Stewart, making sure I had a clear view of the exit. Even if I needed to flee, I wouldn't have been able to. The men and women of the Boston Society crowded the door, Malcolm in front of them all. They appeared harmless, but something about their fascination made my skin crawl.

"Don't mind them. I believe they are fascinated with the only precog they've ever met. Some have met Olivia and even Catherine, but you're a first in our history."

"Please," Veronica sat down, her hands neatly folded on the table. "Will you tell us your story?"

"You're not just proof that precogs exists." Dr. Stewart leaned back in the chair, making himself comfortable. "You're the possibility that a better tomorrow exists."

"I was born the daughter of a farmer..."

Chapter Ten

1943

I couldn't breathe inside the hotel room. The bed had been comfortable and the furniture nicer than expected. Despite that, it felt as if the walls were closing in. I walked down the street until large academic buildings stood high on the side of the street. I hadn't expected spending the night in Boston, so I held my arms close to my side, warding off the chilly wind blowing through the buildings of Harvard.

Even in New York, the name of the university carried a certain weight. I didn't know many people who attended college, but even I had heard of the prestigious institution. When I was younger, I enjoyed school. I had been exceptional at math, especially for a girl, as my teacher would say. Had my mother not dropped me off at the hospital, perhaps I would have been a nurse like her. I couldn't imagine myself studying the human body. No, I'd study literature.

I smiled at the thought, following in the footsteps of Baum, I'd create wild tales about a girl trying to save the people she loved. My life was stranger than anything I could imagine in a novel. Olivia certainly was a wicked witch, even more so, wearing the bright red dress. When this was over, I'd see about returning to school.

"When this is over..." It was strange to think about life after this. For a woman who could see the future, I didn't use my abilities on myself, at least not far into the future.

"Eleanor." The man's voice trembled. "Eleanor Valentine." I turned to see one of the many faces from underneath the arboretum. They had shared their names, but I couldn't remember if he was Tom or Patrick. I had never been good with putting names to a face.

"Yes." Dr. Stewart made it clear that he spread his people throughout Boston. I assumed with me here, he'd brought them close, wanting to monitor my movements. I gave him a slight nod. "Can I help you?"

"Are you really attempting to overthrow Olivia?"

The man inched his way closer. I didn't need to summon the ghosts to know the hand hidden in his trench coat's pocket held a weapon. Did Dr. Stewart send the man to kill me, or had Olivia? It was becoming increasingly difficult to figure out who wanted me dead. Psychic problems, I guess.

"I am. Are you going to stop me?"

He froze. The man feared me. He struggled to maintain eye contact, his eyes darting back and forth. Whatever orders he had been given, he wasn't convinced he should carry them out. Either that or he feared I already knew the outcome of what was about to happen.

"I'm sorry." He shuffled forward, just out of arm's reach. "Olivia—"

The dress slid up my thighs as I spun, kicking him in the chest. I didn't want to hurt this young man, but I would not let one of her minions carve into my flesh. He coughed while he tried to pull the weapon out of his jacket pocket. I didn't have the patience to drag out this fight.

As I stomped toward him, he tried to punch me. I pushed his

fist across his chest, using the momentum to spin him about. Grabbing the coat, I pulled it off his shoulders, dragging it down his body, making it impossible for him to free his hand. Kicking at the back of his leg, he dropped, kneeling on the pavement.

"Did she send you?"

"No," he coughed. "Us."

Dammit.

The rope wrapped around my neck quickly. I didn't have time to stop it. A knee pushed into my back as I clawed at the garrote. I tried to pivot, but the owner held me in place, making it nearly impossible to move. I pushed off the pavement, hard, jumping into the air, and coming down, I raised my legs so the coward had to support all my body weight. Either this worked, or I choked.

My knees almost hit the ground. The attacker stumbled forward. My hand shot up between the rope and my neck. I used the slack to bend my head, sliding out from under the rope. I spun on my knee, bits of gravel digging into the skin. The pain didn't register as my heart started to beat faster.

Malcolm. I suspected his performance earlier had been too convincing. Try as he might, truth had fueled his speech about Dr. Stewart. I crossed my forearms in front of my face, absorbing the knee speeding toward my head. Falling, I tucked my chin to my chest and pushed off, giving me just enough momentum to somersault backward onto my stomach.

"You had your chance," I coughed. Olivia's henchmen had interrupted my evening stroll. The reverie about my future shattered as men attacked. This wasn't about survival, this was about a woman fed up with men inserting themselves where they didn't belong.

I got to my feet as the man came at me. There were no ghosts, I forced them silent, determined to handle the situation on my own. I'd sort out later if it was self-reliance or my ego later. Malcolm swung high, hoping to use his height to lean into the blow. In a fluid motion, I grabbed his wrist, spun my back to him and bent over at the waist. The man had no place to go but over my shoulder.

He landed on his back and I dropped to one knee, driving it into his neck. Still holding his hand, I turned it, popping the limb out of the socket. In New York, the white noise of the city would absorb his cries. In Boston, in front of this beautiful university, his howls echoed like an uncoordinated symphony. There shouldn't be pleasure in another human's agony, but there was. Victorious, I treated his wailing cries as a standing ovation. It quieted as the man slipped into a pain-induced slumber.

Clunk. The pain spread through my shoulder blades and nearly caused my fingertips to burst. Claudette would say it was like the hubris of Icarus. I pivoted, my kneecap moving to Malcolm's shoulder blades. The quick spin didn't end. The world around me continued moving, and I swore the ground tilted back and forth. Frank had checked me for concussions before. For the first time, there was a chance I had one.

I tried standing. The pavement wobbled as if I'd had one too many whiskies. Two men might be an annoyance, but the real foe was gravity. The man blurred, and even in the dark and with fuzzy edges, he displayed confidence. He considered himself the victor, and I was about to be his ticket to fame and fortune. I hoped Olivia put a significant bounty on my head, at least something in the thousands. She better *not add* insult to injury.

"Can't you see the future?" I'm glad to see my ego provided further complexity to my already overwhelming personality.

"I can." Each blink took longer than the last. I could see shadows moving as if they were alive. I wasn't sure if they existed when my eyes were open or closed.

"Then you know what's about to happen next?" He reached into his trench coat pocket and produced a gun.

I laughed. It led to more coughing and a fast-approaching headache. It was worth it. Men, when they're riding an adrenaline high, can be brought crashing down with the mockery of a woman. I assumed it had something to do with their insecurities in the bedroom.

"What the hell are you—"

"You're about to—"

A loud thud sent the man hurling forward. He landed inches away from me. Whatever struck him, hit hard enough to leave him unconscious.

"—to get smacked." I was mildly annoyed that my timing had been off. Rarely did I engage in witty banter with assassins. I would blame it on the pounding inside my skull.

"You looked as if you needed a hand," Dr. Stewart said, holding a wooden plank.

"I had him right where I wanted him." It was as if every hangover I had experienced in my life joined forces. I prepared to hurl, folding over until I was on all fours. It was disgusting enough, but doing it while half straddling a man, made it even more vulgar. It served him right for attacking me.

"I think we need to get you someplace safe." He pulled the jacket off the man, slipping the gun into his pocket. He draped it over my shoulders as he helped me to my feet. With his arm around my waist, he almost carried me as we walked.

"Why didn't you use your gifts? Surely you could have predicted this?"

I tried walking myself but stumbled. Dr. Stewart caught me, holding me upright. The taste of vomit in my mouth had me gagging and at any moment I would have to hurl again.

"I'm more than my abilities." That was all I could manage. There would be no more talking until I brushed my teeth and washed out my mouth.

"I am starting to understand." His curiosity might revolve around the gift of foresight, but for the first time, Dr. Stewart might have seen me as a human.

Maybe.

Chapter Eleven

1943

Dr. Stewart's neck smelled of musky cologne. I tried to ignore it, but with my face pressed against his shoulder, it was impossible. Under different circumstances, I might have enjoyed it, but at this moment, it made my head spin and threatened to make me heave. As he took the steps two at a time, I wrapped my arm tightly around his neck, hoping he'd put me down before I made a mess of his button-down shirt.

He lowered my legs, still supporting me with his arm. His knuckles struck the door. I was unaware of where we were, or how we had gotten there. There had been a fight. Malcolm? He had double-crossed Dr. Stewart and attempted to kill me. He… I couldn't recall what happened. I was seconds away from hurling. I couldn't recall how I wound up with Dr. Stewart carrying me. My eyes narrowed, and I stopped resisting. Then the world turned dark.

"No," he said, "stay awake."

He tapped my face as the door opened. There was a gasp and suddenly we were moving forward. Dr. Stewart didn't want me to fall asleep, but a few minutes with my eyes closed wouldn't hurt. I had been in worse shape before, nothing a night of sleep couldn't fix.

The voices grew muffled, Dr. Stewart's low tenor and another softer voice. I recognized the voice, but I couldn't place it. He set me down on a soft surface. There was a smell, a faint memory of a time long ago. I felt safe, as if I were home.

The farm.

The house hadn't been painted in years. Paint flaked, falling from the wall around the rear door. Poppa always said he would scrape the paint and put on a fresh coat. It was a cosmetic job, and it fell to the bottom of his to-do list. There were fences that needed fixing, fields that needed plowing, and livestock that needed tending to. We didn't have the prettiest house on the road, but it was ours.

"Is this where you grew up?"

She stepped from the air like a magician putting on a magic trick. One moment it was nothing more than a voice. A second later, Veronica stood at my side. She spun about, her eyes narrowing as she took in her surroundings.

"I was born here."

"Describe it to me," she said.

"You can't see it?" Edward and Olivia had been able to partake in the images in my head.

"I'm not a telepath. I get impressions and sometimes glimpses. It's not reliable. I can see you, but everything else is like seeing through fog on the harbor."

"It's the farm I was born on. I spent my younger years here."

"Tell me about it." Veronica stopped trying to see and instead focused on me. The girl's eyes were soft. I couldn't tell if they made her look older or younger than her years. I imagined that like me, her gift required her to grow up quicker than she should have.

"How long have you known you—"

"The house, please and thank you." Veronica's tone was harsh and a moment of anger flashed across those soft eyes. I couldn't blame her. I might not know her secrets, but we shared a pain we'd rather not discuss. Except, we were standing in a location where pain happened a hundred feet away in any direction.

"It's an old farmhouse, white. The barn is a ways from the house. It's really nothing to talk about. I'm sure there are many more like it across the Midwest."

"You're unconscious on my couch."

"What about your parents?"

Veronica didn't reply. There was no need. Through some supernatural way, there came an understanding when you found a person who shared your pain. I could have said sorry or offered my condolences, but we both knew it would be hollow.

I offered a slight nod. "Mine too."

"I know. After you spoke, I scribbled my notes as quickly as possible. I didn't want to leave anything out." I found it disturbing that she found me important enough to record for her history book. "Most people wouldn't call their fathers by their first names."

"He served with my father in the military. Before he died, that is. Frank promised to watch over Benjie and me."

"Your brother? Does he—" Veronica spotted the language of a broken heart. She wrapped her arms around my shoulders, giving me a powerful squeeze. Unlike the white room, or even in the actual world, it felt more like a memory than an actual embracing. It was the hug of sisters-in-arms, worn women who thought they were alone. Her arms tightened like the veterans at the gym. Without words, she spoke volumes. I see you. You see me. We.

"Why come to a place with so many terrible memories? You could be anywhere right now. Why come to a place that hurts?"

"This is a moment that continues to pull at my heart."

She cocked her head to the side. Earlier she had made a simple statement, something so naïve that I passed it off as the ramblings of a child. But Gregory had made a similar statement about me holding myself back. Even Claudette urged me to connect with my emotions. It was hard to explain, but in the last year, I connected more with myself than I had since I was a child. The cold, hard Eleanor, the girl carried from the hospital had peeled away. Now I struggled to discover who remained.

"I predicted my father's death. I knew the time and location. The ghosts showed me Frank delivering the letter to my mother. I've lived every tragedy twice. Back then, there was no way to change the outcome. Even now, if I push too hard, fate corrects the natural course of the universe."

Veronica held her tongue. She stopped looking and now studied me. In her head she must be drawing connections. Had I been her age, I don't think we would have been friends. Something about her demeanor said sweet, but at that age, I was busy bartering drugs with inmates at the asylum. Regardless, she waited and listened for the details.

"I wanted to die, for the ghosts to leave me be. If the Devil demanded his minions torture me, I wanted to face him myself."

I gasped, and the breath hung in the air. The bitter winter of New York didn't have the same crisp quality it did on the farm. My skin should be cold, shivering, but it remained a distant sensation. This wasn't like the white room where I experienced each movement. This was a memory, my brain trying to solve life's riddles.

"Eleanor." I faced the house while she faced the pond. I didn't need to turn around to understand the look of confusion on her face as it transitioned into terror. She had glimpsed at my memories.

"It's best you look away." I didn't need a dream to replay the scene. I had etched it into my mind. Veronica, like a defiant teenager, stood her ground, watching in horror.

"You didn't even try. Why didn't you at least try?"

Only Frank knew the horrors I witnessed. I shielded my reality from Susan Lee and even Edward. Whatever divine entity granted me these gifts, in that moment, the Devil had won. He left me a victim and a bystander in my own life.

"You watched him die." Veronica cried, the tears freezing along her cheeks. It must be the moment I ran to the pond. She turned and faced me, taking a step back. The horror intensified as she stopped seeing me as a scientific curiosity. To this young woman, I had become a monster.

My eyes shot open. I gasped for air, forcing my lungs to suck it in as if it were a precious commodity. Veronica fell backward, crawling away from me. From the corner of my eye, I caught her wide eyes and slack jaw.

Where was I? The last thing I remembered was the smell of Dr. Stewart. I was in an unfamiliar room. He entered, pausing at the doorway, trying to sort out why Veronica cowered as I coughed. I might be a curiosity, to the doctor and his people. But I could see in Veronica's eyes why the world feared Olivia, me, our kind.

On the surface, they may treat us like gods. But our abilities, they tortured us until we became twisted versions of ourselves. We were monsters. The only difference is some of us resisted.

"Eleanor, are you up here?"

I didn't answer Dr. Stewart. I wasn't sure of the hour, but Veronica had long since gone to bed. Even he had fallen asleep on the floor with a pillow tucked under his head. Her apartment had grown stuffy, and I needed to get out into the open. Much like my apartment, metal stairs outside the window beckoned me.

I couldn't put my finger on it, but the air in Boston had a unique quality to it. There was an element of history to it, like the first sniff of an old book being opened. I thought it might have a hint of salt, the breeze rolling in from the ocean, but I wasn't that lucky. Much like New York, the city at night was a spectacle.

The buildings were mostly dark and without the moon overhead, it was impossible to see far. Veronica's apartment didn't offer a view into the city proper, not to the tall buildings tucked between smaller brownstones. But it showed the diversity of architecture. When this was over and I didn't have a blood thirty banshee trying to rule my city, I'd see about taking an architecture class at NYU. I might have to bribe my way in, but it'd be worth it. Then I'd take an art class. Of course, I'd take a course in basic medicine, so it wouldn't be up to Claudette and Susan Lee to bandage my wounds.

"I want to go to university," I said.

Dr. Stewart's steps slowed. He hadn't grown accustomed to my offhanded comments. He still didn't understand me. Yes, he knew about my abilities and what that entailed. But he didn't comprehend the woman behind the visions.

"To better understand your abilities?"

I pulled the blanket tighter about my shoulders. "No. Nothing so boring. I want to learn about the world. I think I'd like to learn about architecture. Why do men insist on creating buildings that reach to the heavens?"

"I see." He didn't, but eventually the academic would study me until he did. "I suppose I can help you enroll."

"I never finished grade school."

"Ah yes, the hospital."

"And religion, maybe philosophy too. I know how to fight. I have the meanest right hook you've ever seen. But I want to know why the world is this way."

"You and me both." I believed him. Dr. Stewart might house enough secrets to fill a baseball stadium, but beneath it all he was

a professor, an educator, a student of life. I envied that, his identity. Beneath my powers, I still didn't quite know who I was.

"Why did you come up here?"

"I wanted to hear Boston breathe. It's foolish, I know."

He walked up to the edge of the roof, standing next to me.
Without his glasses, he didn't quite look like an academic. He was
attractive, with a chiseled jawline and the start of scruff coloring
the lower half of his face. I would dare to even call him
handsome.

Dr. Stewart never stopped studying. Even in the dim light, I
could see his eyes darting back and forth as he absorbed whatever information Boston fed him. Not only did I understand that
distant gaze, but I had been known to do the same. Seeing the
future made it nearly impossible to focus on the now. I was glad
to know that it wasn't a trait unique to mentalists.

"It's not." He coughed, another tell he was uncomfortable.
"Foolish, I mean."

"Are you always this uncomfortable around women? Or am I
special?"

I grinned when he put his finger to his nose, prepared to push
up the glasses he forgot two stories below. The man would never
be a worthy poker player, but it was good to know his body gave
away what his mouth didn't.

"It's okay. I'm starting to understand. Whenever I reveal my
gifts to somebody, they get awkward. It's hard to talk to a woman
who already had the conversation. Or worse yet, a woman who
knows every decision you're about to make."

"It is rather odd. At least with a telepath they only know the
here and now. With you," glanced in my direction, eyes burning a
hole in the side of my head. "It appears as if social conventions go
right out the window."

"What can I say? I like to break the rules."

"I'm learning that."

"You don't need to be awkward. I'm still a person. For you, if you stop thinking so hard about it, it's like every other conversation."

"And for you, you've had this conversation. You've had every conversation we will exchange. It's a bit unsettling. You must give me time to adjust."

"Live in the moment, Doctor."

"I suppose I should say the same. It is difficult not to ask you about every image you see of me. I wonder if I would live life differently if I knew the outcome of my choices. Would it push away the fear of the unknown? Or would it leave me suffocated knowing there was no room for negotiation? You provide—"

There were no ghosts when I grabbed him by the front of his shirt. I pulled him close. He didn't resist as I pushed up onto my toes. My lips touched his, and he stopped being an academic. The years of rigorous studies fell away, and he reacted in a purely instinctive manner. His arm reached behind the blanket to the small of my back and he pulled me closer.

The man's stubble was coarse, scratching along my face as I bit at his lower lip. He held me tight as I let go of the blanket and put both hands on his chest. The man's button-down hid a chest with muscle hidden behind a bit of softness. He parted my lips and his tongue grazed mine. It only lasted a few seconds before he pulled his head away.

"Did you know—"

"Stop it," I commanded. "Some things are best left to chance."

"Sorry," he said, forcing a smile.

I gave him a pat on the chest before securing the blanket around my shoulders again. I didn't know if the vision of the two of us in bed would come to pass. A few days ago, I'd have said it was destiny. Now, I pondered the rigidity of fate. It wouldn't be bad to find a man who didn't ally himself with an egotistical maniac.

"Living in the moment?"

I smiled. He saw through the kiss to the lesson I'd attempted to illustrate.

"That wasn't so bad, now was it?" I let the ambiguity hang in the hair.

"I would say not." Even in the middle of the night, I knew that his cheeks burned a bright red.

"Indeed."

"Very much indeed," he added.

Chapter Twelve

1943

The train pulled into Grand Central and hissed as it came to a stop. Boston had proven more beneficial than I had expected. I had the pleasure of taking in museums, the arboretum, and even enjoying a drink with the locals. Besides that, I found myself with allies. I spent hours the night before telling my story, including every detail that led me to Boston. They listened, gasping occasionally as I went into detail about my confrontation with Olivia.

It was what happened next that endeared me to Stewart's ilk. They shared their stories of how they came to be a part of the organization. More than half of them had been part of the Society, members who joined to be a part of this intellectual group. One by one they recounted their dealings with the men and women in charge.

Fear.

Those at the top terrified them, and more than that, they feared the influence Olivia exerted over them. Dr. Stewart offered them a place to pursue their research beyond science, free of judgment. They spoke of ghost stories, hauntings, prophetic dreams, and an overwhelming sense of déjà vu. One by one, I understood why they gathered underneath the arboretum, hidden away from the world.

"We're here," Dr. Stewart said.

He stood, firmly wedging his bowler hat over his head. The man reached out, offering a hand as we stepped off the train. He was a gentleman. I could see the allure. I didn't find him irresistible enough to bed, but I could think of worse partners to undress.

"Do you think it is wise for you to be in New York?"

He shook his head. "Wise? No. Necessary? Yes."

"Will she know you're here?"

He shook his head again. "I might not have any gifts of my own, but research provides solutions occasionally. I might not withstand the full might of the witch's intrusions, but we're skilled at cloaking ourselves."

We. Dr. Stewart spoke about the necessity of stopping Olivia and putting an end to her growing network. Even if I chopped off the head, figuratively that is, the organization would find a new leader and it would continue. Dr. Stewart didn't want to see the mentalists fall apart, he wanted the entire organization disassembled, or at least redirected. I hadn't decided if his pursuits were entirely noble. One leader stopping another usually meant growing their own power base.

Somewhere, hidden amongst the throngs of mundane people, his followers were doing what they did best. Gathering intel, they hid in plain sight. His network had proven themselves more than able in that regard. It would be necessary to know all we could before confronting Olivia.

We walked past a newsstand and a gentleman held up the newspaper, reading an article on the inside. I slowed to scan the headlines, delighted to see the jewelry heist had a small article on the front page. Little by little, we made the city a safer place, but now it was time to make a grand gesture, something that would ensure New York wouldn't fall victim to a tyrant.

I picked up a newspaper to inspect the article. I reached into my purse, grabbing a nickel, and set it on the counter. It mentioned the men were dead when police discovered the robbers. But it was the ramblings of the survivor that interested me most.

"A man and woman in masks killed the robbers." Dr. Stewart read aloud. "I must say, Boston is by far a safer city than New York. Perhaps you should consider moving."

"Never," I said, "This is my city."

I tucked the paper under my arm as we walked from the beautiful building onto the street. He was as captivated by the scenery as I had been in Boston. He stopped to inspect the buildings and commented on New York's way of showing off its wealth. I couldn't argue with the observation, we were far more loud than Boston.

"Where do we go first?"

"First, Claudette. Then Frank."

"You want her to provide insight into me, is that right?"

I nodded. "You come with a great story and appear to have noble intentions. But let's be honest, so does Olivia. Claudette will know what I need to hear."

"It's only fair. You passed my test, I should do the same for you."

I opted for walking, letting him enjoy the best of New York. The streets weren't particularly busy. Every time we passed another soul, I inspected their arms, looking for the three wavy lines. I was convinced they were watching, and I'd be ready if they acted against Edward's treaty.

"What exactly are you a doctor of?"

"Psychology."

I had a flashback to the hospital and the men preparing to cut into my skull. They claimed it was for my own good. I tried to keep my thoughts to myself. It was difficult to concentrate as I thought of the man drilling holes into the heads of women. I needed to start a mental ledger, a list of all the men who needed to be brought to justice. Everybody at that hospital made the list.

"You don't approve?"

Dr. Stewart might be many things, but it was his power of observation that worried me. With the slightest furrow of the brow or downturned gaze, he seemed to read my thoughts. I found it almost as alarming as when Edward did it.

"I spent years around Olivia. When somebody can hear your every thought, you learn to read the physical expressions. Eleanor, you must speak freely. My profession by definition reserves judgment."

"Your profession attempted to peel back my scalp, saw through my skull, and prod at my brain. So, pardon me if I experience a chill when I hear my unlikely bedfellow is cut from the same cloth."

He didn't hide the look of anger on his face. The elegant manner in which he spoke broke as he tripped over his words. "My profession has its," —I found it almost amusing to watch this collected man turn flustered,— "darker moments. It's young. But I assure you, we should be studying, but not in such a barbaric manner."

"Good." The man didn't fear me. He hardly displayed emotion of any kind. "I wouldn't want to kill you and end this partnership."

Dr. Theodore Stewart flinched at the words. I hope he processed the threat, believing I would deliver. I would never be put in a helpless position again. He gave a slight nod, acknowledging my words as we continued walking. Did Olivia make the same threat to him once upon a time? The thought I had something in common with that witch made my skin crawl.

"I don't mean to alarm you, but we're being followed."

"One of yours?" I asked, maintaining an unsuspecting smile.

He smiled, taking my hand as if we were a couple strolling through the streets of New York. "No, most certainly not."

"Good," I said, "I have some aggression I need to deal with."

The headache persisted despite a steady regimen of aspirin. I longed for one of Claudette's bitter teas and the healing herbs she steeped in the scalding water. I could muscle my way through the pain, knowing she'd make me better within the hour. However, this time, I couldn't risk any amount of bravado. I imagined the flame burning in the palm of my hand and the ghosts started walking on the street alongside us.

"Slow your pace." I tugged at his arm. Steadily we slowed until we appeared to be two lovers enjoying one another's company. "I want them to catch us."

"Never have I met a woman quite like you."

"Enough with the flirting, Theodore." It flattered me that he found me wonderful in an academic manner. But a woman can only handle so much objectivity before she reaches the end of her rope. "When they reach us, I want you to stay out of the way."

"I'm capable—"

"Let me rephrase," I interrupted. "You *will* stay out of the way."

I took his silence as agreement.

We turned down the first alley leading toward Claudette's shop. It was wide enough to drive a car, but it provided the security of only two directions for confrontation. Their steps echoed in the enclosed space. Any attempts at discretion faded as I turned around to face our stalkers.

Two large, very large men followed us. I had spent years working in a gym, watching men strive to achieve this level of musculature. Soldiers were mostly lean beasts, but these two probably worked out every day and spent their free time picking up boulders.

"Did Olivia send you?"

The men chuckled. The taller of the two continued approaching. Buttons on his shirt strained to hide the overdeveloped pecs. I met men like him, they were overcompensating. He had either been rejected by too many women or when he finally lured them to his bedroom they laughed at a tiny penis. I bet the former. There was no way a man this ugly seduced women.

"You offed our boss." For dramatic effect, he ground the fist of one hand into the palm of his other. They were used to being intimidating.

"Bertolucci?" I was surprised. That was a problem over six months old. I had recent problems to deal with. "I suggest not dwelling on the past."

"We saw you and your pops that night."

I laughed. Partly to bait him, but also because it meant they fled before Edward showed and murdered their comrades. "So, you're the cowards who ran away? Oh dear Lord."

The laughing did the trick. The shorter man pushed his way past his friend, charging with his arms stretched wide. I didn't need the ghosts, but I didn't want to risk another disaster. Theodore wanted to see my abilities in action. I'd put on a show for the professor.

He slowed until he held still. His ghost launched forward, and I watched as he approached, and at the last moment, my ghost stepped to the side. Hooking his foot with hers, my ghost shoved him, sending him into a skid down the alley. That had been obvious, but it was the tall man who stepped into an uppercut that I needed to be concerned with. My ghost leaned back, the punch missing by inches. She tried to land a kick in his groin, but the man caught it. Twisting her leg, she spun to prevent a dislocated hip, landing hard while he crawled on top of her. Certainly not the outcome I hoped for.

The world sped up. The short man tripped, skid and I turned to the big man in front of me. I leaned out of the way of his punch. He froze again as I summoned the ghosts, determined to find an alternative outcome. My ghost stepped forward, then a second, and a third version followed. One his ghost twisted to the ground, another he managed an elbow to the nose, the third, however, managed to deflect a punch and land a jab in the kidney. That one, I wanted that outcome.

Time sped up. I followed the ghost's movements. The force of the blow shook my body as I tried to redirect his momentum. I wouldn't be able to deflect as many strikes as I could from Koji, but it provided me the first opening. Knuckles out, I jabbed hard at his kidney. Before he could recoil, or even shout, I let the ghosts guide me.

There were more this time, more versions of me. Had Theodore or Veronica done something the night before? Did they grant me access to the infinite possibilities the future held? The ghosts faded as I lost focus. It didn't matter, I saw the future I wanted, and where it would lead. He tried to drive his elbow into my head. I ducked, balled my fists together and launched upright. I caught him under the jaw. The snap of his teeth was loud enough it made mine hurt. He fell back, giving me the opportunity to focus on the short man.

Theodore held the gun out, prepared to fire if necessary. I waved him off, preferring my workout. The headache returned in force, thumping in time with my heartbeat. It was time to drop the short man, and my ghost sussed out the easiest way to achieve that goal.

The man tried the same move again. How dense was he? He lowered his center of gravity, making it more difficult to trip. But I had something flashier in mind. I took two steps toward him, sliding under his grasping paw. I grabbed his shoulder, swinging about until I landed on his back. I tightened my arms across his neck, squeezed, locking my arms in place. He hadn't seen it coming, but the desperate man was determined to get me off.

He leaned back, threatening to pin me between him and the wall. When we got close, I braced my feet against the wall and shoved off, sending us both forward. He tried to keep from falling, almost running headfirst into the wall across the alley. Flailing, he tried to reach over his back. His fingers wove into my hair and would have yanked me off except his body relaxed and he tumbled. One down, one to go.

"I'll need my knives in a moment." I huffed, trying to regain my breath. Theodore could have easily shot the men, ending the assault. But I wasn't done showing the benefits of my abilities. If he wanted to study me, I wanted him to see the full extent of the ghosts.

I forced the flame to stay lit. It struggled, dancing in time to the pounding in my head. I had been incapacitated before, cut off from my abilities. There was a fear that it might happen again if I wasn't careful. I couldn't match his strength, and I probably couldn't handle another deflection. Koji's training was useful, but at heart, I would always be a boxer. Frank would tell me to use my speed and wear them down. So I did.

The ghosts were only a second or two into the future. As the large man jabbed at my face, I rolled to the side. When he attempted a hook, I leaned back. I repeated the action, making him even more furious. Theodore continued to back up as I danced about the man, each blow only missing me by inches. A man didn't get that big by endurance training, he simply lifted weights. Each strike came slower and slower. Dodging each of them, I waited for the opening.

"We're out of room." Theodore must have backed himself against the intersection of the alley.

Jab. Jab. Hook. Predictable, even for a person unable to see the future. My hands tucked behind my dress, proving a point. It wasn't enough to win, I wanted to humiliate the man. After constant attempts on my life, I needed vindication.

Hook. I snapped my foot forward, driving the toe of my shoe into his groin. The man buckled over, clutching at his manhood. Hands together, I brought them down, clubbing the man on the back of the neck. I'm sure it hurt, but he was too concerned with his tiny package to even register the blow. He whimpered as he rolled onto his side.

"Knives."

Theodore handed me my bag. I grabbed one of the knives and thrust my purse into his chest.

"You're not going to kill them, are you?"

It was good to know the man had some level of compassion. That already made him the lesser of the evils. I started with the shorter man. It felt dirty, as if I were cheating, but I couldn't have either man follow me. There were enough bad guys. A few less would make my work easier down the road.

I knelt next to the shorter man, and with a fast swipe, I cut the tendon behind his ankle. I repeated it to the other. He woke and started screaming again. I stalked to his taller companion, his eyes tightly shut. I jabbed the knife into his ankle and turned. Now he wailed as he tried to swat at me.

Theodore's eyes were wide as I reached out for my purse. I didn't let the man see the pain spreading across my face. The night before left a red ring around my neck, and now my vision blurred as I snatched my purse. I tossed the bloody knife inside and moved quickly to Claudette's shop. At least once I was inside, she'd keep me from falling apart.

Chapter Thirteen

1943

"Theodore," Claudette said again. She rolled the word about in her mouth as if she were sipping wine. Her cautious tone made it clear she was as suspicious as I was. Frank would hate the man, and Susan Lee would be enamored with a professor. I needed the angels to give me a sign that I was on the right path.

"Is this wormwood?" Theodore raised a glass jar, inspecting the herbs inside.

"You know botany?" she asked.

"It can kill a man."

"Many things," she fought the curve of her lips, "can kill a man. But I do not partake in such brutalities, monsieur. This is a house of healing."

"Creole? No," he picked up another jar, opening it and taking a sniff. "Haitian."

"Oui." I sipped my tea, trying to read Claudette. The woman didn't like another person in the room being as knowledgeable as her. She provided me answers, spiritual guidance. I had never taken a moment to ponder her reaction if the roles were reversed.

The headache subsided and the salve along my neck eased the

rope burn. At some point, I wanted Claudette and Susan Lee to come together to discuss medicine. Perhaps between the two of them, there could be a discovery that benefitted all of mankind. I didn't pretend to know enough about either of their jobs to understand the potential.

"Eleanor mentioned you have," he searched for the right word, "gifts?"

I avoided her glare by taking a long sip of tea. We had never spoken about the rules of our relationship and if we could divulge secrets to another. Just because I had stopped hiding and confessed to any willing allies, it wasn't my place to give up Claudette. I would have to apologize.

"That child, she speaks before she thinks." Yes, I would have to apologize profusely.

"My name is Dr. Theodore Stewart. At one point, the Boston Paranormal Society was part of..." he paused. When the man grew nervous, he pushed up his glasses. He'd never survive a game of poker. "We were partners with the Society once. I do not believe in their methods. Yes, I believe in studying mentalists, but as partners, not as subordinates."

"He speaks the truth," Claudette said. "But he also comes with secrets so deep that not even the Loa dare speak them."

"I partook in a secret organization hundreds of years old. There are plenty of things I haven't said. I'm more than happy to—"

"No." Claudette waved him off. Whatever the spirits said to her gave her a slight smile. She glanced down at me and then back to Theodore. The rise of her lip gave away her amusement. I had a sneaking feeling that my vision of us in bed was now on display for her as well. Damn her spirits for revealing my sex life.

"He believes he is doing good work, but often so do bad people. But," the intensity of her stare forced me to shrink, "he will not do you harm."

"Thank you," I whispered. She gave me a light pat on the

back. When this was over, I wanted a dinner party. It would have New York's finest meals with hints of Haitian spices. We'd sit down and eat and enjoy each other's company. I filled my life with tiny compartments, and with this newfound honesty, I wanted them to blend. They may not become friends, but we'd sit, tell stories and perhaps find a new normal. Yes. I wanted something normal.

"Do you have a plan?" Coming from Claudette, the question held a thousand possibilities. Did she want to know about how we would deal with Olivia? Or did she want to know about his grand schemes? I knew her long enough that she chose her words carefully and allowed a person to interpret. Other than the Lao, it was the fastest way for a person to reveal their true selves.

"Ultimately, the Society has the potential to change the world. There could be innovations in medicine, psychology, even help us prevent wars. The possibilities are endless."

"And you're the person to usher in this era of change?"

He shook his head. "The interests of one man can be corrupt. Even the best of intentions can create discord for the masses. No, this has to be a group effort. I only stand here with you because my people requested it. We voted. The good ol' democratic system at work."

"Isn't that exactly what the Society attempted to do?" Claudette refused to relent. The woman had no problem putting the man on a stage, bombarding him with theoreticals. It made me wonder how much the spirits whispered. Did they leave room for her to question the man? Or did she take pleasure in watching him defend his ideologies?

"Attempted and failed. Mentalists aren't people to be revered. They're not test subjects. They're humans and should be treated as such. We ask them to use their gifts as if it were a day job. But we must be willing to support them and at the end of the day, all workers deserve compensation."

I had never thought of my abilities as being part of a job.

While women were assembling airplanes and building warships, I could use my gifts to change the course of the future. I had mild success with seeing the probabilities of different futures, but not enough that I felt as if I could change large events. I was close. Very close. Once that happened, I'd gladly use my abilities for the betterment of mankind. It'd be like cleaning up the streets of New York on a global scale.

"That's all well and good," Claudette sat down on a stool next to me. She pushed the herbs back and leaned on the counter, stirring crushed mint with her finger. "But what about Olivia? She won't relinquish her power easily."

Theodore pulled out a stool across the table and took a seat. The man pushed up his glasses. Since yesterday, his face had grown a shadow, and I couldn't tell if he'd be more or less attractive with a beard. While I wasn't a fan of facial hair, something about it added to his charm as an academic.

"First, we need intelligence. If we're going to confront Olivia and her ilk, we need to know what we're getting ourselves into."

"Why now?" I needed to know. If this was possible all along, why hadn't he taken the opportunity to stop her before?

"At this point, the Society has made no move to affect us. But if she's expanding her power base, how long before she seeks to reclaim our organization? She's a telepath, we'd have no ability to resist."

"That's not an answer."

He leaned forward. "You, Eleanor. You're the reason."

Flattered, absolutely, but that didn't make it any easier to understand. Claudette seemed satisfied with the answer. She grabbed the mortar and pestle, poured the excess herbs into the bowl and made her way back to her apartment.

"I'm not following," I said it low, as if that somehow voided my inability to fathom his words.

"I don't like to separate this into your people and mine, but we could never take on Olivia. It'd only require a nudge and one by one we'd bend to her will. But you, you've stood against her and survived."

"Hardly. Do I need to show you the scar?"

"What did you come to Boston in search of?"

"Allies."

"Did you think for a moment," he reached across the table. His hand hesitated for a moment before it rested over mine. "You're not the only one who needed an ally."

Chapter Fourteen

1943

Frank terrified me more than a woman capable of speaking to angels. In our years together, we remained open and honest with one another. However, we never broached the subject of boys. I had my flings, and I'm sure he had his, but that was different from introducing him to a guy. I should note, the last guy he met had joined an evil cabal and may have been privy to a woman attempting to kill me. My track record did not bode well.

The gym had become a second home for many who came daily. Whether fighting an opponent or an unseen enemy, there was safety inside those walls. For more than one soldier, the gym was the only thing keeping them from eating lead.

I gasped. "Oh, no."

In letters almost as tall as myself, "DIE JAP" had been painted across the windows. They had violated our sanctuary.

Koji. Something in my gut tightened. I left Theodore behind as I ran across the street. Similar slurs had been etched into the doors of the gym, and they had broken one of the windows. I panicked.

"Frank," I yelled. There were several men milling about. Their heads turned as I burst through the doors. Through the men stood a woman with tightly curled hair. Frank had called Susan Lee. Everything must be alright if they had called her to bandage the wounds.

"Eleanor." With a single word, Frank relayed the severity. I couldn't see what was wrong. I missed something. Frank attempted to cut me off. I should have let him. But no, always stubborn, I had to see. One of the vets stepped out of the way and I glimpsed his foot.

"Eleanor, no," Frank stood between me and Susan Lee. "You don't need to see this."

There was no reply. I stepped around Frank as if he didn't matter. Koji's feet were small for a man, almost normal size for a woman. The soles were covered in grime, as if he had been walking without shoes. None of the black covered up the streak of red on his left foot, or the stain on his heel. More than once I inspected them closely as he held a kick close to my face.

Susan Lee had the man's shirt torn open. I avoided watching her medical care, fearful I'd catch a glimpse of Koji's still face. As long as she continued moving frantically, there was hope. I wanted her to clasp her hands together and thank God. Anything, I just needed a sign that Koji would survive.

"I can't—" Susan Lee started, "I need a doctor."

"Did somebody call the hospital? An ambulance?" Why was he still on the floor and not being rushed to a hospital?

"No good," Michael said. "If he goes to the hospital, they'll put him in one of those camps. Poor bastard." Michael, a black man in a wheelchair made sure I understood the consequences of being born a different skin color. But even he admitted that he'd rather be black than Japanese. The war had elevated American's fear to a point where humanity melted away.

I almost screamed, but footsteps moving fast behind me had my hands balled into fists. I prepared to spin and punch when Theodore ran past. The man pushed his way between two taller men. He pulled off his jacket and started rolling his sleeves. He dipped low, putting his ear to Koji's chest before asking Susan Lee for a scalpel.

"I'm not prepared for—"

"Would these do?" I pulled a knife from my purse.

"Hurry," Theodore said, waving me closer. Frank took the blade from my hand and handed it to the doctor. I had assumed he had been a doctor, like the men at the hospital. It hadn't dawned on me that perhaps he had medical knowledge as well. I had questions, but first and foremost, I needed Koji to survive.

His eyes were closed while Theodore cut into his torso. I had seen plenty of blood before, never this much from a living person. One of his eyes was swollen shut and by the angle of his arm, I'd assume it was fractured. It must have been people, many of them. I couldn't imagine one person beating Koji in a fight, much less beating him to death's door.

"What happened?" There was nothing I could do for the man, no medical knowledge to help save his life. The muscles in my arms tightened and my hands clenched tightly, nails biting into the flesh of my palm. I couldn't heal him, but I *could* avenge him.

"It was those purist punks," Vinny said.

Michael wheeled closer, stealing a glance at Koji. "I've had run-ins with them before. It's a bunch of racist thugs. I've come home to 'Die Nigger,' on my door more than once because of them."

They had desecrated our home. These men attacked my family. Frank put his hand on my shoulder. I tried to shrug him off. His grip tightened. I looked at the man and where I expected to see sorrow, perhaps even sadness, I saw the same fire burning in my stomach. He nodded. Approval to do what I must.

"I'll go with you." I started to protest, and he shook his head. "They're my family too."

"Got it," Theodore dropped something on the gym floor. I didn't need to see it to know the sound of a lead round.

"Does anybody have thread and needle?"

Susan Lee opened her bag and pulled out a small metal tin. At home, she used it for stitching up the holes in a dress or socks. I had to commend the woman on her ability to be ready for even the scariest of situations.

Michael took ahold of my hand, giving it a light squeeze. Unlike Frank, or any other man in the room, the atrocity unfolding on the floor hit home for him. His eyes held a glimmer of kindness, but even he had angry tension balled between his brows.

Theodore sat back on his heels, wiping his forehead, careful to not smear blood on his own face. "The wound is closed. But he's going to need antibiotics. Do you—"

"Claudette," Susan Lee said. "I'll go."

"Get them," Michael whispered. The whisper had a tone to it. Show no mercy resonated under his encouragement.

Whatever rumors floated about the gym, about my masked hobbies, I confirmed. I squeezed his hand and gave him a reassuring nod. I had been on a journey, stepping out of the shadows and revealing my truth, a secret I guarded for so long. There was no point, not with the men in the gym. If Theodore and I were going to usurp Olivia, then we would play by new rules.

No more secrets.

"I will."

They gathered on the stoop as if they hadn't committed a crime. Cans of beer littered the steps. All four were loud and obnoxious. As an elderly woman passed, they whooped and hollered at her as if she were a piece of meat. With their tendency of harassing people, I was surprised they didn't hassle her more. Perhaps the whiteness of her skin offered a level of protection not awarded to Michael or Koji.

"Are you ready?" Frank asked. He served as the voice of reason, the deep bass sound that often pointed out when I stepped outside the moral black and white. I had drowned it beneath the anger.

"Yes." I pulled the mask over my face, tying it above my ponytail. Frank pulled a ski mask over his face, looking far too much like a bank robber. I wanted to go in the daylight, to drive my fists into their soft tender spots, but Frank forced me to wait until sunset. We were willing to be seen, but he demanded we remain anonymous to protect those at the gym.

Climbing down the fire escape, between the two buildings, I concentrated on Koji, the black and blue of his face. We had been tailing these men since this afternoon. I feared when we returned Koji might be dead. No, I couldn't think like that. I'd watch over him when I returned, but not until I assured it wouldn't happen again, at least not from these four men.

I spun about on the metal landing, reaching the ladder that'd drop to the alley. Each step down, I thought of Koji's feet. He practiced martial arts to find his inner calm, something I respected though I never managed. Even though he could fight, he chose not to. I hadn't known the word pacifist until I met Koji. I knew it, but I would never *be* it.

Frank followed, loudly clanking as he stepped down the ladder two at a time. Before I could charge from the space, he grabbed the collar of my jacket. He dipped down, so we were staring face-to-face.

"No killing."

Normally, I'd argue. This time, my idea of revenge held equal parts violence and humiliation. I wanted them to survive and wonder which of their crimes led to the retribution. I assume there was a long list. Even if they knew we were there to avenge Koji, I wanted fear beaten into them. But more than that, I wanted them to live with the ramifications every day of their lives.

"No killing," I said.

There were people on the street, few, but enough. An elderly couple walked hand in hand across the road, while a young man carried groceries to his door. Plenty of people had seen me fight, but most had been the victim and I, the savior. Now, we were about to look like thugs committing a crime.

Frank stood at my back as I approached the base of the stoop. All four men lowered their beers, trying to sort out what was happening.

"What the hell is this?" The man on the lowest step stood, crushing the can and chucking it to the side.

I held my tongue. I didn't want to let slip that I was going to batter their bodies in Koji's name. Silence, I learned, disturbed most people. They found when the gap between words drew out too long to be as threatening as raised fists.

"You threatening us? You come to our neighborhood, thinking you're going to what?"

I didn't want to rely on the ghosts, but after continuous fights and a knock to the head, adrenaline alone wouldn't make this easy. I set aside my ego and summoned the phantoms. The fight spilled out onto the sidewalk, and more than one passerby stopped to watch. Nobody stopped to interfere and more than a few turned their heads away, ignoring the men.

The goon at the top of the stairs stepped down, reaching out to hold on to his buddy for support. I wanted them sober for this. I wanted there to be no question that I brought hell to their stoop and that I won, not because I was sober, but because I was better.

"Let's have a little look-see," he reached for my mask. "Maybe she's a looker, guys."

His finger grazed my cheek. I held my ground. The ghosts emerged. One set grappled back and forth. As he extended his hand, I had a moment to catch the tattoo on the inside of his forearm. Where there should have been a half-naked lady or a sailor, there were only three wavy lines. These men believed themselves safe under the watchful eye of the Society.

They believed wrong.

I snatched his hand. Spinning it about, I forced him off the last step and onto his knees. I turned it further until his shoulder cracked. He screamed until I slammed my knee under his chin. I drew my fist back, prepared to drive my knuckles into his face when one of the men jumped, trying to wrap his arms around me.

"Goddamned broad." I stepped to the side, kicking him in the gut. Before he could spit the breath from his lungs, Frank clocked him across the face.

The man with the dislocated shoulder pulled himself to his feet while his bloody companion decided on Frank or me. The two men on the stoop charged Frank, throwing punches left and right as he blocked and jabbed back. I'd get back to saving him in a moment, once these two men were savagely beaten.

"Frankie, get her." His fists came up, guarding his face as he started dancing back and forth on the balls of his feet. Frankie had boxed. Good, it meant he could take punch after punch without going down.

The ghosts revealed his actions seconds before they happened. I turned back and forth, each of his jabs missing their mark by a hair. He wouldn't tire as easily as the man from this morning. As he pressed forward, punching with the usual combo, I slapped his fists away, redirecting his momentum. He tried to kick, but I pushed his knee down. Surprised, his eyes dropped, and I jabbed him in the nose. Broken.

"You bitch." Blood worked its way through his fingers as he cradled his face. If that made him mad, then this would ruin his day. I smashed my heel into his groin, getting as much contact with his manhood as I could muster. I'm sure it was like poking at marbles with straw. It forced him to spit, spraying blood up and down my body.

He buckled, and I grabbed him by the hair, pulling him to the sidewalk. He rolled onto his side, groaning. I slammed the toe of my boot into his stomach and repeated it until the man curled into a ball. I'd continue the fun of making him urinate blood before I finished with his friend.

"Can't fight fair?" His companion apparently believed there were rules when they were losing. Leave it to a weak man to dictate the rules of his defeat.

Inside my pocket, my fingers snaked into the holes of the brass knuckles. Frank had one man on the ground while another waved about a knife, thinking the tiny switchblade would somehow intimidate Frank. If it were anybody else, I might be worried. Frank had the smarts and the strength to take down two men.

Distraction would be my undoing someday. My ears rang and my jaw hurt as the man struck me. He grabbed the back of my neck and prepared to drive his knuckles into my face. This close, I couldn't manage a punch, and like every man I fought, he held me by my hair. I kneed his groin. This time it didn't work.

I snapped my other arm around, striking his forearm and pushing the punch wide. I jerked my head forward, my forehead smashing against his nose. When he started to step back, I hooked the toe of my boot on his foot, causing him to stumble and fall.

I tightened my grip on the brass knuckles.

"Serves them right," yelled a woman.

I stepped over the man before dropping to straddle his chest. He pushed at my face, trying to keep me away. I pushed at the inside of his elbow. He didn't know it, but he had lost. The first strike against his face tore at his cheek. The second struck his skull. His eyes rolled about in his head and his arm stopped trying to push me away. With the third strike, the bone of his jaw gave way. They'd need to wire his mouth shut. Good.

A crowd gathered on the street. While some of them appeared mortified, more and more of them were nodding their approval. I caught the stare of an older black man with his wife. He held a stoic face, unmoved by the violence. It was the wife holding him who startled me. With a slight nod from the woman, I struck the man a final time.

Frank had a lick of blood on his cheek. I was surprised the goon had got that close. Frank grabbed his wrist, stopping the weapon from plunging into his stomach. He jabbed the man, once, twice, and finally, he roared. Frank ducked low, grabbing the man by the crotch and raising him off his feet. He didn't quite manage to get him overhead. He ignored the other man who jabbed him in the side. Driving the man down, he slammed him onto the cement hard enough he bounced.

The last man standing was prepared to surrender. He held his fists up, debating if he had any hope of taking both of us at once. Frank grabbed the man. The goon responded with a solid punch to the face. Nothing deterred Frank. He'd been hit harder by bigger men.

He held the man in a bear hug. Olivia had taken on the scum of New York as her henchmen. We had broken the truce. I had a feeling our actions here were going to start something, a feud that only ended when one of us fell. I'd deal with the future when it came, but for now, we wanted victory.

"Confess your sins." I hissed the words.

"What? You're both—" I punched with my bare hand. With Frank holding him, it almost seemed cruel. Good.

"Confess." I drew my fist back, prepared to hit him again.

Without his companions, his bravado faded. He rattled off a list of wrongdoings from beating up Asians to harassing the black woman in his building. Stealing from the store. Robbing a woman at knifepoint. He didn't deserve mercy.

"Now apologize." Pointing to the crowd, I grabbed his face. "Apologize to them."

"I—" The man cried. "I'm sorry."

The woman let go of her husband and clapped. More than one repeated the gesture. Those terrorized by the man's bigotry finally received vindication. Never had I felt so satisfied as I struck the man with the brass knuckles. Frank hurled him to the side.

"The tattoos," he said, "did you see?"

I nodded.

"They're going to come for us."

"Good," I slid the knuckles into my pocket as I stormed toward the alley. "This is war."

Chapter Fifteen

1943

New York had become a battlefield for an invisible war. Theodore and Susan Lee had taken Koji to Claudette's shop. My roommate assured me over the phone that if Koji's wounds didn't become infected, he'd survive. Theodore offered to keep watch while Vinny and Michael escorted Susan Lee home. They had attacked one of our own, and we closed ranks, protecting our own if it happened again.

Knowing the goons served Olivia, it wasn't if, so much as when.

The window a story below slid open. I left my jacket in the kitchen, giving her the signal I was home. Frank waited until Susan Lee climbed the stairs before he gave up his perch next to me. With a pat on the back, he moved toward the ladder.

"Nobody goes out alone," he pointed at me, "this includes you."

"I can—"

"It includes you."

I held my tongue. As Susan Lee reached the top, Frank offered her a hand, helping her onto the roof. She gave him a slight hug, and he returned the gesture. She might not be happy with either of us right now, but those differences vanished as we reaffirmed the things that bound us together.

Frank hopped up onto the ledge and then descended the stairs and crawled in my window.

As she approached, I didn't know whether she wanted me to reach out and hug her, or if we were still in an awkward place. I kicked at a clump of tar on the ground, unsure of what to say. I was tempted to skirt past the oddities and summon the ghosts. Then she charged at me.

Arms wrapped around my chest. She squeezed until it was difficult to breathe. I snaked my arms free and returned the gesture. Normally she smelled of lilac, but the scent of herbs masked it. Right now, she reeked of Claudette's shop. When she started crying, I held her tighter, rubbing my hands along her back.

"It's horrible," she whispered.

"You were amazing," I whispered, "you saved his life."

She pulled back, wiping the tears from under her eyes. Her head shook back and forth. "Not Koji," she said. "*Them*. The men who did it. How can people do such horrible things?"

Part of me longed to wipe the memory from Susan Lee's memory. A woman with such optimism and hope for the future saw behind the curtain. It was bad enough that Koji had been beaten, but the reasoning, the logic built by fear, that was a darkness she had never encountered. I worried for her and how this reality would beat her down.

"There are bad people sprinkled in with the good."

"I hope somebody does to them what they did to Koji," she said.

Normally, I'd hold my tongue and let her request fall away. However, Susan Lee wasn't asking for a person to exact justice. She was asking me if I would avenge Koji. The innocent girl might not think the same of me, but I owed her the truth.

"They already did. Frank and I beat them to a pulp."

"Good."

The Susan Lee who first answered my ad for a roommate hid behind this cold woman. Behind smeared makeup and stains of blood along her clothes. The innocent Susan Lee had seen the darkness of New York City. I couldn't quite put my finger on why, but having her robbed of that made me sad. I wanted her optimism to balance out my realistic views of the world. The fact she slid into my realm of moral ambiguity worried me about her future.

She reached into her pocket and produced a cigarette. It hardly seemed like the time to harp on her health. When she handed me one I didn't object. My lungs would hurt in the morning, but I felt as doling out more punishment was the right thing to do. Not my best logic, but today had been one battle after another.

She flipped open the zippo and lit mine before her own. With a deep drag, I forced my lungs to hold the smoke despite their attempts to cough. Like countless nights before, we leaned onto the ledge and stared into the vastness of New York City. With the threat of German submarines or Japanese planes, the city went dark at night. I didn't believe we were in any real danger, but we played along as the country looked to us as a source of inspiration.

"Why?"

I took a drag before tapping the filter with my pointer. I watched as the burning ash vanished as it fell to the alley below. Susan Lee mulled over her question. If I waited long enough, I was sure she'd provide me enough context to offer an answer.

Nobody referred to me as patient. "Why what?"

"Why do you do it? Get dressed up and go out there." She was trying to understand.

"It all started because of you."

Even at night, I could see the white of her eyes as they

widened. I didn't know if this was one of those moments when I should break the tension with humor or be heartfelt. I went with heartfelt.

"You spend your days saving lives, then you go aid in the war effort. You're doing your part making sure our boys come home. I wanted to make sure there was a home waiting for them."

"You make me sound like a superhero."

I laughed. The coughing started. Once my lungs calmed, I put a hand on her shoulder. "You know what we say about you?"

"Send Susan Lee, she'll end the war," she recited.

My cheeks turned red from embarrassment. "You heard that, huh?"

"You're not exactly subtle."

"No, I guess I'm not."

Our relationship might never be the same, not since she discovered that her average roommate with no fashion sense fought crime at night. I resisted for years, refusing to know her more than a stranger on the street. What we had was simple, uncomplicated. Somewhere along the way, I realized our cordial agreement had blossomed into friendship. It might not be the same as before, but anything was a step in the right direction.

"Why you?"

"Why should a woman capable of seeing the future be the one to fight crime?"

"Foolish question, I know."

"Not foolish," I dropped the fag and ground at it with my heel. "Frank was the only person who knew about me for years. Sometimes I forget nobody sees the world the way I do. I've been like this since I was a child. But back then, I thought the Devil worked through me. He cursed me. When bad things happened, I would see them. Nobody would listen to me when I warned them."

"Then they came true." Susan Lee's tone gave away the underlying horror.

"Then they came true." This was the first time I spoke of my past with somebody other than Frank. Even as I lay curled around Edward's naked body, we spoke of happier times. "I watched Poppa die. Even when I tried, I couldn't change the future. Then the demons showed me Benjie drowning in the pond. But I couldn't change the future," I wiped the tears from my eyes. "So, I didn't even try."

Susan Lee gasped. She tossed her cigarette over the ledge of the building and covered her gaping mouth. For the longest time, I had numbed myself to my brother's death. Fate made it impossible to intercede and save him. Instead, I watched the boy who idolized me descend into an icy grave.

"There was nothing you could do."

A stifled a sob as I thought of the multiple versions of my ghost. That might have been the truth once upon a time, but now I wasn't quite so sure. "I think I can change the future." Saying the words out loud should have been empowering. Having the gift of premonition and the ability to alter events made me one of the most influential people on the planet. But it also meant Benjie didn't have to die.

"Stop it, Eleanor. Stop it right this instant. You were a girl. Stop wondering what might have been. You'll drive yourself crazy."

"But—"

"Be the woman Benjie would admire."

She used her thumbs to wipe the tears away from my eyes. Wiping them on her blouse, she came in for a hug. Normally only Frank had the opportunity to see me cry. But now, there were more shoulders for me to lean on. I gave her a squeeze before letting go.

"You asked why I do it. If you can spend all day saving lives and then save soldiers, I guessed I had to do my part, too."

"I'm delighted that I can guilt you into making questionable life choices, Eleanor."

"Did you just sass me?" This morning I was wearing a dress by choice, and now Susan Lee was giving me grief. The tables had turned. The slight giggle from the woman drowned the sadness and filled my heart with hope. Perhaps we'd emerge on the other side of this better friends.

"What about the Society? And do you care to tell me where you found that handsome Theodore?"

"Go get the cookies out of the cupboard and I'll meet you in your room. Then I'll tell you all about the handsome Dr. Stewart."

"He's the most rugged doctor—"

"Go," I shooed her away.

I followed her to the fire escape. Staring out into the city, I rolled over Susan Lee's statement. Being able to change the future meant I could have prevented Benjie's death. But dwelling on the past seemed counterintuitive for a psychic. I imagined if he were standing next to me now, he'd be proud of the woman I became. Sure, I had experienced bumps and bruises along the way, but I maintained the heart of a Bouvier.

"Benjie, I hope I make you proud."

Chapter Sixteen

1932

"You can join me, you know?"

I eased my way around the corner of the hall. It had been almost a month of avoiding the man. He had proven himself harmless. The clanging of metal was the same as every night, almost down to the minute. He set the table and ate dinner, and when I didn't join him, he'd bring the plate to my door. Most nights I ate, trying to understand how a man could be so bad at cooking.

"It's meatloaf again tonight. Probably not your favorite, but money is tight. I figure any food on the table these days is a good thing."

I sniffed the air. It didn't have the same burned smell as usual. Frank had taken more care with this meal, ensuring it didn't char in the oven. Perhaps he could learn. The least I could do was sit at the table and eat with him face-to-face.

"At some point, we have to figure out some more appropriate clothes for you. Wearing hand-me-downs probably isn't the best way to dress a young lady."

I had wondered where he was getting the clothes. They were

loose on me, but I had tied them tight enough they didn't fall off my hips. It made sense. Despite being clean, they still held a scent of sweat. I had grown used to it.

"I don't know what else you need. But I was thinking of going to the library and seeing if they had another of Baum's books. I think there are more?"

"No," I whispered.

I inched my way through the kitchen. Frank didn't stare, he hardly made eye contact as he cut into his food. Even from here, I could see bits of food sticking to the tips of his mustache. He was bulkier than I remembered, not fat, but thick. The muscle along his shoulders and arms was obvious under his shirt.

He finished chewing before replying. "No? Would something else be better?" He pushed the book across the table. "You can have it. I got it for you."

Frank didn't have children. The decor and belongings made it clear nobody had lived with him in a long time. I wondered if he had a girlfriend or if he was a bachelor. He raised a bottle of beer, taking a long swig.

"I like that book." I pulled out the table chair and sat. Touching the metal of the fork, I marveled at the trust. At the hospital they never gave us knives, and even our forks were often plastic, that is, if they gave them to us at all. But here, he had a napkin folded neatly under a fork and a knife as if it were nothing.

He had poured the glass of milk, hopeful I'd join him. Night after night the man repeated the ritual. Consistent, he gave me space, never pushing me.

"It's yours," he said simply. We ate in silence. Now and then he glanced up from his plate and I averted my eyes. I focused on the book. The last time I had finished it myself, I had been sitting in a tree in our yard. The cover of this copy wasn't nearly as worn and hadn't been read a dozen of times.

Frank was the tin woodman. It wasn't hard to imagine the

burly man swinging an ax. But he also had elements of the Scarecrow, simple, lovable. For a man willing to burst into a hospital operating room, he had more courage than the lion could muster.

He finished his food while I continued shoveling meatloaf into my mouth. Compared to the lackluster food of the hospital, this was delicious. I looked up to see Frank sitting back in his chair, watching me with a raised eyebrow.

"It's not fair that I know about you, but you must have plenty of questions about me. Is there anything you want to ask?"

I had hundreds of questions, but none of them I wanted to voice in that moment. I feared if I said the wrong thing, I might mess up our arrangement. At an early age, I learned, if I didn't know what to say, it was best to remain silent. Frank, however, had never learned that lesson.

"I got out of the military after an explosion caused a roof to collapse. My back isn't what it used to be. A couple of months ago, I would have joined the local firefighters, but we had a bit of a falling out. It took a while for me to get out of a funk, but I decided I need to do something with my life."

I didn't quite understand how I fit into this awakening. Was I going to be a project for him to work on while he discovered a new era of his life?

"I decided I needed to do some good. You know, help people somehow?" I didn't know. I did not understand what he might be getting at. "But first, I had to make good on a promise. I figured I'd first make sure you were okay, then I could worry about the next steps."

Frank collected his dishes and placed them in the sink. He opened the fridge and pulled out another bottle. Popping the cap, he sat down at the table. After a long swig, he started in again.

"I never had a family of my own." He laughed for a moment, making a gesture toward the rest of the apartment. "But you're smart enough to figure that out. So I'm not used to having somebody in the house. We'll probably bump into one another, but I think we can make it work. You can keep the bedroom, I'm more comfortable on the couch. It keeps the back from aching."

I sipped milk from the glass. Frank had a sweet nature about him. Perhaps a bit lost, but he tried his best to make me feel comfortable. In one meal, he spoke more than the orderlies had my entire stay at the hospital. Unlike them, he didn't bark commands or make threats. I commended his attempts to put me at ease. Bit by bit, I believed his plan had worked.

"I'm not going to lie, this is scary for me too. Look at me," he drank the rest of the bottle, "I'm not good parenting material. So, we're going to need to figure this out together. I'm going to make a lot of mistakes. You'll have to forgive me. But I'll do my best, Eleanor. I can promise you that. Is that okay with you?"

I eyed the book sitting on the table. He had the book before he rescued me from the hospital. The man had gone out of his way before carrying me from hell. I didn't know what to say. I gave a slight nod.

Frank smiled at my response. "My pops owned a building in the city where he worked on cabs. When he died, he left it to me. I've been thinking of doing something with it. There must be something I can do. I haven't figured it out yet. But I need to go check on it. Maybe you can come with me."

Over my shoulder, the door to his apartment led to a strange world. There were thousands of people, and more people meant more demons. I feared the number of specters that would fight for my attention. I didn't know if I was ready. My fingers brushed through my hair, reminding me that I wasn't a scared girl anymore.

"Eleanor, there is something," Frank said. His tone changed, going from the bumbling man to a more serious concern. I tensed at the shift. Ghosts roamed the living room, versions of him lying on the couch and walking to the fridge. He listened to the radio while he drank his beer before packing up and walking out the door. Hundreds of transparent Franks filled the room. "Your father told me a lot of things about you."

He followed my eyes into the empty space. He tried to hide his alarm, but it was there none the less. "You're seeing them, aren't you? The ghosts?"

I wanted to be angry with my father for revealing our secret. But I found it comforting to know he believed enough to tell his closest friend. Momma hadn't been capable of coping with the reality of the demons, and I feared Frank might run. I lowered my head, ashamed.

"I've seen some crazy shi—stuff in my life. Even watched a man lift a truck to save a buddy. I don't know what I believe, but I like to think there are things we can't explain all around us. That there's a bit of magic in our lives."

Hell. It's hell. Demons violating my mind day after day, promising to show me horrible things I can't change. Frank might believe what my father revealed to him, but he didn't understand. The man couldn't fathom watching your brother die—not once, but twice. No amount of explaining could make him understand the helplessness.

"I won't pretend to understand, but your father believed it was true. I believe him, Eleanor. It's not a burden you have to carry on your own."

I gave him a slight nod and pushed my chair back. I walked my dishes to the sink, stacking them as he had. Then I started toward my bedroom. Frank held up the book.

"Don't forget this."

I paused as he extended his arm, offering me the paperback. Shaking my head, I kept on walking.

"I like your woodman."

Chapter Seventeen

1943

The images were horrifying. Newspapers hadn't prepared me. The men and women housed in the concentration camps would haunt me, but that was only the beginning of the atrocities. Mothers withered away to nothing, cradling their children. Each time the vision slowed, allowing me to focus on their faces, I caught flashes of firing squads, brutality, and—

"Fire," I gasped. I dug my nails into my palm, reminding myself I remained kneeling in my bedroom.

I woke this morning, and something had changed. The conversation with Susan Lee hung in the air. It was time to admit there was a possibility I could change the future. The guilt tried to grapple with my heart, but I believed Benjie wanted me to move forward. More than that, Poppa would demand I let go of the heartache.

In the past, the visions had controlled me. Not today. Eyes closed and focused on the war, I found it almost easy to step into a future thousands of miles away. The soldiers were dirty, tired, and the wounded were too many to count. Susan Lee made it her mission to help them. But perhaps there was more I could do than protect New York.

Once the visions took me to Germany I shuddered. It was like blinking and each time I opened my eyes I found myself in a new location. I couldn't tell the time or date. I could be seeing the Nazi troops minutes into the future, or perhaps decades. Gregory believed I would know the when, but no, my internal clock spun out of time.

It was when I saw the emaciated men in stripes I discovered why we fought this war. The smell of smoke filled my nostrils. Burning hair, no…

I opened my eyes. I choked back bile and swatted at the smell permeating my nose. My heart raced, threatening to work its way into my throat. The words on a printed page didn't prepare me. They marched them into furnaces and burned them alive. Men. Women. Children. Nazis were monsters without humanity.

"Hitler," I whispered. He was the heart of the Nazi regime. I needed to see him.

Closing my eyes, I focused on the smell in my nose. I didn't want to see the horrors, but I summoned the visions. I had something to prove, a mission fueled by the memory of my father. He gave his life for this country. I couldn't save him, but perhaps I could save tens of thousands of Americans. If I could endure the worst of mankind, I could change its course.

"Poppa," I whispered, "guide me."

The doctor stood to one side of the hospital bed. The bright lights didn't stop the room from feeling cramped. I don't know what I expected, but when I laid eyes on him, the man responsible for genocide, he seemed, weak, even insecure. The illustrations in the newspaper were mostly accurate. The signature mustache and slicked over hair. He was shorter than I expected, which explained the underlying insecurities. One man had done this. Left to his own devices, he waged a global war. By comparison, Olivia was insignificant, but left alone, could this be her future?

The doctor held a syringe, injecting it into something on the table. It took a moment before the dog materialized. The two men watched, checking the clock. The dog whimpered and seconds later it stilled. Neither of them flinched at the animal's death. Neither were human. They had expunged any part of them that claimed to be part of this species.

A moment later I stood in a bedroom while Hitler sat on the bed next to an unmoving woman. I didn't know her name, but someday she'd go down in history as well. Attractive, her face held its tension as the life drained from her body. Worry was scribbled along her brow. Her glassy eyes remained fixed on him. He popped a pill in his mouth and brought a gun to his temple. I jumped as he pulled the trigger.

It was over. The great Hitler had committed suicide.

I knew the ending of their story, but I needed to turn around and look backward. I needed an opening. It was her, she was the only one with him at the end. I wanted to see her life and what choices led her to this point. I sat on the bed, occupying where her lower body draped off the edge. My hand passed through her face as if each of us were ghosts.

Ghosts stepped out of my body. It started with a handful, six maybe. They moved as if they were going to walk out of the room and vanished. Then they poured from me in a steady stream. Hundreds, perhaps thousands scattered about the room, running to some unseen destination. I followed the woman's death, her entering the bunker, her romance with this tyrant. The timeline wasn't linear, each moment consisted of infinite possibilities. For a split second I saw her entire life, but more than that, I saw every version of what her life would or could be.

I devoured her entirety.

Her relationship with *him* had been kept a secret. They had known one another for years before they committed suicide. Her sister married one of his trusted companions. She had taken photographs of his home and sold them to another man. She worked as a photographer and traveled. At some point, she attempted suicide after being neglected by her murderous boyfriend. Yes, there was trouble in paradise and there I had found an in, a plan of attack on how to get to the tyrant.

She attended a wedding, delighted to be in his home. But they hid their relationship from the public, and he refused to grant her the respect she felt she had earned. From that moment, I watched as the timeline fractured. Flashes worked backward, branching like the roots of a tree. There were so many it was almost impossible to actually look at what happened. I didn't so much see them as write the moments to memory as if I dreamed I was there.

Sipping coffee at a cafe, a woman sat across from her. It seemed innocent enough until the woman slid a paper to the secret mistress. I watched as the timeline expanded in both directions. The mistress held a gun. Hitler laying at her feet in a puddle of his own blood. Then she killed herself.

I fell to the floor, gasping. There were so many futures, endless possibilities. I crawled to the side of my bed and pulled out my journal. I started documenting the memories. Drawing a line, I could connect one event to the next. Working backward, I found the connection to me, to where I sat in my room writing in a journal.

"Eleanor," Susan Lee's voice was soft as she opened the door. "I heard a noise, are you okay?"

"Yes, yes," I continued scribbling.

"What happened?"

I finished the last note. I raised my journal, baring the open book to Susan Lee. To anybody else I might sound mad, like I was a victim of delusions. But for the first time since my father died, I didn't feel helpless, the victim of a deity torturing me.

"I know how to end the war."
I would kill Hitler.

Chapter Eighteen

1943

"Frank will kill us."

Susan Lee was probably right. This was bigger than a telepath recruiting hoodlums to do her dirty work. In my pocket I held a letter with information about Hitler that nobody but his closest allies would know. Even if we managed to deliver it, we'd fall under the watchful eye of the government who might deem us Nazi sympathizers.

"What about Olivia? She's out there."

Susan Lee was correct, the telepath tightening her hold on the city remained a problem. The visions had never come so easily. I wanted to believe it was a sign, and if I could protect more lives by ending the war early, I had to risk it. Olivia would have to wait for her justice.

"We'll deal with her soon enough."

"I have an uneasy feeling about this," Susan Lee said.

"You wanted to help our soldiers overseas. This could end the war."

"Are you sure?"

I shook my head. "I wrote everything I could. But I don't

know the dates and times. I tried to trust my gut. But," I shrugged, "this isn't a science."

"So, we're going to a Naval shipyard with information about a secret relationship. It may or may not be correct and could potentially land us in prison. Am I correct?"

When she put it like that, it was hard to see the validity of this plan. I wished the visions came with a timestamp and calendar. If I could pinpoint the information, it'd help our claim. Right now, I didn't know the woman's name, just that she worked for Hoffmann, the exclusive photographer for the Reich.

Unlike Brooklyn, Manhattan served as New York's polished gem. There were strips of stores and at the center, hidden away by skyscrapers was a park big enough to be considered a forest. It had a veneer that left it feeling fake, almost as if it were a postcard that only showed the best. Residents of Manhattan turned their nose at Brooklyn and as we meandered through the shipyard I understood why.

Brooklyn housed the working class. In every direction, women not only pulled their weight but picked up the slack left by men. They were no longer the daughters, sisters, and mothers, they transcended society's limitation of our sex. I caught Susan Lee's smile as she spotted a group of women carrying a large plate of metal. I might know the future, but so did Susan Lee. These hardworking ladies served as hope. Me and Susan Lee were charging in, determined to join this movement.

We turned past a warehouse and the sight became even more impressive. Past the boxes of parts and stacked sheets of metal, one of the war vessels had been set in the water. Welders continued working, suspended from the side by ropes as they sealed the ship airtight. While the work being done on land was mind-boggling, it was only when I saw the immensity of the war machine in the water that I comprehended why all of New York's resources had become scarce.

Susan Lee poked my shoulder. "Go over the plan again."

"We're just two lovely ladies taking a stroll through the shipyard. If anybody asks, we're looking for ways to support the war effort."

"And Mayor La Guardia?"

"He works with President Roosevelt. I can get word to the president through the mayor. He only spends three days in the city and always comes to the shipyard."

"Then you hand him a letter. He goes to President Roosevelt, who alerts people overseas, and then they set up a rendezvous with this mysterious woman? Then we hope she turns on her boyfriend who just happens to be the most paranoid man in the world?"

"Susan Lee." My expression soured at the dissection. "Have a little faith."

"In my roommate who can see the future?"

Now she was just mocking me. I should have been insulted, but I took it as a sign that our relationship was mending. She had been apprehensive at first, but I needed her. With our hair in curlers and expertly applied makeup, she'd be more than capable of charming any man who tried to see us out of the shipyard. In fact, I was relying on it. The soft-spoken nurse with uncanny determination and skills of persuasion was part of the vision. I needed Susan Lee.

We had shipped the men to war. What was left was those unable to fight and women. It was a sight to see, so many women in overalls and jumpsuits walking about. In a massive hangar, it was women building the war boats to be sent overseas. The papers had reported about the female workforce, but it made it seem as if they were playing make-believe. There was none of that as we walked up to a group of women sitting in the business end of a bucket loader.

"You ladies look lost," said one of the women. They had their lunch boxes out, sandwiches in hand. The three of them were covered in grease. I wanted to congratulate them, not because they were fighting a war, but because they would be the pioneers of a movement that granted women equality throughout the United States. All in due time.

"We're hoping to catch a glimpse of Mayor La Guardia. We heard he comes to the shipyard." Susan Lee could befriend even the most begrudging human. I swore, it was a superpower.

One of the women hopped down from her perch. She didn't hide the disappointment on her face. Here she was, working her butt off and two women of leisure stroll into her workplace acting like harlots. I think I would be annoyed with me as well. I almost respected her more for the look of annoyance.

"You shouldn't be here," she said, "go home before you get your dress dirty."

The other women gave approving nods. "Homemakers," another said dismissively.

"We will, but we really want to meet La Guardia," Susan Lee stepped in closer, "we're hoping he'll help fund the food kitchen we run."

Their leader's expression changed quickly. Susan Lee didn't relent. "We're providing food for kids and honestly, we can't keep up. You know what it's like. They pay us nothing and then expect us to survive. We want to help. I'm certain if we can get some face time with him, he'll support struggling New Yorkers."

I'd have to congratulate her on the swift thinking. This hadn't been part of the vision, but Susan Lee already made herself invaluable.

One of the other women jumped down. "I'm barely making thirty dollars a week and I have three mouths to feed."

"At least you're not taking care of your parents too," added the third.

Susan Lee tapped into a universal sentiment shared by all women. When the first woman pointed toward the piers, I almost jumped. "He'll be down there. They're launching a ship later today and Mayor LaGuardia likes to be in front of the cameras when it happens."

"Don't let his people see you. They'll escort you out so fast your head will spin." The second woman laughed when Susan Lee reached into the collar of her dress and lifted her breasts.

"We've got this," Susan Lee said.

Who was this woman who slept under the same roof as me? Never would I guess that she'd use her sex to her advantage. I had seriously underestimated the marvelous Susan Lee. I looked down at my chest, I'd adjust as we walked.

With a quick thank you, we were on our way.

"That was amazing, Susan Lee."

"For years you've said I could end this war. Well, the girls and I are going to do just that."

Could a letter change the course of mankind? I spent the morning carefully penning the note, using my best penmanship. Momma would be appalled at how bad my calligraphy had become. Her grandmother had taught her, and she insisted I learn the skill. It was silly to think swooping descenders and carefully punctuated sentences might make a difference. I wrote President Roosevelt's name on the envelope. I prayed he appreciated the marks.

"It's massive," she whispered.

The ship Susan Lee point at was indeed enormous. We had seen plenty of photographs from the deck of the ships, with men smiling for the camera. None of them prepared me for the immensity when standing close. How many sailors would man the ship as it prepared for war? My hand went to my purse, squeezing it against my torso. If all went well, no men would be needed and the ship would become part of an era long passed.

"If this works, they won't need another warship."

Susan Lee spoke and then paused. Something troubled the woman. "Have you thought this through?"

"I—"

"No, not the war thing. I am certain you saw these changes. But, are we doing the right thing? Should we be tampering with the future? What if this makes things worse?"

"Susan Lee, this could end the war."

"But what if it brings about another war? What if changing this, changes more? And what if it isn't good?"

She had a point. Frank often ran hypotheticals when I first tried to change the outcome of the future. Back then, fate course-corrected and happened regardless of my meddling. But that had been different, I hadn't been capable of seeing multiple versions of the future. The branches had shown me thousands of outcomes, and this was the one to make the biggest impact.

"What if by playing God, we make it worse?"

"When you're operating on a patient, do you worry about tomorrow? Or do you make sure they survive today?"

Susan Lee held up her finger, prepared to protest. Her eyes grew distant as she lost herself in thought. I could only imagine she was dwelling on the last patient to enter the hospital. She would have jumped into action, making sure she stabilized them with a chance to see another morning. If something bad happened again, she'd act, doing everything in her power to keep them alive.

She nodded. "Save them now. If necessary, save them again tomorrow."

We weren't Gods. In the pit of my stomach, this felt right. While Olivia raised an army of New Yorkers, she only cared about elevating herself. We were two women fighting a mammoth injustice. Every fiber of my being said this was right. Neither of us had anything to gain except the satisfaction of doing our part for the war effort. This beat Susan Lee yelling at my inability to knit socks for the troops.

As we approached the ship, fewer women milled about. The ratio of women to men tipped. More men carried equipment about this part of the shipyard. Our presence turned awkward, and we received more than one raised eyebrow. It wouldn't be long before somebody asked why we roamed about.

"That must be where they are." Susan Lee pointed toward a sizable gathering of people. Some were wearing plain clothes, looking almost as out of sorts as we did. They must be press, which meant La Guardia would be somewhere nearby.

Despite there being bits and pieces of the war machines scattered about, this area was almost entirely empty. The press stood in a cleared-out area that offered the perfect opportunity for photographs of the big ships. Had Mayor La Guardia intentionally left it empty so he could have his photo taken? I prayed the man's vanity could be used to our advantage, otherwise this would become a fool's errand.

"Ladies, can we help you?"

There were knives in my purse. My first instinct was sliding my hand inside. Despite insisting on doing good deeds, I maintained a certain level of pessimism. Getting stabbed by Olivia left a woman jumpy and quick to the draw.

I let my hand slip from my purse, suddenly aware of how fast I allowed myself to resort to violence. During the night when I stalked the streets, I considered myself a vigilante, much like Robin Hood. And yet, I prepared to dispatch the voice before assessing the situation. I found myself on a slippery slope and with every death, I fear I was losing ground.

I plastered a large smile on my face, falling into character. Their tan suits made them stand out, but the guns at their side made them military. Both men wore white helmets with the letters "MP" stamped on their forehead. Later I'd learn it stood for military police, but right now, they were in the way.

"I'm so sorry, officer," I started.

Susan Lee gave a slight curtsey. "Gentlemen, we're here to see Mayor La Guardia."

"You can't be here, ma'am." The man on the right looked us over. Usually that meant he was looking at the exposed skin, but as he hovered over my purse, I understood. The man scanned for threats, careful of any hidden guns. The knives weren't the scariest thing, but if he opened my purse, I could bet we'd spend the night in jail.

"Mayor La Guardia was supposed to send a car for us," Susan Lee huffed. "He should fire his assistant."

The men paused. Had we rushed them, I'm sure both would have given us a workout. But a scorned woman is a different type of threatening. Susan Lee leaned in close, pointing back at me.

"We started an auxiliary station to support the troops. Mayor La Guardia stopped by himself to say thank you. You know how he likes the cameras. But," she looked over her shoulder, giving me a wink, "he likes her more than the cameras."

Both men broke into a smile. What is it about men and their communal support for their gender getting laid? While Susan Lee and I talked about the future of Edward and me, never did she inquire about his prowess in the bedroom. But when it came to men, their minds lived in the gutter. Susan Lee must have telepathic abilities to read people this well.

"He offered to fund our operation if he got some alone time with Ms. Lenore." She stood up straight, brushing off her dress and giving her hair a light fluffing. "Now are you going to be the men who ruin my war efforts, or are you going to help me help Mayor La Guardia?"

They looked at each other. The man on the right turned around, attempting some sort of privacy. "They're two dames, how dangerous can they be?"

"Do you want to be cleaning latrines?" The other didn't seem as convinced.

"What are your names?" Susan Lee had no patience for their

nonsense. "I'll make sure to mention your names to the mayor. Being in his favor will benefit both of you."

"If it gets us out of shipyard duty," the man urged the other, "I'm willing to risk it."

"Or I could tell him you two got in the way of his indiscretions."

"Fine." The man caved. That's it, she's a telepath. There is no other way this calm and timid woman who nagged me about being civilized was capable of this. I regretted not enlisting her services sooner.

"We'll escort you," he added.

She curtsied again. "We'd be honored."

For a woman able to see the future, I felt less than useful right now. Susan Lee had taken control of the situation. When Frank heard about this, he'd roar with laughter. Just like that, she proved she could single-handedly end the war.

Reporters impatiently waited with microphones and notepads for the mayor to begin speaking. We stood in the back; the soldiers waiting for the event to be over. Several officers were standing near the mayor, none of them appearing happy to be there. We had seen this photo in the paper a dozen times, but still La Guardia insisted on turning it into a spectacle.

He wasn't tall, but he was a thick man. The suit he wore framed his body, making it obvious he had packed on a bit of weight. The man's slicked hair parted down the middle. Everything about the man said politician. Had we been walking down the street and passed him by, I'd assume he worked for the government. The consensus of New York was that he was a good man, and I hoped that meant he'd be willing to speak with President Roosevelt.

The presentation of the newest carrier, the Kearsarge, was

ready for the water. It wouldn't be sent to war for another few months as they finished working. It seemed premature to be congratulating the hard work of the Brooklyn Naval Yard, but in these trying times, I suppose we should celebrate any good news.

The reporters asked questions, almost none of them relating to the launch of the ship. Reporters wanted to know what insight he might have about the war. They asked about his position in Washington and if he felt he had undertaken too much responsibility. They were ruthless, but La Guardia didn't flinch. The man was articulate, thorough, and more than willing to stand up against the reporters. At first, I wasn't sure what to make of the man, but my respect grew as he answered each question with a sense of honesty and patriotic pride.

He called an end to the ceremony and posed for photographs with the two officers at his side. It would be in the newspaper tomorrow, and if no word of the war came in, he might even make the front page.

Before the reporters broke away, Susan Lee grabbed my hand and pulled me through the crowd. We bumped and pushed, putting some distance between us and the military police. The ghosts stepped from the reporters, dozens turned into hundreds. It had become rare that they appeared without being summoned. The hair on the back of my neck stood on end. They served as a warning that something bad rested on the horizon.

Susan Lee continued pulling. I scoured the area looking for a ghost giving away the source of danger. Even staring up to the platform of the ship, I couldn't find anything out of the ordinary. Something was off, I couldn't pinpoint it. If I had a moment to collect myself, I might see my own ghost long enough to sort it out. But Susan Lee's mission didn't leave time for meditation.

"Mayor La Guardia," she said, loud enough to be heard over a grinding sound from a nearby shipyard worker.

"Hi," she continued, "if we could have a moment of your time. Hi, Mr. La Guardia," she started waving her hands. He brushed us off, continuing a conversation with one of the officers. Both men wore uniforms, their chests riddled with pins and trinkets.

Susan Lee wouldn't be dismissed. "Mayor La Guardia, we need to speak."

"You'll have to make an appointment with my secretary."

I gasped as she stepped between the mayor and the officers. "Your secretary won't want to hear about these indiscretions."

"Ma'am—"

"The last thing you need is a scandal," her gaze was like steel, unbending. "I'd be happy to talk to the reporters instead."

Did Susan Lee know something about the man or was she bluffing? She couldn't maintain a straight face while playing cards, but right now, I believed every word. When this was over, Susan Lee and I would have a heart-to-heart conversation about this other woman tucked away behind a civilized appearance.

"Ma'am, I have no idea what you mean." It was common knowledge that he married his last secretary. Women spoke about it like he seduced her or abused his power. However, their marriage had been public, and the two appeared madly in love.

He excused himself and put his hand on Susan Lee's back, guiding her away from the reporters and officers. Spinning about, I watched the ghosts, sure that nobody came behind us. Even the soldiers who escorted us over gave a slight wave, making sure we included them in our discussions. I gave a slight nod and quickly followed Susan Lee and La Guardia.

We walked until we were more than a safe distance away from the crowd. We stood next to a parked car and several large trucks. The only ghosts I could see were our own and a few workers going about their jobs. The nagging feeling didn't dissipate despite our apparent safety.

"What is it," he asked, the annoyance seeping into his words.

"We have information about the war," Susan Lee blurted out.

"Do you, now?" I couldn't blame him. It was a wild statement. There must have been plenty of people providing their two-cents about how the war could be won. The moment she said it, his arms crossed over his broad chest. This would require convincing.

"Eleanor," she said. His eyes widened. I watched as his ghost made a dismissive gesture, waving us off. As the arm of his suit pulled back, I discovered the warning the ghosts demanded I see.

I grabbed the man's wrist, pulling it away from his body.

"Ma'am, what do you—"

Three wavy lines.

"The Society got to you."

He pulled his arm back, breaking free of my grip. He straightened his jacket, adjusting his tie. Olivia had been busy since sliding a knife into my gut. If she reached the mayor, I didn't know where it might end. Perhaps the reporters or soldiers were also her minions.

"I don't know what you're talking about."

I wanted to punch the man. Whatever she offered, he had agreed to her terms. Did the mayor demand power, fame, maybe even fortunes? The longer she roamed without opposition, the more I saw why the Society originally feared mentalists. If she reached him, would the president be next?

"We don't care what she offered you," Susan Lee interjected. "If you're involved with Olivia and her kin, they surely told you about Eleanor."

"The future seer," he said with a bit of ire in his voice. Olivia not only recruited, but she tainted them. On a steady stream of lies and perversions, she turned me into the enemy.

"That's me."

For the leader of New York, he quickly took a step back. It was only after giving me the once over the tension in his shoulders relaxed. I scowled, more disappointed that I didn't live up to the fear Olivia instilled in the man. A lovely dress and flawless rouge left me looking like a pampered homemaker. Thankfully, the shark that was Susan Lee didn't relent.

"We're serious, we have information that could end the war," she said.

Mayor La Guardia stiffened as I reached into my purse. I had no idea what Olivia had said about me, but there was something useful about being feared. The letter had wrinkled. Straightening it, smoothing the letters of Roosevelt's name, I held it out.

"We don't care what she offered you. This has nothing to do with that vile woman. We want to stop the war. We think we know how." I spoke bluntly. I hoped his heart, or at least his ambitions, overrode his greed.

He made no move to take the letter from my hand. The man was right to fear her. But to do it at the cost of human lives? I resisted the urge to spit on him. Olivia's recruitment could be costing soldiers their lives.

"Whatever she offered you, is it enough to jeopardize the lives of millions? You know what is happening in those camps. The Germans are…" I couldn't find a word to describe the horrors I had witnessed. "It's monstrous."

Susan Lee took the man's hand. "This needs to go to Roosevelt. Nobody cares about your reasoning. Do it for the soldiers or do it so Roosevelt owes you. Either way, the war needs to end."

Smart. Susan Lee drove a wedge between the man's allegiance with the Society by offering a more powerful ally. She took his hand, placing it on her chest. "You'll be a hero to this nation. Mr. La Guardia, please, for the love of God, get this letter to President Roosevelt."

The man's stern face softened at the mention of the word, "hero." It wasn't enough to tempt a man's good character. The promise of being worshipped by the masses had put it over the edge. He snatched the letter from my hand. Spinning it over, he stared at the seal on the back. "What makes you think I won't read it?"

"Read it," I said, "then you'll know I'm correct."

"Which do I do?" he asked.

There was no way to hide rolling my eyes. Even though his queen had warned him about my abilities, he wanted me to prove myself. "You could have asked if you win the election, or how you'll die. You want me to prove my gifts with that?"

"Do I win?"

I turned around, taking Susan Lee's hand. "You're on your own, good sir." The letter had reached his hands. If destiny had loosened the reins, then two young women from New York City may have just ended the war. I didn't want to celebrate too soon, but if this worked, what else could we do to help mankind?

The possibilities were endless.

Chapter Nineteen

1943

"Tell him where you've been," Theodore said.

"Excuse me," I snapped at the professor, "I don't care that you have your spies following me. But do not think you have the right to put my business on the table like that."

"Eleanor." Frank didn't hide the knowing tone. I tried to keep secrets. He was the only man able to force a confession with a single word.

"Susan Lee and I went to the shipyard in Brooklyn to meet with Mayor La Guardia."

"What in the Lord's name were you doing?"

"Stopping the war," Susan Lee chimed in.

"Eleanor dragged you into this too?"

"She did no such thing," Susan Lee said. "She needed help. And it's not like we were going to wait for men to save the day. Besides, it worked."

Frank couldn't compete with her outburst. I had feared our relationship was in danger. But perhaps it took her longer to adjust to the changes I thrust on her. Sisterhood hadn't been a concept I believed in. I steadily changed my tune.

"I had a vision. But something's different now. I saw more than the future. I saw them all."

"The Everett theory?" Theodore had technical terms, and a bit of excitement. But only Frank understood the weight of the statement and the turbulent emotions buried just beneath my skin.

Frank stepped around his desk, pushing Theodore out of the way. He didn't ask if I needed it, but he enveloped me in a bear hug. "Are you okay?"

"Am I missing something?" Theodore asked.

"Yes, yes you are," Susan Lee scolded.

Frank stepped back, sitting on the edge of his desk. He had listened to me cry countless nights. While reading to me from the hallway, he patiently waited for me to come to terms with my past. We talked about what happened, but it usually ended with me frustrated that I couldn't save my brother. I had just admitted to performing the only thing I ever wanted. But Susan Lee had reminded me to move forward and become the person who made Benjie proud.

I scooted to the end of the rickety wooden chair, straightening my back and lifting my chin. If my little brother was in Heaven, I had faith he'd be proud. Not of my survival, or even my next statement, but that I was learning to pull myself free from a pit filled with regrets.

"I think I just killed Hitler."

Frank burst out laughing at my statement. Even Susan Lee stifled a slight laugh. Only Theodore missed the humor in the statement. He still wore his suit from yesterday, and despite being the smartest person in the room, he couldn't uncover the punchline.

"Theodore," I said, "I've been trying my entire life to fight fate. I," I took Susan Lee's hand, "we might have finally done it."

"What changed? Are there any variables between then and now you can pinpoint?"

Truly an academic, he siphoned the joy out of the moment.

"Gregory had been right. It was me all along. I was stopping myself." I squeezed her hand. "It took a swift kick in the pants to realize it."

"Does that mean it'll be easier to stop Olivia?" asked Susan Lee.

Frank, always the pragmatic one. I hadn't considered turning this extension of my abilities on the harpy. "The visions don't always come when I want them. Even the ghosts, it's new. Maybe? Is this the time to rely on an unreliable gift?"

"It could be the secret weapon we need to kill Olivia." I agreed with his words.

Susan Lee stiffened at the comment. "Kill? You're going to kill her?"

The woman had attempted to kill me once already. Twice, no three times if you consider her goons. It was never a pleasant situation when I forgot how many times somebody attempted to assassinate me. In all the time I considered stopping her, I had given little thought as to how. Fighting muggers in the park only required humiliating them. Olivia wouldn't stop, bruising her ego would only make this worse.

"It's not my first choice," I admitted. "But I don't see any other way? If we put her in jail, she'll just control the police. If we dump her in a field, she'll come back. How do you stop a woman who can manipulate those around her?"

"You don't *stop* her," Theodore said. "I don't say this lightly. The Boston Paranormal Society has always been about the pursuit of knowledge. We're not fighters. We study and research. But she managed to run amok and take over the entire organization. Conventional means can't stop her."

"There has to be a way."

All day, Susan Lee had paved the way on a mission to save lives. There was no surprise that it persisted, even with Olivia, a woman determined to bring down hellfire on the city. "Perhaps Edward can help us."

"You mean her newest addition?" Theodore's network had already given him information about her cabal. "He's just as bad as the rest of them."

"No," I got in the man's face, "he's not."

I stood at the door, watching the veterans at a table on the other side of the gym. The mood had been somber since last night. They quietly rolled bandages for Susan Lee's brigade.

"What did I miss?" asked Theodore.

"Edward Valentine is her boyfriend," Susan Lee whispered.

"Husband."

"What?" She jumped to her feet, the shock stretching her face as she attempted to process the statement. Yes, the woman with little interest in a relationship had fast-tracked her way to a husband. I'd be shocked if it were the first time I said the word.

"It's not legal or anything, but we had a small ceremony on the rooftop."

"Eleanor, how dare you? I thought you were being honest with me last night." I don't think the fact I had married upset her. She was more disappointed she didn't get to partake in the planning, dress picking, and minute details that came along with a wedding.

"You were kind of there." It sounded awkward even as I said it.

"What?"

"It's a telepath thing. Don't worry, if we survive this, we'll do something proper." I don't know if the prospect of a legit wedding calmed her, or my casual comment about survival, but she sat down again.

"Valentine?" He mulled over news. Theodore's intelligence couldn't have gathered information about me. For all intents and purposes, I didn't exist. I didn't have a driver's license, I didn't belong to any organizations. Outside of this gym, I was one of the many nameless New Yorkers the system had forgotten.

Theodore didn't have room to pace. He took two steps,

turned, and repeated the motion. He adjusted his glasses as he paused. The man didn't like not knowing all the facts. I guess for an academic, being ill-informed must be a punch to the gut. Or did this have less to do with facts? Did this somehow involve our future tryst? No, for now, I could only focus on one problematic male in my life.

"We're as married as I will ever be." Even saying it sounded absurd at this point. I had tempted fate, throwing a wrench in the gears, hoping it was a big enough gesture to stall his death. Perhaps it was? If I could stop the war, then maybe there was a chance to save Edward from bleeding to death in my arms.

"I don't mean to sound petulant, but don't you think this was worth informing me?" He didn't mean to, but he certainly did. Looking over my shoulder, the shocked expression on his face was almost the same as his face in the vision where I bedded the man. Every future I had seen was now called into question. If they weren't guaranteed, then maybe every future I knew to this point was a lie.

There had been hundreds of random events I spotted in the future. From the march of women on Washington to African American's integrated into schools, I glimpsed a better world. Were they possibilities? And if they were just one version of the future, could everything… I gasped.

"I could die," I mumbled to myself.

"Edward, can you hear me?"

It was foolish speaking to myself in the mirror. I returned to the apartment to drop off Susan Lee before going out for the night. Pulling the dozens of bobby pins from my hair, I had a sudden sense of fatigue. In a moment of weakness, I needed to hear his voice.

"I don't know if you can hear me, Edward. If you can, you

need to leave. Olivia's men attacked a friend of mine. I didn't know it at the time, but I broke the truce. She's going to come for me and you're going to be in the middle."

I know.

I let out a sigh of relief. There had been something magical about sharing thoughts without speaking. He was the first mentalist I ever met, and part of me would always love him for opening my eyes to an unseen world. I didn't expect him to respond. Now that he did, I found myself at a loss for words.

You can run, Eleanor. Flee. It's the only thing—

"We could run away together, Edward. We could start over, be new people."

I imagined his hand touching my cheek, stealing my breath. It could be him reaching out, touching my skin, or it could be the memory of his hands. I missed the way he kissed me, as if it might be his last.

Reaching up, I touched the spot on my face, imagining his hand cupping my cheek. I leaned into it. Our relationship never reached perfection. A psychic vigilante and a telepathic grifter, we should never have worked. I would have taken a ten-to-one bet in the boxing ring before I bet on the success of our relationship.

For a time, we worked. The line in the sand had been drawn, and I didn't like that we were staring at one another from opposite sides. While I fought for the little man, Edward allied himself with an organization bent on what I don't know.

Even you don't believe that it's an option.

He was right. I hated it, but the man was right. "I don't want you in the middle of this."

Nor I, you.

We each saw the other as the willing victim. Try as I might, I couldn't convince him he was working with a woman hell-bent on consuming the city. The only good thing to come out of today, if my visions could be wrong, then perhaps Edward wouldn't die.

"Edward, it's not too late. You can come back to me. Things can be different. We can stand against Olivia together. We can stop the Society."

Olivia is an unfortunate bedfellow, Eleanor. I'm not fond of her either.

"But you," the tears were starting. I gasped, trying to hit the right buttons to make him see my point of view. "Gregory, she killed him."

There must always be four.

I ground my teeth at the statement. "She killed him. She blamed you. Why? Why did she do that, Edward? To make a vacancy for me?"

There was silence. Without saying a word, he confirmed a suspicion Olivia planted. Even if he hadn't caused Gregory's death, he knew of it. Knowing that his queen had killed a man in cold blood, did nothing to deter his allegiance.

We have eradicated the mob. We have infiltrated politicians ensuring they make decisions that benefit their constituents. This will work, Eleanor.

"Twice her henchmen have tried to kill me."

Rogue members. They have been dealt with.

"Killed, you mean. Don't gloss over the details, Edward. They kill those who step out of line. When it comes to it, will you do the same to me?"

I had delivered the ultimatum. He might choose power over my approach of one crime at a time. But when it came to her or me, who would he choose? Could I rely on the memory of an insecure telepath charming me on the merry-go-round to choose me over a cold-blooded woman with power?

I'm sorry it's come to this.

I had my answer.

The sensation along my cheek vanished. I was alone. I turned the sink spigot until water splashed about in the basin. The noise masked the sniffling. I sat on the edge of the tub and let myself cry. I hid my face behind my hands and let my emotions come to the surface. I stopped fighting it. The tears turned into uncontrollable sobbing.

Even if he didn't die, the Edward I had fallen in love with had perished, replaced by a man striving for power. We were over.

My heart hurt. I mourned a death the ghosts couldn't prevent.

Chapter Twenty

1943

Frank didn't trust either secret organization. The man bullied his way into the meeting with Theodore and his people. Two dozen of them had come to Boston, standing behind my mission to stop Olivia. Those who remained behind had done so for wives and children, noble in their own right. Most of all, if things went sidewise in New York, Theodore wanted to make sure the pursuit of knowledge wasn't lost in a massacre.

Both men were stubborn. Perhaps that was the reason Frank didn't trust Theodore? Frank could hurl the academic through the wall, and yet, Theodore continued talking to the man as if he were uneducated. If they threw punches, I would not stop Theodore from losing a tooth.

We gathered in an old restaurant. It looked as if the owners hadn't served food here since before the war. The tables were dusty, and it smelled of stale French fries. It was far away from Olivia, enough to provide relief from her prying eyes. Theodore's people came in waves to prevent suspicion. Once all had arrived, they started unloading all information they had gathered. His people were frightfully efficient.

"It's her, we're sure of it."

Two of his spies had contacted the remnants of Bertolucci's thugs. It seemed Olivia wanted both the politicians and the underbelly of New York. Was she securing herself on both fronts or was she using one to leverage the other? It made my head hurt to follow her logic. Both were going to be problematic, but at least I could beat thugs with my fists. Politicians, I didn't have the social graces to combat them.

"Catherine," Theodore said, "she's been put in charge of your mobster's former colleagues. If we're going to stop Olivia, she's the weak link."

I dared to sound like an amateur. "Why her?"

"Telekinesis, the ability to move objects with your mind. Flashy yes, but not nearly as dangerous as a telepath."

Frank coughed at the statement. "She can move things with her mind? How is that not more dangerous?"

Theodore pushed his glasses up his nose. I could tell by the expression of the rest of his peers, they already knew the answer to the question. Despite having the ability to predict the future, I always felt like the last one to know what was going on?

"She has limitations. But a telepath…" Theodore removed his glasses entirely, massaging the bridge of his nose. "Olivia could trap you in your own body and turn you against the rest of us. You'd be cannon fodder at best. At worst, you'd be another one of her puppets we'd need to put down."

I'm sure only half of that made sense to Frank.

Theodore continued. "I've been on the receiving end of Olivia's manipulations. She can freeze a room of people or get in your head and unravel your reality until you believe up is down and down is up. At least Catherine can't mess with our senses."

Frank nodded. I couldn't tell if Theodore intentionally explained it in a condescending manner, but it didn't make me want to get naked with him. I appreciated a man with a bit of danger, but not so much the attitude.

"Do you know how powerful she is? Can she move a lot of things or are we just talking about a couple of champaign flutes?"

"The only people who can answer that question are dead."

"Noted," I said. I went back to spinning a salt shaker about on the table. I didn't like not knowing the extent of the woman's abilities. How would seeing the future give me the advantage over Catherine? If I couldn't throw a punch or hurl a knife and know they'd land, there wasn't much good in being a precog.

"The journals say most telekinetics have to see an object to move it." The woman was at least ten years my senior. Lines around her eyes had set in, not making her appear old, but definitely making her appear wiser.

With a quick glance at all the faces in the room, one was missing. Veronica hadn't come to New York City. Her abilities weren't battle-ready, but I would have thought she'd have come. If Theodore required her to stay in Boston, I thought more highly of the man. After gallivanting through my memories, I'm not sure she'd ever be my biggest fan.

Frank leaned forward, resting his elbows on the table. "So, we sneak up on her—"

"We must work in concert. With enough of us in play, she won't be able to cover every direction."

To be honest, I liked Frank's idea better. I had never worked with anybody else in the room. None of them appeared to have battle scars or any inclination they had taken part in a scrap before. I couldn't walk into a fight with a bunch of academics. Knowledge might be powerful, but it was no match for brass knuckles to the jaw.

I finally spoke up, "How many of you have been in a fight?"

I waited to see if any of their hands came up. "None of you? Not one of you has been in a fight before. How about guns? Have any of you used a gun before? A knife?"

One man raised his hand. One. No, there was no way I was going into a fight with a woman capable of hurling me across the room and these folks being my backup. The conversation ended with that statement, I didn't need to hear more.

"So it's decided. Frank and I will go in alone. You're liabilities."

"But—"

I held a finger up toward Theodore to silence him. I stood, gently pushing in my chair. "It's been decided. You're better at being our eyes and ears. Keep digging up what you can on Olivia. Frank and I will handle Catherine."

"But—"

I didn't try to be subtle as I put my hand over his mouth. "The next words out of your mouth better be, 'Why yes, Eleanor, I agree to keep my people safe so you can do your job,' or I'm going to slap you."

He gave a slight nod. "Good, you wanted this to be a partnership. All of you, you want this to work, right?"

They nodded. A slightly older lady reached out, placing her hand on mine. "I was there when Olivia took over. We can't let her win. We'll help you."

I made eye contact with Theodore, pointing at the woman. "I like her already."

There was no laughter, no giggling. While we cemented a working relationship, there was still a chance we would die by tomorrow. Thankfully, Theodore had to take out Catherine, the brute muscle of the operation.

The researchers had been crossed before, tossed aside by the Society. They might not be fighters, but they wanted justice. Turning the Society into a benefit for mankind was a noble goal. If it helped me protect New York City, then I welcomed the partnership.

"You're all academics. You know this better than me. I need information. Tell me everything you know about mentalists."

And they did.

Complicated was an understatement. I am the first to admit that I had difficulty cooperating with others. Okay, that was a lie. I despised relying on other people. Frank and Susan Lee had been nothing but reliable confidants, but... I hated that the thought entered my mind. They were human.

Koji had proven that even a skilled fighter could become a victim. He was more than capable of defending himself, and a few goons had nearly killed him. Now I had a room full of academics whose definition of battle meant receiving a paper cut from an aggressive dictionary. Even had they trained with Koji for years, they remained human. Against Olivia, human translated to victim. It was hard to see them as anything other than potential victims.

"I need some air." I pushed away from the table. All eyes turned toward me. Two dozen men and women watched as I made a break for the door. They remained seated, and I'm sure they feared I had a vision. While I saw them as human, they couldn't get past seeing me as nothing more than a woman capable of seeing the future.

For the last three hours we discussed tactics, plans, advantages, and mentalist's weaknesses. The last part came as a shock. Theodore couldn't make eye contact as he outlined the details of each mentalist's abilities. He ranked them in order of danger, and I found it surprising when he cited Gregory as being the most dangerous man he ever met. It might be impossible to resist his abilities, but while he was alive, he was nothing but kind. If he had survived, I had no doubt he'd be here working to stop Olivia's tyranny.

Had Susan Lee been here, I'd be snatching the cigarette from her mouth and taking a drag myself. All the talk of strategy had me itching to drill my fists into the jaw of a cretin. It'd only take a sideways glance, and I'd be feeding them my knuckles. Yes, a cigarette might be the safest decision right now.

I laid my head back against the red brick, staring up at the sky. It was a beautiful day by New York standards. A breeze passed through the streets, just cool enough to want a jacket but not *need* one. The clouds hung frozen, stretching across the sky like somebody had hurled a can of white paint against a blue ceiling. It was perfect, *too* perfect.

In either direction, not a single person walked along the street. We were in the city that never slept, and to see an entire street empty was odd on its own. More than emptiness was the lack of sound. No birds chirping, no whooshing of the wind, and none of the white noise created by the biggest city on the east coast.

"Edward," I knew the signs of a mentalist. I waited for the echo of the world around me to bleed into the infinite stretches of the white room.

"Edward?" If he wanted to speak, he used to snatch me away. Slamming the walls into place around my flame, I wondered if he was still capable? Olivia had wormed her way into my mind once. Was he being polite or were his powers unable?

I watched as my ghost pulled away from my body. She turned, staring me in the face, and as we blinked in unison, my eyes opened to see I had shifted positions. No longer seeing from my ghost's perspective came off as jarring. My body and brain had an agreement. I knew I remained leaning against the wall, but my mind was free to explore. But unlike before, I wasn't seeing New York City, I had stepped into the white room of my own accord.

"Curious," I whispered.

"I didn't want to be presumptuous."

"You didn't want to make me mad," I corrected.

"I'm going to do that no matter how this conversation goes."

I worried he had seen me outside of the restaurant. He had never expressed knowing where my body lived while in the white room. I hadn't thought to ask Theodore if that was one of their gifts. The more I feared the answer, the more my heart sank. I wanted to save Edward, but it wasn't possible to stop his destructive path. As I let go of the idea I could, a sadness pulled my heart into my stomach.

"What do you want, Edward?"

"I want you safe, away from the city. You can go to the cities you've talked about. Rome? France? I can pay for you…"

"You made your choice, Edward. From the start, you knew that I was dead set on protecting the city. You're the one who sided with Olivia."

"Eleanor, you can't make the city safe. One brawl after another? It would take more than a lifetime for you to change the course of New York." He might be right about that. Thanks to a vision and the gumption of Susan Lee, we might have changed the course of mankind.

"And you'd rather strip them of free will to set things right?"

"I—"

"Don't bother answering. We will not agree. We didn't then, and we certainly won't now. You've sided with a woman who attempted to kill your wife. I know where I fall on your list of importance."

Edward's face hung low. Despite his aspirations, he knew. That bastard knew he picked the wrong side. He refused to back down. I wanted to scream. I wanted to unleash a string of obscenities that would make Frank blush.

"He did, didn't he?"

Olivia stepped from behind Edward as if by magic. She hung on his shoulder, like a schoolyard crush. When she ran his hands through his hair, I nearly lost my composure. I wasn't a jealous woman, not by any stretch, but Olivia was not a random floozy.

"I don't know what I can say to fix this, 'Nore?"

"He can't, can he?"

She might have invaded our private conversation, but the way she moved about Edward, caressing his chest, seemed off. Edward never faltered, his eyes fixed on me. It was the first time I stood in the white room with two people. I didn't understand how it might be different for telepaths, but it turned obvious that he was unaware of her fondling.

"I'd throw her in prison if it were an option."

"It's not." Even he understood. There was a single option. Either she died, or I died trying. There was no middle ground in this situation.

"Despite the riches. Despite New York City under his reign. He still thinks of you."

Her words hurt. It'd be easy if Edward had become an egomaniacal killer. It'd be easy if he cast me away for the Society. But even with all of her hopes and promises, part of him clung to our relationship. It wasn't enough.

"It's hard to imagine he thinks of you," her finger touched his lips, "when he's with me."

She baited me.

"Edward, this will be fixed when she's dead."

Olivia leaned in close to Edward's face, her eyes darting between me and him. With one graceful swoop, her tongue slid across his cheek. I am not a jealous woman. No, I lied, I'm jealous.

"It's fine, Eleanor," she taunted me. Half-truths and misdirection, these are the weapons of a telepath. I recited Theodore's warnings, trying to keep my anger in check. My clenched teeth and balled fists were less than calm.

"Regardless, he does a fine job of keeping me happy."

The flame roared to life and pressed against the barriers I put in place to keep her at bay. Edward and I didn't have a typical relationship, how could we. If he mentioned an indiscretion, I don't believe I'd have been jealous. I knew his heart, and as mentalists, we simply *know*. But Olivia, I couldn't, no, not today, not ever.

The walls didn't crumble, they exploded. The flame poured

out and a legion of ghosts shot from my body. Slamming into Edward and Olivia. Her facade broke and for a moment she had a look of panic. It was all I needed. Underneath that flawless mask, Olivia was scared. She should be.

"Is everything alright?" Theodore glanced across the street, trying to find what had caught my attention. He removed his glasses, polishing them. Without them, he appeared almost dashing, his stubble attempting to mask the fine line of his jaw.

"It will be."

I had seen this bedroom.

As Theodore opened the door, offering a slight bow, I had decided. He was a handsome man, thicker than many of my suitors, with a bit of a roundness starting in his midsection. If I hadn't already seen his naked chest, I'd be curious if he was one of those gorilla-like men or if it was as smooth as my own. There was no mystery, at least for me.

He stepped into the room, shutting the door behind him. Hesitating, with his forehead leaning against the door, he had more on his mind than he was saying.

"Spill it already."

"You've seen this."

I don't know if the idea excited him. He turned slowly, his eyes not giving away his emotions. I didn't want to be a mentalist. I didn't want to be a precog. Right now, I wanted nothing more than to be a woman, an object of desire. But Theodore wasn't like any man I had seduced before, he thought before he acted.

I opted for honesty. "I have."

"Are you doing this because of the visions?"

Why was I doing this? Revenge? Jealousy? Was I about to taint our relationship because of Olivia? Dang it, Theodore's intellectual nature seemed infectious and already I felt myself getting lost in a series of what-ifs.

My cheeks warmed as I found myself embarrassed. I turned away, trying to hide my confusion. Even before Edward, if I bedded a man it was for the thrill or at least the gratification. But right now, the emotions weren't so easily labeled. Whatever drove me, it was at the center of a knot so complicated I wasn't sure if I acted of my own accord.

Then it struck me, and the sheer simplicity caused a slight chuckle.

"Are you okay?"

"That's why," I said.

"Eleanor, I think you might need to elaborate. I'm smart, but let's say women aren't my field of study."

"When you look at me, what do you see?" I had never asked a man to analyze me.

"You're a…" His voice trailed off. I feared the next word out of his mouth. In the time it took him to collect himself, I could have bested a man in the ring. He took a step closer, and then a smaller step. They grew shorter as he stepped within reach.

"You're a determined woman. I have never met somebody willing to put themselves in danger like you. You claim to not believe in a higher power, but you answer a calling. Eleanor, your heart." His hand reached my face, inches from my cheek. "I'm an academic. I want to understand what makes it beat."

There were few who thought of me as a woman first and foremost. My identity revolved around this gift and little else. My breath stuttered as his finger grazed my cheek. There were so many labels I had assumed, but to be seen as a woman, that caught my breath.

His eyes had softened. They no longer darted back and forth as he tried to write something to memory. Theodore Stewart had cut through my macho bull. I fanned my face as tears pooled along the bottom of my eyes.

"Oh no, did I say something… what can I do?"

"I'll be fine."

He brushed his thumb against each of my cheeks, wiping away the tears. "That's not what I asked."

Whether his words held a deeper sultry meaning or not, I didn't care. I grabbed him by the jacket, pulling until my body pressed against his. He wasn't passive, not in the least. His hand went to the back of my head and he pushed his lips against mine. His other hand worked to the small of my back and he pulled me in tight. I forgot this quiet man had taken a piece of wood and beaten a man to protect me. Believing him shy vanished as he broke our kiss to kiss from behind my ear to the collar of my blouse.

I bit my bottom lip, trying to hold back a gasp.

He stood straight, reaching for his glasses. In a well-practiced motion, he pulled them from his face and tucked them into his interior breast pocket. He pulled his jacket from his shoulders and I stopped him.

"This is my favorite part."

I slipped his jacket off, letting my arms brush against him. With a flick of the wrist, it fell to the floor. I wanted his shirt off him, but he hadn't brought a suitcase from the city. I respected that he might only have a single shirt. Painfully, one button at a time, opened, revealing a chest coated in short hair.

"Your favorite part?"

I pulled the shirt from over his shoulders, trapping his arms at his side. Holding the fabric tight, I kissed along his chest. Moving to the left, I flicked my tongue across his nipple. Each time I made contact, his body tensed. I didn't need to be psychic to be one-of-a-kind. Theodore wouldn't forget this tryst.

The teasing ended as he pulled his arms free and tossed the shirt. I stepped back, leaning against the bed as I unfastened the buckle of my jacket. He stopped fumbling with his belt as I pulled off my jacket and moved on to unbuttoning my blouse. He chewed his bottom lip.

I took my time, tracing a finger over my skin as I pulled the shirt open. As I removed my slacks, he did the same. In seconds we were left in only our unmentionables. I sat on the foot of the bed, scooting myself backward.

Theodore stared. No longer did an academic ask questions about my abilities or about the future. As he stood at the edge of the bed, there was nothing intellectual happening. The bulge in his briefs made it clear which head was doing the thinking. There were no theatrics, no imaginary scenarios played out, just a man excited by the woman in his bed.

Without ceremony, he pulled down his underwear. It might not be polite to stare, but Theodore was full of secrets. A lady knows that a man's prowess in bed had little to do with his penis. Those ladies had never seen this man naked. I might be fearful that he relied on the size of manhood, but I recalled the vigor he displayed in my vision.

Spinning about on the bed, I sat on the side, with him pressed against my breasts. I kissed just above his navel, the tiny hairs across his abdomen tickling my nose. I don't know what passive response I expected, but as he reached down, grabbing my hips, I let out a laugh. He lifted me from the bed, my breasts in line with his face.

"I've never met somebody this confident." The words were breathy. He could have commented on the breasts in his face, or the curvature of my hips. My confidence, of all the assets at my disposal, that was what he thought about?

"Don't ruin the moment." I prepared to put a finger to his lips.

"In the museum…" I lowered my finger, giving him a chance to finish his thought. "When you walked into the room, I hoped you weren't the voice from the phone. Seeing the future? We've prepared our whole lives for that. But a beautiful woman? There weren't enough written words to prepare—"

I'm sure his sentiment was elegant, perhaps poetic. But something in my chest broke, and the ghosts filled the inches between our mouths. I smashed my lips against his. He supported me with one hand while he unclasped my bra with a deft hand. I pulled it the rest of the way off and tossed it aside.

He dropped me onto the bed and crawled over me, between my legs. Supporting himself on his elbows, he kissed his way up my body until he reached the space just beneath my breath. He let the stubble graze my skin while his tongue studied my body like there would be a surprise test in the morning. I wrapped my legs around his waist, feeling him hard through my underwear.

"We're on a schedule, skip the foreplay." I'd regret it with his girth, but I couldn't roll around the sheets and save New York City.

"I'm not one to rush."

Theodore did not lie.

Chapter Twenty-One

1943

Hell's Kitchen. It earned its name. Years ago it served as a bastion for organized crime, rumrunners, and hidden distilleries. When alcohol became legal, crooks found new methods to make money, always at a cost to the poor. Bertolucci's name might have sparked fear throughout Manhattan, but here, he might only be a small-time criminal.

The warehouses lining the pier had once been a sign of a functioning commerce. That faded as mobsters seized control of the ports. I roamed these streets often and never did I come away without confrontation. Bruised and battered, I could fight my way through street-level mobsters, but the true victory was taking out the head. Even I knew the limits of my abilities. Thankfully, the rest of the gangs kept to a small section of the city. Had Bertolucci stayed in Hell's Kitchen, he might be alive today.

The Hudson smelled of rot. With the tide going out, the smell permeated every fiber of the piers. It clung to my nostrils, and I'm sure it'd continue long after I showered. If Mobsters were going to hide in New York, this struck me as fitting. Images of bodies found along the Hudson with ropes tied to their ankles and cement blocks often reached the papers.

I checked my pocket for the brass knuckles and the back of my jacket for the knives. Three weapons on my body. I reached into my left pocket, feeling the charcoal. I didn't need to disguise myself, not when the only person who mattered knew me by name, but the ritual steadied my nerves. The powder coated my eyes, creating a mask, providing a secret identity. There was something powerful about being anonymous.

I no longer needed to focus on the flame. The visualization technique had become second nature, another simple comfort reminding me how far I had come. The scar along my torso did the same, but not in a good way. Years ago, I considered the ghosts a burden, cruel manifestations of the Devil. With the flame lit, the pier came alive with phantom men and women.

I lifted the mask to complete the costume, securing it on my face. I might not have a cape like Superman or a shield like Captain America, but I wasn't looking to be a beacon of hope. Right now, I wanted to instill fear. When this was over I'd consider changing my image, maybe.

A row of massive buildings separated the street from the water. Running almost the full length of the pier, it stood four stories tall. The doors were almost as massive, with a bank of windows high above, reminding me of the doors to a church. It had a new feeling to it with the well-maintained brick, but the lack of lighting and vehicles going to and from the building made it appear deserted. For any New Yorker walking by, entering would have been foolish.

I was a foolish New Yorker.

None of the ghosts paid me any attention. I continued looking over my shoulder, ensuring I didn't miss anything. I had fallen prey to my own ego before. This time I kept my blind spots front and center in my mind. They would not knock me over the head tonight, at least not from behind.

The sun had set an hour earlier. There was no need in trying to duck and hide. I crossed the street, careful to avoid the single light shining from a nearby pole. Even if mobsters hid inside watching through the window, they'd never be able to see me.

Olivia might be capable of entering my mind and waging an unseen war, but Catherine relied on the physical world. Even if she could hurl me into the sky and strike me from a distance, I would much rather be here than dealing with her boss. Much like a boxing match, this powerhouse was the warm-up. I longed for the simpler days of just punching and getting punched.

I eased the door open. Peering inside, I let my ghost enter. Observing through its eyes, I could see the vast empty space. Benches lined the middle of the room, where passengers waited to board the boats. The stillness made me nervous. Theodore had been certain of his intel. The ghost knelt down, running its hand along the floor, looking for dust. In the dim light, it was hard to see anything but the ghosts, footprints revealed there had been plenty of traffic. They were here.

"Time to save the city," I whispered.

While this section housed the passengers, I assumed one wing was where the supply boats deposited their wares. I didn't have the time to waste searching for them. The question, do I go left or right sprung to mind. My ghost turned in one direction, then the other. I didn't fear the outcome. I shoved the urge to save the city, my terror of failure, and shoved it into the flame.

My ghost split, one left and one right. I caught glimpses through their eyes. Time quickened in-between blinks. The ghost on the left ducked as a man stepped out of the door. The one on the right entered an empty section of the building. I breathed a sigh of relief. This newfound freedom with my abilities opened a new world of possibilities. I wish I had the time to explore, to practice as Gregory would have wanted.

"No time like the present says the psychic." It'd be humorous if I survived.

Following in my ghost's footsteps, I caught sight of the guard before he arrived. I ducked into a stairwell leading to the second level. The space had more than enough equipment, tables, and crates to weave through and stay hidden.

My concern wasn't for the men with guns, it was for the telepath potentially listening to my every thought. I tried calming my brain, focusing on my body as Koji instructed. But knowing somebody could follow my every action upped the stakes. Perhaps she had already alerted Catherine, and I was about to walk into a firing squad. Theodore's people tried to explain how to become a shadow. It wasn't a tactic learned in a single lesson.

I reached into my pocket and pulled out the brass knuckles, looping the fingers on my left hand into the holes. It wasn't my strong hand, but I needed my right for the knives at my back. The plan was to eliminate her guards, reduce the number of mobsters, and then take her out. I might be a brute in the ring, but right now I needed the lay of the land before I picked off the mobsters. I didn't want them to find bodies until I was ready to reveal myself. Unfortunately, the future had different plans.

I followed my ghost. One timeline, one direction. The mobster was smoking a cigarette, moving through the empty space in a predictable pattern. Up one aisle and down the next. I moved from one crate to the side of a table, ducking out of sight. In a few minutes, we'd meet. I watched as my ghost stood behind his, grabbing him by the head, plunging a knife into his throat. Messy, but effective.

Hurry.

Chapter Twenty-Two

1943

Edward. I would always recognize his mental whispers, even from a single word. My heart picked up momentum. There was hope. I might not lose him. With a simple suggestion, I hoped the young grifter I first met had returned.

I waited for the mobster to pass. Without fanfare, my hand darted out, the knife sliding through the flesh of his neck. I stepped behind him, covering his muffled, gurgling sounds. Before the body went limp, I tucked him away to prevent his buddies from finding him.

My feet moved, thrusting the ghost from my body, watching down the service hallway separating this part of the warehouse from the next. Narrow, barely wide enough for two people shoulder to shoulder, the passage connected to a space near the pier. One of her men hid in a doorway on the right, fighting to stay awake. Another stood at the end, blocking the exit that would lead to the part of the building extending to the water.

The brass knuckles slipped into my pocket. I slid the knives from their holsters. Spinning one around in my right hand, I prepared to throw. I watched as my ghost hurled the blade. I cursed under my breath as I watched the phantom blade strike the man in a dozen different spots. Even if I could follow the flick of my wrist, it was far too fine a movement to repeat. I steadied my breath, praying I could time the throw.

I started down the hall. The man didn't notice me at first. I paused just before I reached the man hidden on the right. I exhaled and threw the knife. Spinning faster than I could see, it struck the man, stopped short by the strap holding his gun.

"Damn."

He looked down, confused. "What the hell?"

"Bruno, did you say something?"

I stepped into the doorway with the sleepy mobster. Unsheathing my second blade in a smooth movement and balancing my left hand with my right forearm. I thrust the blade forward, sinking into the space just below his Adam's apple. With a twist, I pulled it free.

I jumped into the hallway. The man at the end raised his gun. It was desperate, but I chucked the blade. I stepped into the doorway to avoid the barrage of bullets. The sleepy mobster was bleeding out and sank to the ground, trying to keep the blood from spilling out of his neck.

"Improvise." I pulled the gun from around his neck. Frank had taken me shooting, but the weapon felt alien in my hands. This was far larger than the pistol he'd taught me to use. I knew the basics. Point. Pull the trigger. Hope the bad guy dies before he shoots you. Easy.

I leaned out of the doorway, the gun leading the way. Prepared to jerk the trigger, I froze. The second knife had found its way into the man's neck and like his partner, he struggled to stem the bleeding. He pulled the knife free. Spurts of red shot between his fingers. It was almost too easy. Then the man fell backward, bursting through the double doors into the room on the other side.

Ghosts filled the next room, mobsters of all shapes and sizes using the corridor to travel between the warehouse and the delivery area. I looked back and forward. Clear. I stormed down the hallway, picking up the first blade and then pulling my other free from the dead man. I wiped them on his jacket before looking up.

Catherine, flanked by two cronies.

"What do…" My ghost stepped out of my body and time stood still. The fight needed to end before she realized a plan was already in motion. For that matter, I had yet to realize the plan. Theodore's men disseminated the plan, providing just enough information to those who needed to know. Should Olivia invade my mind, or Frank's, we were only pieces of a bigger puzzle.

I watched my ghost chuck the first knife. It would have landed in her left eye. Precision I only found while practicing. But it never reached its mark. An unseen force pushed the killing blow to the side, and it scraped along her goon's cheek, splitting it in half. I gathered my fear and let it seep into the flame. Another ghost stepped out of my body, and another. I watched the blade thrown a hundred different ways, none of them landing where I wanted.

I picked the best alternative and hurled the knife low. Even before she batted it to the side with her abilities, I slowed time again. Pushing past the ghosts, glimpses of a thousand outcomes flooding in. In none of them did I get the knife in my left hand to my right and hurl it before I ran out of time. In some futures she knocked it to the side, others she spun it around, hurling it back. In at least a dozen of those possibilities, she killed me.

I let time resume. The knife sank into the groin of the mobster while I raised my hands.

The mobster cursed. Catherine waited a moment before growing tired of his shrieking. The blade pulled free. Quickly and with deadly accuracy it flung into his neck, replacing his screaming with a gurgling sound.

"You win."

Catherine's smile grew, spanning the width of her face. "You couldn't find an outcome where you won?"

"Not with violence." Whatever parts of the plan that were supposed to fall into place had yet to reveal themselves. I waited for a sign, hoping it arrived before she crushed me.

"I wished Edward hadn't found other business. He'd absolutely love to see you without options."

Was he supposed to be here? Again, the man perplexed me. He had urged me forward. If he wanted to lead me into a trap, why not be there to see his handiwork? Or did Edward being absent somehow benefit me? For a woman capable of seeing the future, there were things the ghosts couldn't reveal.

"A psychic who sees the future and can do nothing to change it. That almost seems cruel."

She didn't know. If Catherine didn't know my abilities had evolved, I still had a glove in the ring. I would need every advantage if I was going to take on a telepath. Or was that telepaths?

Catherine lifted off the ground. It was hard to believe a person could float like magic. I couldn't best her with a blade. I needed to distract her. Thankfully, she offered me a narrative to delay having my neck snapped.

"Wait, you believe there is another option, don't you?"

"Join me." It wasn't part of the script, but I needed a chance to sort through the timeline. I wouldn't die here.

She didn't laugh. I assumed she was as egotistical as Olivia. She considered my offer. Slowly, Catherine came closer, leaving the remaining mobster holding his gun, nervous as he watched the woman. Her toes skid along the ground, hovering almost a foot above the ground. This was by far more impressive than floating a champaign flute across the room.

"What do you see, precog?" Her eyebrow raised slightly. Catherine was willing to hear my offer.

"Olivia is going to die." I hadn't seen it in a vision, but it was on my list of things to do in the next few days. "Without her influence, the Society will implode."

"Telepaths are a dime a dozen. I am their muscle and you," she considered it a viable option, "with your foresight, the Society could be something bigger."

"Money? Power? Play by my rules and you can say goodbye to managing the mob. We can build something good and remain powerful."

Now she chuckled. Unlike Olivia's condescending laugh, Catherine almost giggled at the notion. "You speak like a dreamer. Good and powerful, do not go hand in hand, Eleanor. You're showing your naivety."

"We can make it what we want."

"Mankind has to be molded, persuaded even. If not by power, or by money, then might. I don't think you have it in you."

It was almost humorous, the blood staining my hands this very moment. "Theodore said—"

"That is who's been putting these foolish ideas in your head. Theo, I should have crushed his skull when he defected. Be careful of that one, Eleanor. He'll get you killed with his ideology."

She hovered close enough I could see the folds of her clothes fluttering as if a breeze swept through the room. Knowing I came here to kill her, she moved dangerously close, well within arm's reach. I only needed to find a crack in her guard, a way to plunge the knife into her chest. I tightened my grip, preparing my muscles.

There were plenty of ghosts in the room. With Catherine overseeing the underworld of the Society, there should have been mobsters in the room. The other pieces of the plan came into sight. I tried to shove my ghost forward, to find a kink in her armor. Despite the specters in the room, I couldn't conjure my own, or if I did, it didn't move from this spot for the foreseeable future.

I acted on instinct. Even if she pushed the knife aside, I'd be ready to drive my knee into her gut. But my arm didn't flinch. Every muscle tensed as I tried to will myself forward. I could only blink. Whatever cursed gift she wielded, Catherine held me in place.

"A knife? Precog, you must have seen this."

I grinned.

"I did."

Chapter Twenty-Three

1943

The snap and echo of gunshots filled the room. While Theodore's men might be experts at collecting information, they weren't fighters. I needed an army. It just so happened, some of the United States' finest had raised me. I had never been so happy to see Vinny.

The mobster to her side didn't have time to raise his gun. His body jerked as somebody fired into his back. Vinny sat in the rafters, hugging one of the steel beams. With grace only mustered by a soldier, he fell three more mobsters as they barreled into the room.

Nicholas stepped out from a side door, holding a gun similar to the mobsters. Even Tony, that sweet sweet asshole Tony, joined them. Covered in blood, he had already seen action this evening.

"Give up," I offered her a last chance to live.

Vinny turned his attention on Catherine and fired. She spun about, throwing her hand to the side. Tony and Nicholas pulled back their triggers, sending bullet after bullet at the woman. Growling, she threw up both of her hands. I gasped. Dozens of little black dots hung suspended in the air. With a grunt, the bullets flung at Tony like a kid throwing rocks, enough to sting, but not to kill.

"How dare you?" With one hand raised toward me, she clenched her fist. The wind squeezed from my lungs. My arms tightened against my body. She raised the hand while Vinny and Nicholas continued shooting. I raised off my feet, frozen solid.

Catherine's abilities were awesome. With her other hand, she merely held it up, palm facing out. The bullets struck an invisible surface, flattening and falling to the floor. Had she not worked for the bad guys, I could see this as an amazing ability to fight crime.

Just as Theodore had said, her abilities had a limited range. While she squeezed my chest, threatening to break a rib, the veterans stayed far out of reach. Another jerk of her hand and my lungs stopped struggling for air.

"You thought you and three old men could stop me? Save you?"

"F—" no air, "our."

"I'm sorry, I couldn't hear you."

"Four," came a deep bass voice.

The bang of the shotgun made my teeth rattle. Her powers didn't require her hands. The pellets of the shotgun blast hovered just behind her back. Catherine spun about, her toes still inches from the cement. A few feet away, Michael held a shotgun. Silently, he wheeled in with a clear shot at the back of her head. His witty banter cost him the shot.

Catherine didn't move a muscle. I fell to one knee as she hurled Michael backward. He swore as he struck the side of a truck, hands clutching his head to soften the impact.

"Foolish—"

I lunged. The knife sank into her back. I turned the blade and jerked it free. A scream tore from her lips while I prepared to repeat the blow. Catherine fell onto all fours. She fought to stay upright. I grabbed her by the hair, pulling until she got to her knees. She flailed with her arm, trying to bat me away.

"Ooph." It was like a truck hit me. I couldn't stop from soaring through the air, striking the ground and rolling. She hadn't merely lifted me, she smacked me with an invisible force. Every bone in my body vibrated with ache.

I crawled away from her on my elbows, hoping to reach the magical border and escape her abilities. She let out a blood-curdling scream, trying to bend her arm in a way to reach the wound. It bordered on cruel as she writhed, her lungs failing her as she wheezed.

I had been prepared to cut her neck and make it a fast, painless death. Part of me preferred the suffering. I hated that it came to this, but I didn't want her to die quickly. I didn't care how horrific it might be, I had been pushed too far. I imagined the slippery slope I approached, staring down into a dark void. As she screamed, I realized I was more than prepared to risk that descent.

The men could have pulled the trigger, ending her misery with a single shot. The silence in the building made it clear they mirrored my feelings. Blood poured from the wound and Catherine wobbled until she fell, her chin driving onto the cement. The woman had been part of a cabal attempting to seize control of New York. These were the same people who nearly killed Koji and six months earlier, me. Relishing in her whimpers and cries, a part of my soul turned black. Worse, I didn't care.

It took minutes before Catherine's body stopped twitching. Tony ran across the room, traveling in a wide arc to stay away from the mentalist. He grabbed Michael's wheelchair, pushing it toward the fallen vet. With a quick check of Michael's head, Tony helped him into the chair. I couldn't believe Tony checked the man's skull for injury. A year ago, he'd shamed the man for being black. We might not always get along, but Frank transformed us into a family.

Nobody fucked with our family.

I grabbed the knife, tightening my grip until my fingers hurt. I moved up behind Catherine, straddling her body. Pressing my knee into her back, I drove the blade into the crown of her skull. It didn't sink nearly as far as expected, but far enough to know it struck her brain. With a hard jerk, and then a wiggle of the blade, I yanked it free.

"What the hell was that? How—how did she do that?"

Tony couldn't hide his disbelief. He pushed Michael in his wheelchair, coming close enough to confirm Catherine was dead. "How did she do that? How did you do *that?*"

Nicholas hung back, staying clear of the dead woman. "Those men Frank sent, they warned us…"

"Nothing prepared us for *this*." Tony gestured to the dead woman.

"You're like her?" Michael asked.

I shook my head. "No," I said, "I'm nothing like her."

I wiped my blade on the back of her blouse, leaving red streaks on the fabric. I slid the knife behind me, working it into the sheath. As I stood over the dead body, staring at the hole in her skull, the statement didn't quite hold the same weight. I was more like her than I wanted to admit. If offering my humanity protected New York, I'd face the consequences later.

"I appreciate your help, but you need to go home. This is only going to get worse."

"Worse than this?"

I gave Michael a nod. "Catherine was…" I didn't quite know how to explain it to people without abilities, "she was the least lethal."

"We're coming with you." It started with Tony, and one by one they raised their hands to their foreheads in a salute.

I held up my hand, "No."

There were no words to voice my appreciation. They wore their uniforms, ready for a war they didn't understand. These men set aside their differences and blindly followed Frank's orders. They were obedient soldiers. I would be honored to have them at my back. But our enemy had the ability to turn them on one another.

"You can't go where I'm going."

"Eleanor, we've got your back." Michael would have followed me without question. These were the uncles every girl needed. They were loud, vulgar, and often I wanted to scream at them. But they'd put their lives on the line to protect me.

"I know you do. But Olivia isn't like Catherine." They looked to the body on the ground. Her powers were impressive. "It's not the same as ambushing mobsters. She can read your minds," I took a deep breath, "she can control people. One second you're fighting with me, the next you're holding a gun to my head."

"We'd never—"

"I know, Michael. But you wouldn't have a choice. It doesn't sound as impressive as moving things with your mind. But it's far more terrifying."

Vinny had made it down from the rafters and jogged over to us. "Not bragging, but taking out New York mobsters is way easier than Russians."

Older than the others, Vinny would have gladly returned to service if it wasn't for his hearing. Everybody froze as I gave Vinny a hug. Unfamiliar with my affection, the man stiffened, his arms tight at his sides. I had boxed with him a hundred times, but never had we hugged. In the future, I would change that.

"I have to do this alone." I let go of Vinny and stepped back. They didn't like that option, they were soldiers and needed orders. "Go home and wait for the all-clear. This is certainly going to make Olivia angry. I don't want her attacking our people."

"But—"

"That's an order." Thanks to Frank, I went from a grunt on the streets to a commanding officer. There was no comfort or satisfaction in this newfound position. I never wanted to be the leader.

"Yes, sir," Tony said. My disdain for the man waned as he fell in line.

"Be safe," Michael added.

Catherine had been the warm-up. Now the actual battle was about to begin. I could heal from bumps and bruises. Having my mind torn apart by Olivia, I could think of better ways to spend my evening.

"Be the last man standing," Tony said.

I'm coming for you, Olivia.

In the back of my mind, a distant echo responded. *I know.*

Chapter Twenty-Four

1943

I hadn't driven in years. The gears whined as I shifted, nearly stalling the car. I parked blocks away from Olivia's brownstone. Her abilities obviously could reach as far as the piers, but she hadn't interceded. Perhaps killing Catherine was as inconsequential as murdering Gregory. Something didn't make sense, and I didn't like not knowing the woman's motives.

She might not read my mind, but she had made it clear she was powerful enough to manipulate me. Trapping me within the white room while she moved freely in both places made her dangerous. Even sitting here, I grew leery. Was this real? Could I already be moving toward the door and she somehow forced me to think I was still in the car?

"I hate telepaths," I cursed. Edward had taught me the basics, what a telepath could do. But it was Olivia who showed me the magnitude of their abilities.

I stared out the window in the brownstone's direction. "Edward, I hope you stay out of the way." It was bad enough I had to worry about the others, but I didn't want this night to end with him and me on opposite sides. Part of me hoped when this was over, he'd see the error of his ways. That part steadily shrunk.

"Let's do this."

I pushed the door open and stepped out. In the next hour, I'd either be getting back in the car, or I'd be dead. The knives were neatly tucked away in their sheaths and the brass knuckles tugged at my right pocket. My eyes were already blackened, but I reached into the left pocket, grinding charcoal between my fingers.

I'm waiting, Eleanor.

Olivia believed she already won. There was no mention of killing Catherine or that I steadily interrupted her influence. Even if I had abided by the truce and steered far away from her men, it would have come to this. I didn't need to be a psychic to know that our destinies always lead to this moment.

Shut up, you cow.

She started to respond, but I slammed shut the doors to my mind. As I rubbed the charcoal over my eyes, I pictured the flame surrounded by material stronger than steel. It burned brightly, protected away from the mind witch. I could summon the ghosts without it, but returning to the basics provided a sense of calm. Gregory would be proud.

My pointer and middle finger were black, covered in the dark powder. Pulling the collar upward, covering my nose, I tied the straps to the mask behind my head. Foolish concealing my identity, but I needed to embrace whatever brought me a sense of power. Tonight, it'd be as much a battle of wills as it would fists. God, I hoped I had the chance to beat her pretty face with my fists.

I froze under a street lamp. Curfew would begin any minute, and the power to the lights would be cut. Somebody in a window to my left stared. By the silhouette, I assumed it was an elderly woman. I paused, turning in her direction, staring at where her eyes would have been. Grabbing the curtains, she promptly pulled them shut, hiding herself.

The last time I had set foot on this street, I'd struggled to keep myself alive. Susan Lee was at home being watched by Frank's men. Tonight, she wouldn't be coming to my rescue. It bothered her, but I couldn't put Susan Lee in harm's way, not with Olivia looking for any method to strike me down.

Stealing a glance at the future, ghosts milled about the street, the early walkers taking their dogs outside to relieve themselves. I avoided looking at the brownstone. While I had been freed from the shackles of fate, I didn't trust myself enough to tempt the cruel mistress. I didn't want to see a future I couldn't change. Gregory would have forced me to practice day in and out. Two days would have to do it.

Poppa and Benjie had been a delusion, a symptom of blood loss, that I hoped to see again. Poppa had spoken to me while I'd danced the fine line between life and death. Part of me wished it were real. Considering my friendship with Claudette, perhaps seeing the deceased wasn't so far-fetched. When this was over, I'd visit the farm and put my demons to rest.

Until then, I imagined the anger of unfinished business rolling down my skin. The liquid fury soaked into the sphere around the flame and inside, it grew brighter, hotter, threatening to cause an explosion. It only grew more intense as I thought of Edward inside those walls. Admitting I couldn't change the past allowed me the luxury of manipulating the future. It was a beautiful balance, one that had been vastly one-sided throughout my life.

I stepped onto the sidewalk. It was only another few feet, then twelve steps before I reached the door. Inside, a woman was going to try to kill me. For a moment, I contemplated taking the easy route and setting the building on fire and watching it burn. I'd revel in the sound of Olivia screaming.

With each step, I swore the pressure on my skull increased. More than once in a fight with Edward, he tried to bypass my walls to speak with me. He had never been this insistent, nor had he succeeded. Every stair toward the front door, I celebrated a minor victory. Try as she might, I wouldn't allow her in my head.

The door was ajar, a slight crack between it and the frame. The threshold was still stained a dark black from where Olivia attempted to gut me. She had thought me dead, that she finally defeated a psychic. For all I knew, I was in another mirage and everything since the car was fake…

No. Unlike before, I was prepared for her.

I took the last step. I stood in the doorway, the door creaking open. It was just as I recalled. The study waited off to the left. Inside remained quiet, and I could only assume she hid, knife in hand, prepared to carve a matching scar on my other side.

With one last glance over my shoulder, I entered the house. I reached into my pocket, sliding the brass knuckles over my fingers. Everything Koji had ever said passed through my mind. Be aware of your feet. Watch your center of gravity. Narrow your gait. None of it mattered fighting a telepath, but it helped keep me focused.

Something was amiss, a scent in the air or maybe a rumbling under my feet. My gut tightened, and the scar ached. I had walked into the proverbial lion's den, but I refused to be reduced to a mouse. No, I was a lioness, and it was me doing the hunting.

Or so I thought until the door slammed shut.

Bomber jacket creepiness. The hollow husk of a human stepped out of the shadows leading into the sitting room. Only ten feet down the hall, another stepped from the study. It limited my options. Run up the stairs and hide, or trade blows with two men in close quarters?

"Boys, ring the bell."

The ghosts materialized seconds into the future and rippled

outward. I focused on the future, allowing time to slow as my brain processed the information. I only needed to be a moment ahead of them, a fraction of a moment. I watched the fight unfold, and then I forced the ghosts to replay the timeline again. Each ended resulted in my death.

I refused to accept my demise. I pushed past the headache, beyond the doubt. The pressure in my skull grew more painful, but I saw them, versions of the future. I found several where they lay broken on the floor. I worked my way back, finding the path that ended with me the champion.

I snapped to the present. I leaned back, the swipe of the blade passing dangerously close to my neck. I pushed his arm further, crossing his body so he couldn't swing back in the other direction. I used the man for leverage, pivoting, a sidekick struck the other husk in the chest.

Before I lowered my foot, I drove my knuckles into the kidney of the first Barren. For any other man, there'd be a grunt, a groan, but he hardly reacted. Their terrifying determination and inability to feel pain made them dangerous. The blades were scary, too.

Unable to swipe with his knife hand, he spun, putting his back to me. The elbow would have struck me in the nose had it not been for the ghosts. I kicked the back of his leg, robbing him of momentum and sending him to one knee. With a swift kick to the back, I sent him to the hardwood.

I turned in time to see the sheen of the blade. I used my forearm to take the blow. It cut through the fabric. The metal on metal sound made me thankful for the wire running through the sleeves. The ghosts gave me options. Unfortunately, the one that resulted in a dead Barren would hurt.

They preferred to slice, but they were capable fighters. He dropped to one knee, changing direction, I grit my teeth in preparation. The blade slid across my thigh, cutting through my trousers and biting into the flesh. I'd need stitches, but it offered me an end to this man.

I kicked his knee, pushing it out wide, cracking the bone and possibly knocking his hip out of joint. He flailed with the blade as he collapsed on his side. Down, but not out. But, he would be, soon as I killed his friend.

They were like a fighter in the ring that favored the same combination or only tried for final blows. The first Barren had clamored to his feet. His blade had slid down the hall, I partly expected him to go for it. Koji always made it a point to ensure I didn't rely on weapons. He believed that the body was the only weapon necessary during a fight.

"Come on, Olivia," I goaded at the man, "I know you're in there. Is this the best you've got?"

The pain in my head pulsed in response. I took it as a sign of desperation. For her to send men to kill me meant fear. When I had a moment to breathe, I'd let my ghosts run loose through the house and see just how many of these puppets she had created. First order of business when Theodore took over was to promise none of these things were created again.

The Barren proceeded with his fists. I raised my hands, ready to spar. Punch redirected, knee blocked, jab thrown high, he moved quickly, faster than most, but at this rate he'd never land a blow. I had enough of him, of them, and of Olivia's games. It was time to go on the offensive.

I blocked his swipe with my left arm and jabbed him in the face. The brass knuckles broke his nose, causing an explosion of blood. Now, even more menacing, his smile persisted, white teeth shining despite the crimson. A tiny bubble of snot and blood expanded from one nostril, making my stomach turn.

He grabbed me around the neck with his free arm. A cross to hit the inside of his elbow knocked his hand away. I jabbed again with the knuckles, over and over. Teeth broke free as his skin tore along his upper lip. I leaned forward, using my elbow to push the man back. I pinned him to the wall, drawing my hand back to finish the fight.

He struck me in the torso. I nearly doubled over. But I continued hitting him. Each jab I brought my fist back further until I had pulverized the man's skull. Whoever he might have been, the identity he had before Olivia had long since vanished. Now, I finished the process she had started. He was dead before I killed him.

My hand dripped, slick with blood and bits of gore. I tried not to think about it, but I could feel it clinging to my fingertips. Now, to slaughter another poor soul before I went looking for their master. The dull ache in the back of my head turned to a pounding. Olivia banged at my mind with both fists, but she would not get in, not until I wanted.

The other Barren attempted to stand. He braced himself against the wall, but when he lunged, the weight of his body caused his leg to buckle. It was almost pathetic enough so that killing him seemed like a mercy. I stood over him as he got to his knees. My fingers cradled his cheeks as I spun. The first two were easy, but I struggled to reach the final click. Jerking hard, his neck snapped.

"Olivia, you coward. Stop sending goons to do your dirty work."

I'd need to bandage my leg before going any further into the house. My ghosts stepped out of my body. From there, dozens of versions moved through the halls. They ran upstairs, into the study, and down the stairs to the basement. The woman was nowhere to be found.

With no more Barren to stop, I grabbed one of the curtains in the living room and started tearing. Once in a long strip, I tied it around my leg. I grit my teeth as I tightened the bandage. The last thing I needed was a handicap dealing with blade-wielding killers. It needed stitches, Susan Lee would get to save me again. There must be part of her that took pleasure in being the hero.

"Where are you, Olivia?"

I walked into the study, keeping watch over my back. I imagined we'd replay our last fight. She'd use the study as an opportunity to beat me again. I expected a certain sense of poetry to her madness, but she had vanished.

"What are you up to?"

On the mantle, I found the photograph of Theodore. He hardly aged. The younger version of him had a bit of innocence in his face. There was a dashing quality to the man, and wooing him didn't seem so ridiculous. I broke the glass and took the photograph, folding it in half and shoving it inside my breast pocket.

While Olivia roamed freely through the city, it was possible she gathered her minions and threatened those close to me. I turned to leave when my foot kicked something, sending it under a high-back chair. Curiosity got the best of me. Searching around on my hands and knees, I grabbed onto something cold, hard, and…

"Oh no." I pulled the gun from under the chair. Could it be? Did he dare?

I had seen Frank's revolver a dozen times. He rarely took it out of his apartment, but as of late, it stayed on him even at the gym. His only job was to protect Susan Lee, but it appeared he tried to be the protector even when he was out of his league. I flipped open the cylinder and found five bullets remaining. He had gotten off a single shot.

"If you hurt Frank…"

I put my hand on the table between the chairs to push myself to my feet. I paused, my hand resting on something hard, but not the table. A large book took up the majority of the surface. Holding the gun in one hand and the book in the other, it was as if fate put me here. My fingers traced over the three wavy lines.

A need to know drove my hand to open the cover. Lives were

at stake. I didn't have time to read every page. But I needed to peek.

"Charged with the responsibility of recording history, I am the secretary of the Paranormal Research Society and this is our legacy..."

Theodore wanted the position of overseeing the Society. I had been reluctant, but here, under the tips of my fingers, was a history of what went wrong. In these pages, I could find a roadmap and pinpoint where they failed as an organization. With this, we could remake the Society and be a force to change the world for the better. Perhaps this was how Edward and I reunited.

Did fate offer me a gift? Or did Olivia offer me a temptation that would continue her plague long after I killed the murderous tyrant? I tucked the gun in my belt and stole the book. Normally one might say, "Only time will tell." No longer did fate control me, I'd traverse the timeline and one deed at a time, I'd ensure I did better.

"Now to end this."

Chapter Twenty-Five

1934

I sneezed. The room was more spacious than the barn where Poppa stored the hay. There were shells of cars littering one wall, while parts were scattered about the floor. Believing it had been a repair shop was easy, with so many vehicles filling the space. The car graveyard hadn't been cleaned in ages.

"It's disgusting in here."

"'Nore, have some imagination." Frank walked through the room, pointing to the far wall. "This is where the weights could go. And over there, I was thinking of building a ring for boxers. I know it's not exactly the best place, but it's what we have to work with."

I roamed past the dead cars, trying to let Frank's enthusiasm wash over me. It had been a year since he'd rescued me. Despite his apprehension, he wasn't bad at being a father figure. He swore too much and threw his hands up in defeat too soon. But of course, I hadn't made it easy. The first time I swore at him during one of our heated disagreements, I thought he'd slap me. No, Frank laughed. He might raise his voice, but the man was kind, rough around the edges, but a gentle soul.

"Can you ask the ghosts to show you how it turns out?"

The demons had become less vicious. They still didn't listen to me, but now they appeared from time to time when bad things weren't looming over my head. I took it as a victory. The future had to be more than unfortunate events. Despite my inability to summon them, Frank always asked for their opinion. I think he did it less because he expected an answer and more to make the ghosts less of a taboo subject between us.

"They said it's still dirty," I yelled back at him.

Frank dragged car parts across the building while I wandered toward the back. His father had erected a small room, separate from the large one we'd first entered. I didn't know what to expect. No, I lied, I expected more dust. Covering my nose and mouth as I walked, I tried not to sneeze.

"I thought you were going to help me."

"Frank, I'm straightening up back here."

"I should have had a boy."

The banter came naturally. It surprised me when Frank revealed himself as an only child. He had no problem trading jabs with me, and I did not make it easy. For the first few months, he treated me with kid gloves, fearful I might break. Each night he read to me from the same book, and when he reached the end, he'd start again. It must have been on the third read through before he finally barged into my room, tossing the book on the bed. He had never set foot in my room at night, and for a moment I thought this might be where things turned bad.

"Tomorrow we're getting the next damned book in the series." Then he stormed out in a huff.

I laughed at the humor of that night. He stopped worrying about making the wrong decision. The next night, true to form, he started in on the next book. It wasn't long before I sat on the couch while he read. I'd fall asleep, and he'd carry me to bed. He might be rough around the edges, but he did right by my father.

"There's an office back here," I shouted.

Something dropped with a bang and I jumped. Frank wiped his greasy hands on his shirt and headed in my direction. "The old man's office. This is where he did all the bookkeeping."

Newspaper clippings hung in a frame on the wall. A man stood out in front of the building next to a cab. The image had faded, but if I hadn't known by the date, I'd have said it was Frank. I plopped down in the wooden chair, staring at the pages filled with numbers and dates.

"I'll probably tear it out. It doesn't serve much purpose in a gym."

I reached for a picture frame on the corner of the desk. A man and woman stood behind a young child. Frank's firm jaw had been a gift from his father. "No, you can't do that. You'll need an office."

"To do what?"

I shrugged. "To do business stuff, I guess."

"It's a gym, what kind of business stuff do you think is going to happen?"

The ghosts tended to respond when I was at a loss for words. There were dozens in the room, but only two people. I saw versions of Frank and me, the two of us talking intensely while he poured over papers. I wasn't much older than I was now. Further into the future had me sweaty, dripping as we argued back and forth. At multiple points Frank lay with his head on the desk, an open bottle of whiskey sitting next to his head.

"Looks like we'll be doing plenty here."

"We?"

I nodded my head. "Apparently you spend too much time here."

"Are you going to be okay without me around the apartment as much?"

I let out a laugh. Frank raised his eyebrow. Hopping out of the chair, I snatched the frame from the desk. I stood only a foot away from the man. I sized him up. The thought of spending time in the gym hadn't appealed to me at first, but it could have its benefits. "You think I'm not going to be here as much as you?"

"What do you see yourself doing?" He eyed the room. Frank didn't think I had noticed, but whenever I mentioned knowing the future, he looked for the ghosts. He accepted it without question. Never once did he oppose me when I mentioned them. But I knew the man wanted a sign, something other than me speaking to make it true.

"Working out of course."

"A man's gym isn't any place for a woman."

"Then I guess this isn't going to be a typical gym for men, now is it?"

He tried to snag the frame from my hands, but I ducked out the door. It was alarming that he had no photos of him and his family. I wanted to add this to the photograph of him and my father. If Frank was like my father, then the man and woman in the picture were like grandparents. Having a family made me smile.

Frank chased me across the room. The man might be strong, but his bulk stood no chance of catching me. I ducked behind a taxi, working my way to the far end of the room. If he was going to open a gym, then perhaps I could start lifting weights. Maybe I'd get as strong as him. Had I been older, and stronger, then perhaps I would have been able to fight off the orderlies myself. Yes, I could see a reason to work out with Frank.

I slowed as I came up on a lone punching bag. Slightly deflated, and with a long gash in the side, it had seen better days. I poked at it with my fist, listening to the chain rattle as it creaked back and forth. I punched it, startled when it swung back.

It wasn't the first time I had seen a punching bag. There had been one when Momma and I had visited Poppa at the base. It had been in a gym where the men trained. One man held it while the other wailed on it with his fists. Their bag had been in much better condition.

"That belonged to my pops. He liked to get in a workout after all day behind a desk. Sometimes he'd let me hold the bag while he boxed."

"Do you know how to box?"

"I did some overseas."

"Can you show me?"

Frank approached the bag, both of his hands clenched in a fist. He gave it one firm punch, causing it to swing back.

"No, not you," I set the picture on the ground. "I want you to show *me*."

"You want to learn to box?"

I held my fists up like he had. I had never thrown a punch in my life. Even when Benjie nagged me all day, I never thought of hitting him. Since then, I had seen a much scarier world. I didn't want to rely on Frank to protect me. If learning how to box made me feel safer, I'd beg until he gave in.

I punched the bag. Frank put a hand in front of me, backing me away from the equipment. "No, that's not how you learn to box."

"I can hit the bag—"

Frank shook his head. "Boxing isn't about hitting a bag. It's about being the last man standing. A bag doesn't hit back, but your opponent? They do hit back, and they hit hard."

I wanted to be the last man standing. Each time the orderlies had fetched me, my body went rigid with fear. I didn't expect to wrestle them to the floor, but if I had been able to resist, or put up a fight, then maybe I could have escaped on my own.

"Teach me."

I lowered my fists and Frank reached over and gave me a light slap on the face. My jaw dropped. He had been the gentlest of men. We might not have always seen eye-to-eye, but for him to hit me was appalling. And yet, here I stood, frozen, unsure of what to do next.

"First lesson," he said, "never lower your guard."

I raised my fists again. He reached under my elbow, lifting them higher than I expected. He held me by the shoulders as he kicked my feet, forcing me to narrow my stance. When he finished, he stepped back, admiring his handiwork.

"Go ahead," he pointed to the bag, "might as well see how you handle yourself."

I tried to remember the posture as I got closer. With my left shoulder closest to the bag, I punched. It was a quick punch, knuckles striking just right of the tear. After another jab with my left, I swung hard with my right, hitting the bag hard enough it swung back and forth.

"You said something earlier," Frank got behind the bag, holding it. "Hands up," he corrected. "You said not a typical gym. I think you might have been onto something." He braced himself as I repeated the left and right combination. "What if I did it for ex-military? For wounded veterans with no other options, you know? I could give back."

"That's delightful," I said. Frank didn't need to hold the bag. It was more for show as he kept it from swinging back and forth.

"Elbows."

As my right fist struck the bag, I could feel the ache in my knuckles. My arm vibrated from blow after blow, and I found myself sweaty. I hadn't imagined in all my life, I'd learn to fight. But with each strike, the racing thoughts in my head slowed. There were no ghosts as I unleashed my anger.

"You'll get the hang of it. Once you've been hit a few times, you won't be scared."

My fingernails bit into my palms. My muscles ached and my breathing grew ragged. In all the years I had carried the burden of the ghosts, I had become angry, scared of what they might show me. I didn't have to like knowing the future, but in that moment, I decided they would no longer ruin my life. I would not be scared.

Chapter Twenty-Six

1943

Frank's apartment had been the closest. My heart had jumped into my chest when I discovered the door nearly torn off the hinges. While we plotted and planned for Olivia's execution, the wicked witch had a scheme of her own. By the time I stepped into his apartment, my ghosts had already revealed every nook and cranny. It didn't matter if I turned left, right, or didn't enter at all. There was no future in which I found Olivia or Frank inside.

At this hour traffic was minimal. I reminded myself to ease up off the gas pedal, worried I might get in an accident. Frank had been told to protect Susan Lee. That was his role in this plan. When I found my apartment in a similar manner, door broken in, I panicked. It was one thing to worry that the Barren had hijacked my father, but I'd never forgive myself if something happened to Susan Lee.

I assumed Frank was in charge of protecting Susan Lee. I demanded our best man keep watch over her. But perhaps he was also in charge of watching Claudette as well? The healer could handle herself, but I didn't want anybody close to me alone. With Olivia trying to drive her thoughts into my head, I needed somebody with gifts of their own. Whether or not she could speak to the angels, I needed guidance in finding Frank.

Olivia sacrificed Catherine. While we stormed the warehouse and dispatched mobsters, Theodore and I hadn't imagined ourselves in a chess match with Olivia. We played chess with a grandmaster, and she predicted every move we made. I found it unsettling that somebody was interpreting the future better than me.

I parked the car on the main road and headed for the alley leading to Claudette's shop. I hugged the book against my chest. Spinning about, I kept an eye on my rear. The longer Olivia pressed at my defenses, the shorter I saw into the future. The ghosts moved a few seconds ahead of me and then tapered off. I urged them further, pushing them through narrowed eyes and tightened jaw, but to no avail.

There was no mistaking it, Olivia learned that the tighter I locked away my mind, the harder it was to use my gifts. I didn't know if this was a new trick, or if she was pulling it from her repertoire. If I couldn't predict her moves, every shadow suddenly transformed into a hideout for the boogeyman.

"Dammit," I cursed.

A scream trampled my self-doubt. I had heard Claudette's scream before. A serial killer had first brought me to her door. It seemed dangerously poetic that it might be a nearly identical encounter. My legs couldn't pump fast enough.

I skipped the brass knuckles and reached for the gun. I'd empty all five rounds into any Barren who dared to attack Claudette.

A broken door. Light shone through the cracked entryway. The shadow of a man spilled across the pavement. More shouting. I charged for the door. Needed to make it in time. Cocking the hammer. Lifting the gun, I stared down the sight. I wouldn't aim for his torso. I'd shoot him in the head. He'd bleed out on the floor of her shop, just like his predecessor.

The shot fired.

Not my shot.

The air shook, my heart holding still. A second shot fired, and a figure launched backward through the door. The bomber jacket made it clear the Barren were attacking. I was about to rush in and save the day when Claudette stepped out of her shop, shotgun braced against her shoulder. The barrels were smoking as she pointed it at the thing on the ground.

She ignored me as she gave the Barren a slight kick. The barrel remained fixed on his face, ready to fire if he moved. If she were the front lines, I didn't need to ask, Frank wasn't here.

"Claudette, are you okay? Eleanor?" Susan Lee stepped out of the door. Her face lit up as she stepped around Claudette and wrapped me in a tight hug.

"Is it over?" I appreciated the woman's naivety, her hope that everything would turn out fine. She pulled away, and I caught Claudette's face and Theodore in the doorway. They knew the reality. "It's not over," she whispered.

"Catherine is dead," I said.

"Well thank God, for small favors." I sneered at Theodore. I wasn't in the mood for him to congratulate me on killing my own. It might have been a delay tactic, but had Catherine offered to join us, I would have made good on my offer. Join me or die. Another step toward becoming Olivia. I growled as I sorted through our similarities.

"What's wrong?" asked Theodore.

I heaved the book in his direction. He caught it as if he had never played catch before. With a quick spin, he stared at the cover. "Eleanor, do you know what this is?"

"It's the history of the Society, the private journal of the four."

Claudette kicked the Barren one last time before lowering her gun. "The angels speak quickly tonight."

"Angels?"

I forgot that speaking to beings from Heaven was new for Susan Lee. "Claudette hears voices, they know things."

"Like," Susan Lee tapered off, not wanting to appear rude to a woman who just killed a man to save them.

"She's no more crazy than me." This was our new normal. "What are they saying?"

"There will be more. If not these beasts, then police. Eleanor, they *will* keep coming."

It was my biggest fear. Stopping a serial killer last year had been a one-time event. Now, even if we somehow killed dozens or hundreds, there would be more. However, the next wave might not be these empty husks. They would be those she influenced and corrupted. If we survived that, it would become our loved ones. Nobody would be safe from the tyranny of a telepath hungry for my flesh.

"Where's Frank? Wasn't he protecting Susan Lee?"

Theodore's eyebrow rose. Something hadn't gone according to the plan. "He brought her here and said he had to go. I assumed his part in this was to join you at the warehouse?"

"I thought he was supposed to stay with me," Susan Lee added.

Segment the responsibilities. Break up the plan. If Olivia read any of our minds, we were safe. We operated blindly to prevent her from piecing together our intentions. Had she infiltrated the mind of Theodore's coven? Had that been what launched her offensive? It seemed desperate for a woman convinced she was superior, but it didn't change the facts.

"Did you try his apartment?"

"I did. I went to ours as well. They had ransacked both. Claudette, can the angels help?"

"They grow louder," Claudette said. Her eyes were open wide, as if she were surprised. We all jumped when she dropped the gun.

Her jaw dropped as if she saw something unspeakable. A

moment passed before her lips turned up, smiling. The light from the doorway reflected in the tears streaming down her cheeks. She might be cryptic, but even this seemed out of sorts for Claudette.

"What's happening?" asked Susan Lee.

"Olivia? Did she get to Claudette?" Theodore studied the woman's face and took a step back.

I had difficulty reading the Haitian woman. There were moments when she spoke bluntly, and others when she reverted to her cryptic double-speak. I think part of her enjoyed playing the sagely elder, but it made it impossible to comprehend her connections to the angels. Edward had said when his powers first developed, he thought God spoke to him. At times I fear something similar for Claudette, but then others, she knew things, impossible things.

"Claudette, are you okay?"

"They no longer whisper," she said, with a slight sob. In the light from her shop, I could follow her eyes, darting back and forth. Whatever she watched moved in a smooth pattern. I checked over my shoulder to only see Susan Lee's worried face.

"Claudette?"

"Eleanor, what's happening?" Susan Lee clutched my free hand. I squeezed it tightly.

"Eleanor…" Even Theodore wore a look of concern. For all the talk of mentalists with his researchers, none of them had described a person quite like Claudette.

Claudette's body shook, the tremors working through her hands and up her arms. My ghosts stepped out, running to hold on to Claudette as her future self went limp and collapsed. I gasped out loud as hundreds of ghosts filled the street. There were hundreds of people standing still, their right hand resting on the shoulder of the person in front of them until only the person closest to Claudette touched her shoulder.

"What the hell?" I whispered.

Their mouths moved in unison.

"Olivia," she said. Claudette stared at me, vacant eyes that reminded me of the dead. As I retracted my ghost, pushing it away, the people, men, women, and children alike vanished.

"The one you call Olivia, she can not survive," Claudette's voice shifted slightly.

"The angels…" When I summoned my ghost again, they were gone. I caught up to the future and tucked the gun in my belt as I went to Claudette. The tremors had stopped, and she nearly fell as I caught her.

"They spoke to me, Eleanor."

Her mother had a similar gift, and it had driven her mad. I gave Theodore a look. He grabbed under her arms and helped carry her into the shop. We set her on the floor against the counter. I squatted, putting her head between my hands.

"They spoke," she said with a smile.

I couldn't quite understand, not entirely. But if this was the difference between hearing their whispers and being a mouth-piece for the angels, I understood why it consumed her mother. I wiped away the tears streaming down her cheeks.

"What just happened?" asked Theodore. "Was it Olivia?"

Until this moment, I didn't quite believe Claudette had lost her abilities, robbed by an external force. I swallowed my own beliefs. Claudette's smile stretched across her face. I did the same.

"It was the angels." Saying it felt foolish, even from a woman who could see the future. "I think they spoke through her?"

"Like channeling? I've never seen it before. The occultists believed—"

I cut him short. "We don't have time for a history lesson."

"They want her dead," Susan Lee muttered.

I rose to my feet. It still bothered me that one act at a time, Susan Lee fell into our world. Asking about angels speaking through a medicine woman wasn't met with disbelief. Perhaps I had been wrong all the time. Susan Lee was one of those people, like Theodore, who would reside with one foot in my world and the other planted in theirs.

"They're watching us tonight. Whatever they are, they're watching."

Susan Lee made the sign of the cross. My poor roommate had fidgeted, reaching into her pockets fishing for something. When this was over, she and I would have a heart-to-heart. I'd ask how she felt about knowing there was an entire world she couldn't see.

"Even the angels have condemned Olivia," I said. Something about knowing these supposedly pure and well-intentioned deities wanted her dead eased the burden on my shoulders.

"What about Frank?" asked Susan Lee.

"If I find Frank, I'll find Olivia."

Theodore clutched the book to his chest. He'd study and learn. His people would dissect every letter, searching for answers. I needed them to do that, to make sure that nothing like Olivia ever happened again.

"Where could he be?" Susan Lee pulled on a bandage, wrapping it around her hand before unwinding it. First she helps me save the world, now she unknowingly helped me save Frank.

I pointed at the bandage. "The gym."

The final stop this evening.

Neither Theodore nor Susan Lee mentioned the gym as part of the plan they had been told. My stomach continued to tighten as I approached. If Theodore's researchers had gone there, I might face off against good, well-meaning people. Worse, had my workout buddies returned to familiar territory, I might find myself at the end of their guns. Whatever force spoke through Claudette, I hoped it spared them.

I was thankful Koji remained in the shop. He was out of

danger, both from the beating earlier and Olivia. I couldn't imagine squaring off against him if he dropped all reservations. I might be skilled, but I was far from reaching his caliber of fighting. Even with the ghosts, I would have been hard-pressed to stop him.

I opened the car door, stepping onto the sidewalk. The streets were empty, without a single soul hurrying home or walking their pets. It was unusual for any place in New York to feel this abandoned. With a deep breath, I let the cool air fill my lungs. Reaching into my pocket, I rubbed the charcoal, trying to ground myself. With nobody on the street, I might very well already be tangled in Olivia's web of lies.

It was impossible to tell what was and was not real.

The pressure pinching my temples together was the only constant. I assumed that as long as I continued feeling Olivia slamming against my barricades; I was safe. But as I listened to the lack of cars or the hum of conversation from nearby homes, I wasn't entirely sure it was an accurate barometer.

I'm coming for you.

There was no witty retort, no claim she intended to put an end to me. The one benefit of stalking an egomaniac, they made mistakes. She underestimated me. In the ring, she'd think her sheer power and force would best the match. I had downed giants when they attempted the same tactic. Had I been her, there would be police stationed in every shadow and whoever managed the shot would take it. I wouldn't make such a foolish wager.

I tried summoning the ghosts. For a moment it appeared as if they'd fade into view. Nothing. I had my abilities stolen from me before, when I had been clubbed across the back of my head. Then it had felt as if that invisible line I drew to the ghosts had been hard to find. This felt different. I could follow the delicate thread, but at some point, it cut short.

Olivia might not need to see into my mind. If I couldn't step out of my own head and conjure ghosts from the future, I'd be nothing more than a human with metal wrapped around my knuckles. I didn't bother pushing and reconnecting. I wanted Olivia to revel in her false sense of security, then we'd see who would win a match of wills.

Before getting close to the building, I inspected every nook and cranny where a Barren might hide. Nobody hid in the alleys or in darkened doorways, waiting to put a bullet in my chest. I couldn't be too cautious, not with a woman who stayed one step ahead.

I cursed at the sight of a new war poster taped over the front window of the gym. With so much real estate, they insisted on making sure nobody forgot about the biggest war in the history of mankind. It gave me a moment to pause and consider my plan of attack. Barging in the front door and squaring off against a woman who knew I was coming seemed a poor choice.

When Frank first converted the building from a garage to the gym, he required I stay within eyesight. He had never raised a child before. God bless him. He feared for a young girl from the country lose in the wilds of New York. I had gotten adept at sneaking out. There wasn't a window I hadn't shimmied open or fire escape I hadn't climbed.

I jogged down the alley to the windows that led to the locker room. Beneath the window there were a set of oil barrels, placed there years ago during my more defiant years. I hauled myself on top and pulled the bottom of the window out. Before I jumped into danger, I summoned the ghosts, or at least I tried.

"Dammit," I hissed. Each time I reached out to stoke the flame, nothing. I contemplated pushing, sinking my emotions into it for fuel, but I held off. If I was vigilant, I wouldn't need them. I wanted to beat Olivia at her own game, but there would be a time for that. I just needed to find out if she wanted to face me directly or if she brought the Barren to do her dirty work.

The window let out a slight creak as I slid inside. I hung onto the wall and lowered myself. I heard the squeak of boots in the showers.

"That's my answer." They moved quickly.

I pushed off the wall, rolling backward. The floor was wet enough to soak through my pants. Frank always feared men in the shower with me. The irony of this encounter wasn't lost on me. Now that it happened, I'd make sure he never feared for me again.

Their blades struck the wall creating tiny blinding sparks. They turned, and both came at me, determined to be the first to drag the blade across my throat. I didn't have time to drag out toying with the henchmen. Their master needed to be dealt with.

I used my forearm to catch the blade from the left, the metal in the sleeve held firm protecting my flesh. With my right, I drove my knuckles into the man's throat. Even if he didn't yelp, struggling to breathe would break up the attack.

The first Barren couldn't get past my defense. Between Frank and Koji, I'd learned to absorb and redirect any blow. With a fast spin, I dropped, dragging my leg along the ground, kicking his feet out from under him. The moment I stopped turning, I was on him, hands on his neck and my knee holding his knife hand down, I squeezed. I didn't have time for him to suffocate. With a lift of his head, I smashed it on the floor. Two more times and the man's eyes rolled back in his head.

I didn't wait for his friend to gather himself. Jumping, I tackled him, tumbling against the wall. The knife fell from his hand and I clenched his throat. He tried to punch at my face, but I stayed too close for him to gain momentum. The light hits to my temple weren't enough to loosen my grip. Seconds later, his body went limp. I let the corpse fall.

"Olivia, you're next."

Pulling the knife from the back of my jacket, I left the locker room.

Chapter Twenty-Seven

1943

"Eleanor—"

Frank's voice shook the air. He opened his mouth, trying to yell. Swatting at his throat, he tried to fight off an invisible attacker. His palm smacked across his face, hard enough it'd leave a handprint come morning.

"Edward." I could barely believe the audacity of the man. "How could you?"

Frank wasn't tied and his mouth wasn't bound. With a telepath, there was nothing he could do to ward off their intrusions. He forfeited any sense of identity as Edward forced his abilities on my adopted father.

"I didn't want it to come to this."

His voice was calm, collected, and almost void of emotion. Edward had never been an overly emotional person, but he had mastered his poker face. Even if I could turn on the lights and examine the man, I'd be unable to read his emotions. I suspect he didn't like being in this position any more than me.

"If you harm Frank—"

"He tried to shoot me, Eleanor. Your father knows more about us than most humans, and still he doesn't understand. They are toys, playthings created to serve us."

"I... I..." I couldn't fathom the extent he would go. I traded slivers of my soul with each act of brutality. Edward peddled his wholesale. There was no coming back from where he went. I prepared to follow.

"I will kill you, Edward. If you make me decide, I will kill you." The words were easier to say than expected. I maintained my composure as I threatened the man I loved.

"So be it."

The click from the gun echoed throughout the gym. Edward's thumb was slow, deliberate, and steady, as he held up a revolver. I could flip the knife and hurl it. It wasn't likely I'd strike him, and even less so with Frank blocking my path. I thought about dropping the knife and pulling out the gun in my waistband.

"It seems fitting that he die by his own weapon."

With a slight shift of my weight, I could feel the metal against my back. Olivia overplayed her hand. Edward turned the gun around, waiting for Frank to take it. It wasn't enough to best me, or even wound me. She wanted to drag out the torture. I don't know if she thought her mental intrusions were succeeding or if she just didn't care. Either way, she wanted to see me flinch.

Frank put the gun under his chin and without so much as a farewell, he pulled the trigger. It wasn't real. It couldn't be. My opinion of Edward hovered between foolish and stupid, but not even he could be this evil. No, this was the work of a madwoman.

While the body toppled, I eyed the room, looking for anything out of the ordinary. The thing thudding on the floor wasn't Frank. None of this was real. Olivia recycled her earlier play, hoping to catch me off guard. While I was trapped here, I left my body unprotected. I needed to fight back.

"He died because of you," Edward said.

"Fuck off." Was he real? Or just another imaginary person plucked from my memories.

"They will all die because of you, Eleanor."

I had fought valiantly to keep Olivia from invading my mind. But as the puddle of blood pooled about Frank's head, I prayed she had found her way inside my… The entire evening the headache grew from an annoyance to a throbbing pain between my eyes. I assumed it was Olivia pounding at the walls I erected. Hoping this was fake, I prayed she was strong enough to worm her way through my armor.

"I can do better," I whispered. If she bested me tonight, it wouldn't be using the same tricks as before. The last time we met, my bravado outshined my abilities. I'd like to think since Olivia gutted me like a fish, I had grown.

"I will—"

In the past, I'd have shoved my anger into the flame. Gregory had been anything but impressed with my ability to barge through life with brute force. I wasn't the angry young woman I had once been, determined yes, but angry, no.

Fear, the emotion I barricaded against for most of my life. I ignored it as if it wasn't bubbling beneath the surface. I imagined Dr. Gustafson with the drill in hand. Before Frank burst through the door, I had nearly wet myself at the horror. Olivia wanted to instill fear, but that posh woman didn't know I had already survived the worst.

The hair along my arms stood on end as I imagined the liquid fire rolling along my skin. Inside the box, behind the walls I raised to protect my mind, the fire pushed through, gathering. If this was real, it meant Frank was dead on the floor of the very gym created to help those leaving the front lines. If it wasn't real, it meant Frank was still in danger. I wanted to cry, to scream in defiance. I imagined the fear building in my fists.

The walls didn't crumble, they ruptured. Shredding the barriers I put in place for protection, the icy colored fire flew out like an explosion. Edward had taught me to imagine the fire, but never had I felt the heat. It was only the first of several explosions.

The air rippled.

The emptiness, the space we occupied, it warped and bent, distorting my view of the gym. It radiated from my hands and found something in its path. No, not something, someone. Torn from wherever she had been hiding, Olivia flew backward, her arms shielding her face.

"Thank, God." I stood in the white room. The corpse on the floor was nothing more than Olivia playing games.

She stopped rolling, smacking against one of the corner posts of the ring. It wasn't her. Just like Frank was a memory plucked from my mind, so was this victory. It might not do much good, but I tightened my grip on the knives. In the white room, raw emotion acted like a bomb, but it was confidence that defied the realm of science.

"Where are you?" I wanted to believe the body on the ground was really her. Could one accidental flare of power have been enough to fell somebody as powerful as Olivia? I wanted to believe it, to think this nightmare ended as quickly as it started. Edward would be free. I would enlist him to help Theodore and me rebuild the Society.

I spun about on the balls of my feet as I moved toward Olivia's body. Edward's eyes followed, but he didn't speak. I imagined if he were really there, he'd have said something. But if he wasn't here…

I closed my eyes. They weren't to be trusted. Koji could move as elegantly blindfolded as he could with his sight. He insisted I train my senses, that it would make me a better fighter. I thought the exercises childish. But a disturbance in the air caused the tiny hairs on my neck to stand upright while goosebumps rushed along my skin.

I threw a high elbow back. Whatever I struck moved backward. I spun. Instead of going for a killing blow, I ducked, dragging the knife against something. Just as the blade finished slicing through meat, I pivoted my swing, greedily trying to score a second cut.

My eyes shot open when a hand grabbed my wrist. Olivia's fingers dug into my wrist, pressing a muscle that forced me to drop the blade. I shoved the other knife through her forearm, jerking hard, tearing away flesh and scraping bone as I pulled it free.

The wound stitched itself together, healing until her flawless skin returned. Olivia's laugh, the condescending sound of superiority, filled the gym. What started as a pompous snicker turned into a deafening cackle with no origin. I hated her voice, hated her.

I plunged the knife into her chest. Puncturing her blackened heart didn't stop her. My skills relied on muscle, the ability to dodge, deflect, and retaliate. Here, none of that mattered. If she could heal the most lethal attack, I wouldn't win this match with a simple blade.

Slap.

It wasn't skillful or up to the caliber of my boxing skills, but it was satisfying to feel her skin under my hand. She let go of my wrist and touched the side of her face. Why did that matter more than the weapon buried in her chest? Was there something different? I had so many questions. She batted me with the back of her hand. I was learning on the job and I wasn't doing it quick enough to win.

Her knuckles connected with my jaw. The force was like being hit by a monstrous wave. I flew across the gym further than should have been physically possible. Skidding along the floor, I smashed into the wall, loosening the mortar enough for several red bricks to tumble at my side.

"We've done this before, have we not? If my memory serves me correctly, it didn't turn out well for you?"

If I could think it, I could manifest it. I had to play by her rules. Rules written by Olivia. There were no laws here, science and rational understanding didn't matter. I had to remember that. She could appear and vanish as she wanted, her bones could heal, none of it was real. But wherever my body stood, that was real.

I wasn't prepared for this fight, and that fact might cost me my life.

Worse, it would cost Frank his life. The weight of this fight pushed down on my shoulders. I wasn't fighting to get revenge. The winner of this battle would lay claim to New York City. If I lost, it wouldn't just be me on the floor, it'd be anybody who dared to defy Olivia.

Theodore. Susan Lee. Claudette. Koji. Every member of the gym. The good guys. One by one they would stand up and resist her stranglehold on the city they loved. They'd fight.

"Olivia," I shouted. I braced my back against the broken wall and shimmied until I stood upright. "I'm giving you a chance to walk away. Leave New York."

Would she stop with the city? Was this only the first stop on her way to conquering the world? Would it be another war spread across the globe? Would any who stood in her way be subjected to camps as the Nazis had done?

"You forget yourself, Eleanor. I am not some common thug. Your abilities will not do you any favors. You're in a world I created. I'm a god here, and you…" she said with a sneer. —I'd beat her face in until those muscles wouldn't work.— "You're just like them, human."

I was the last defense for them, these humans she loathed. Olivia thought herself above those without gifts, above me. But she hadn't spent her entire life rallying against forces out of her control. The devils came for me and I survived. Fate hammered me until I nearly broke. I emerged victorious. Olivia could be a god if she wanted.

"You're not the first god I've fought."

Chapter Twenty-Eight

1943

The gym didn't belong to Olivia. This is where broken men came to heal. Frank created this gym, this bastion of community. This gym taught me what it meant to fight against the demons. Here, within these walls, I'd stopped being afraid of a past that had long since passed.

This was *my* gym.

The walls rippled, and the lights flickered. If confidence served as a weapon in the white room, she made a fatal mistake bringing me here. Anywhere else in the world, I might have drowned in my insecurities. I grew into a woman in that ring. Each time I dropped my guard, a fast jab connected with my nose. The mats were covered in dark red stains and early on, most of them were mine.

"Once you've been hit a few times, you won't be scared."

"It's not me who should be scared," she replied, believing I spoke to her.

It was my turn to smile. Olivia truly thought the world revolved around her, that we were servants at her beck and call.

No, this wasn't about her. Frank had said those words to me the day he made this our home. Olivia had her chance and my scar throbbed as a reminder. It was my turn to return the favor.

I called the ghosts.

The walls rippled again. As it passed over Frank's body, it faded from view. Even Edward's face reset, staring blankly into the nothingness. Next to him Frank held a similar expression, alive once more. I pushed against Olivia's mind tricks, the headache between my eyes growing until I thought a real spike drove into my head.

"What's wrong, Eleanor?" As Olivia walked forward, the rippling in reality calmed. "No visions? You must know how this ends, no?"

I didn't ask the ghosts, I demanded they answer their master's call.

Dropping to one knee, I struggled to stay upright. The pain moved from my eyes into my shoulders and along my spine. One by one, every part of my body screamed to stop. The room spun. I was about to hurl if I didn't pass out first. Drops of crimson splashed on the floor, working their way into the grooves between the boards. I dropped the knives to touch my nose, unsure if the blood was really mine or not.

"You can't…" Olivia's voice trailed off. Forcing my eyes off the floor, her face was somewhere between shock and disbelief. My bloody nose wasn't what caught her attention. Somewhere above me, something…

I blinked. As my eyes opened I was standing upright, looking through the eyes of my ghost. Despite her confidence in suppressing my abilities, I summoned a single specter. Blood smeared across my hand as I wiped the droplets from my nose. The pain pulsing through my bones transformed into a distant ache. Despite the spinning room, I pushed myself upright, standing until I occupied the exact space of my ghost.

"I can."

My vision split, then split again. I was no longer a single woman trapped in Olivia's prison. The ghosts multiplied until hundreds emerged. My army and I stood still, perfectly aligned. Several broke rank to wipe their noses while one extended its hand, raising a middle finger. For the second time tonight, I raised an army. If she believed this place a holding cell, she had mistaken which of us were the prisoner.

The scream started in my belly and vibrated until my entire chest trembled. The air didn't ripple, it simply tore away like falling bits of shattered glass. My battle-cry spurred the troops into action. Hundreds of Eleanors charged. Some veered to the left or right. More than a few creeped cautiously toward their target. The vast majority took a direct approach, hands reaching for brass knuckles or fists clenching ready to strike.

Only a handful of my ghosts opted to skip the fight and run straight to Frank. Through their eyes, I watched as they slapped him across the face or shook his upper body. One even turned their attention to Edward, holding his face as they tried to wake him from his dreamlike state.

"I think not," she hissed.

Each time I summoned my ghost, time nearly stopped. I had an infinite amount of time to process the future and absorb input from the ghosts. Once I discovered the best path to take, time resumed, and I moved into action. This time was different. Olivia let out a low growl, waving her hand about her head. A ghost lunged, and it evaporated as her fist connected with my future self.

Nobody had ever seen the ghosts like this before. *I* had never seen them behave like this. Instead of hundreds of possibilities, they manifested into living soldiers. I prayed they whittled away at her defenses.

Purple light surged about Olivia's arm and trailed in the air as she swung her hand. The light spun about her body and with a ferocity, she snapped her wrist. The illuminated whip cracked against a ghost, obliterating it into a million shards. Olivia continued the move, using her momentum to pull a knife out of thin air and slice through the next three ghosts.

I could barely comprehend what unfolded. With uncanny speed, she sliced through at least a hundred of the ghosts. Those that evaded her blade found themselves snared by the whip. By the dozen, I watched their minds disappear. At this rate, it would only be seconds before it was just her and me.

"More," I said, "I need more."

More of the room cracked, sounding like bombs going off as panes of reality smashed against the gym floor. Each time my eyelids closed and opened, I saw through a thousand more ghosts. In seconds, I could see every outcome of the next few seconds. Except, instead of telling me how to defeat Olivia, they took matters into their own hands.

Olivia wielded her whip like a frenzied cowboy. Her resolve didn't weaken as more spirits stepped out of the ether. Never had I conjured the ghosts for anything other than seeing events yet to pass. Now they surged forward, an army of myself. Woman after woman tried to tackle Olivia, but with a wide arc of the purple whip, hundreds of allies deteriorated.

My jaw hung loose as I caught sight of the woman standing next to me. The wrinkles from her eyes made her appear soft, but I recognized those eyes. They might be wiser, and perhaps more worldly, but as she reached up, smudging charcoal across her eyes, I realized I wasn't alone in this fight.

Some of them wore my jacket, but others dressed in formal attire, or even in shorts like the men at the gym. They were an army, *my* army. Me. Olivia thought herself untouchable, a titan amongst men, but she stood alone.

I pitied her, or I would after I killed her.

Each time Olivia snuffed out the ghosts, I felt them vanish. It came in waves, her newest weapon keeping them at bay. I charged after my elder self. The whip soared through the air, a hum of electricity as it struck my forearm. The tip bit into flesh, and a look of satisfaction crossed her face.

I grabbed the whip. She tugged and appeared annoyed I didn't fall. Her anger turned into a snarl when I jerked back. Olivia staggered forward, closing the six-foot gap between us. With my right fist, I punched hard at her face. Her attempt to block the blow was the emotional pick-me-up I needed all day.

"Don't lower your guard," I barked.

She had never been coached by Frank. As she grabbed for her nose, the skin along her cheeks glimmered. The smooth skin vanished. I was left staring at a woman scarred from years of acne. Even her hair transformed, and a scar adorned a space above her left eye. For all the pomp and circumstance, Olivia's biggest deceit rested in her vanity.

"Proud of yourself?" She transformed into the ideal version of herself as if it were second nature. "Do you think I can't pull the same trick?" Behind her, four replicas of herself stepped out. She prepared a witty retort when a gym full of ghosts trampled her doppelgängers. Fists beat against their faces. I watched a timeline of infinite possibilities converge with one goal, stopping this vapid harlot.

She tackled, sending us sliding along the ground. I put one hand around her neck, trying to keep her away from my face. She rolled off, and I reached down, prepared to jump to my feet. As my fingers dug into the cold moist earth, I watched a plume of steam hang in the air as I saw my breath.

I held up the snow in my hand.

The gym had vanished and now I sat in a wide-open space covered in snow. Off in the distance, I could make out the farmhouse. I didn't need to turn around to know I was about to find myself caught in a scene that frequently replayed in my mind. Veronica had thought me a monster for this moment. I couldn't blame her. Even Olivia uncovered that it haunted me.

"What is it, Eleanor? I thought you'd enjoy a trip home."

I drew back my fist, but found the snow undisturbed where Olivia should be. This wasn't longer about besting me in a game of wills. Irked that I beat her in the gym, she decided to be a poor loser. It was no longer enough for her to win, or for me to lose. She wanted me to suffer. Unfortunately for her, this moment was so engrained in my mind, watching it again would do nothing.

"You're watching it happen. I recognize that blank look. Frozen, watching it all play out in your head. You knew he would die."

Her voice taunted, the tone urging me to partake. I refused to have a dialogue with the woman. My right hook would speak for itself. But despite spinning in circles, hoping to find her, all I could see was a younger version of myself.

"You might have been young, but you were never innocent."

Olivia stepped from around the tree. Her formal attire was as impractical as it could be. Her hands rested on the shoulders of a younger me. Bending over, she rested her head just above the girl's shoulder, watching Benjie playing on the ice.

"A simple shout could have saved your brother. If you had spoken, he might have grown into a fine, young man. But here yo—"

"I made peace with what happened."

She laughed. Pointing to the lake, I followed her finger to Benjie running back and forth across the ice. It only took a few seconds before it cracked and he fell through. Olivia stepped around my younger self and stared into my face.

"You watched it happen, and you knew. I can see it in your

eyes. You waited for him to die. You call me cold? I didn't murder my brother."

"No, I couldn't stop it," I shouted the words. Olivia had gotten under my skin and received the response she wanted. "I couldn't…"

"Peace? It appears otherwise. I want to watch it again."

The crack vanished and Benjie returned to running back and forth on the ice. We were only feet away from where the hole in the ice would form. With one final skid, the ice broke and in slow motion, I watched his face as the toe of his shoe touched the water.

"Eleanor," he yelled.

"He called for his sister. You should have protected him."

He called my name. I didn't remember if he shouted before vanishing into the darkness below. Benjie, my baby brother died that day and I did nothing but watch. I could have challenged fate, even if I lost, I could have tried. Instead, he died believing I didn't care if he survived.

"No," I whispered.

"Yes," she replied. "What kind of hero watches those she cares about die?"

The off-color of the ice changed as it thinned closer to shore. Frank stood still, unmoving and hardly caring what happened. He'd be the next to die if I didn't stop her. The white-blue tint of the snow snaked its way up his legs until his face transformed into a frosty corpse.

Olivia forced her way into a festering wound. I thought I accepted Benjie's death and moved on with life. Even Poppa urged me forward as I teetered on the verge of death.

A thunderous roar filled the winter day as ice cracked across the pond. Somewhere in the real world, I stood still, a victim for Olivia to dispatch. I waged a war, and even as the general of an army, I couldn't best the woman.

Olivia's hand pushed against my back. The single tap sent me into the air. My arms and legs kicked, trying to turn myself upright to prepare for the inevitable crash into the pond. I covered my face, smashing against the ice. Jagged bits of frozen water cut my arms as I broke through the surface, falling into the water below.

The light faded as I sank deeper. My lungs fought for breath as my body tensed from the frigid water. I couldn't let her win, not without fighting back. My stubborn determination fought against the shock holding my limbs in place. I needed air. First the left arm, and then slowly the right. I pulled at the water, attempting to swim upward.

I craned my neck to see the hole above. My legs refused to kick, so I dragged harder with my hands. Air, I needed air. My lungs burned, threatening to suck in a mouthful of water. I would make it, I had to make it.

I smashed into a wall of ice. The hole had frozen over. I remained trapped in an icy, watery grave. Air, no more air. My fists thumped against the ice, trying to break through. In the light above, the only thing I could see was Olivia standing at the edge of the sealed hole, her body heaving as she laughed at my defeat.

Wisps of red swirled in front of my face. Where the ice had cut me, long thin lines of scarlet bled into the water. They weren't the cuts of a jagged ice, but a long thin blade. I had many similar knife scars on my body. She stood nearby, cutting into my flesh, one knick at a time. I'd die here *and* there. Much like with my brother, I'd also experience my death twice.

Winning wasn't enough, the witch wanted me to suffer. And then I saw it, him, Benjie. The look of terror, frozen on his youthful face. His hair waved about in the water, his body suspended in purgatory. His eyes stared at me, fixated on my face as I tried one last time to pound against the ice.

He drifted in my direction, only an arm's length away. I tried to scream, but there was no air left. No air. When I inhaled I felt the water pouring into my lungs. His hand rose, reaching for me, his fingers only inches from my face.

"Eleanor," the bubbles rolled along his skin as he spoke.

I inhaled again, trying to force a scream. I swallowed water, steadily sinking in the pond, into the darkness. The last thing I could make out was the silhouette of Benjie against the hole, and above him Olivia laughing.

I sank, dying.

I stopped trying to scream. I stopped struggling to swim. I stopped and accepted the inevitable. The water no longer held a chill, my body acclimating to its new home. I sank further than was possible in our lake. I only prayed that Olivia spared Frank, Susan Lee, and Claudette. Trapped in the darkness, I waited for the reaper to claim me. Death had been my bedfellow since childhood, it only made sense that he visit me one last time.

I tried to push away the misery, the horrors sprinkled throughout my life. I wanted my last memory to be something happy, a joyous occasion. I thought of Frank, his hands fidgeting with a cup of coffee as he took a seat at his first Alcoholics Anonymous meeting. He didn't speak during that first meeting, but that night I listened from the hallway as he made a promise to God. He had something to live for, someone. Me.

Even as I died, I smiled.

They were like speckled moments of joy, beacons of light fighting against an all-consuming darkness. If it were not for the water, I'd surely have cried as I recalled Susan Lee standing in the doorway as I nervously answered. I feigned a smile as she gave a slight curtsey. As I elaborated on the newspaper ad, she barged into the apartment and commented on the drab interior. Before I could introduce myself, she was making suggestions for window dressings and the need for a proper table cloth.

The ring Edward handed me. The flowers. I remembered the smell of roses covering my rooftop in a fairytale wedding. The man tried valiantly to create a picture-perfect wedding. The dress, the altar, even the stringed quartet, he had outdone himself. For all the fights, all the angry bickering, I wanted to remember Edward as the dashing man who set aside his insecurities when he said, "I do." I could almost hear our… I gasped.

Pachelbel Canon in D Major filled the air.

Chapter Twenty-Nine

1937

The call came in the middle of the night. I hobbled into the dining room where the phone sat and picked it up. It was Harry, and he needed me to pick up Frank. I feared the day this call would come. It started as Frank having one or two beers with dinner. It grew increasingly worse.

As I walked through the streets long after the lights had shut off, I tried to ignore the ache spreading through my muscles. Today had been my first match in the ring, my first chance to challenge another man at the gym. He'd won fairly, but the boasting afterward, the prancing around the ring claiming he beat another woman, that had angered me.

It had been years since I had been blessed with a vision. In only a few seconds, I watched as he beat a young woman, slapping her across the face. The look of horror on her face was made more disturbing by her lack of resistance. When I snapped back to reality, standing in the ring, I punched him behind the head and then pummeled him. It had taken two men to pull me off.

I regretted nothing.

The air had grown cooler. It wouldn't be long before the snow fell. New York City in the winter remained one of the most miser-able places I could imagine. Instead of white sheets along the ground, business owners shoveled, leaving it dirty. The winds whipped between buildings and people hurried to their destinations without a smile or wave.

I reached the door to Harry's. I had been inside before, even partook in a few drinks. However, most of the time, when I entered, it wasn't in search of good spirits. The massive wooden door with a black handle resisted as I pulled. They had already turned the lights inside on, and it was awkward to see the establishment well lit.

"Sorry, we're cl—" Harry poked his head up above the bar. "Oh, 'Nore, it's you."

"Evening, Harry."

The man had a prosthetic attached to one of his legs. Blown off in the war, he now had to hobble when walking. He retrieved a glass from the sink and toweled it dry before setting it on the counter upside down.

"Sorry to wake you, but—"

"I know the routine, and appreciate you calling." I did, truth-fully. Harry had promised to keep an eye on Frank when his drinking worsened. We discussed cutting him off, but where there was booze, Frank would find a way. At least here, I knew somebody watched over him. Otherwise he'd be walking the streets, mugged, or something far worse.

"Is it still bad at home?"

I leaned against the bar, looking around until I found Frank with his head lying on a table in the rear corner booth. Dealing with an intoxicated Frank was almost enough to make me want a drink. Thanks to indulging in his liquor, I had discovered alcohol helped keep the ghosts at bay. But thanks to his nightly falling asleep with a glass in his hand, I learned to meter myself. I tried not to replace one demon with another.

"It is," I admitted, "he promised he'd watch himself, but..."

Harry flipped another pair of glasses on the counter. They hadn't served together, but Harry and Frank shared a wartime bond I didn't understand. "I've seen it before, 'Nore. Some men can drink themselves to oblivion and then never have another drop. Then there are people like your pops, they can't resist it. It happens more than I'd like to admit."

"Is there help?" Our roles had reversed. Where Frank once took care of me, now it was me carrying him to bed and tucking him in. I referred to him openly as my father. Frank treated the bar as his church and Harry as his priest. He confessed his sins and secrets, all but the ghosts. Even in a drunken stupor, he knew that was not his secret to divulge.

"One of the men mentioned this new group he attends. He says it's helped him turn his life around."

It sounded almost too good to be true. "Do you buy it?"

"That man was one of my best customers. I haven't seen him since he came and apologized for making a fool of himself. It's worth a shot."

I reached for my pocket. "How much is his tab?"

Harry waved me off. At first, I had been upset with the owner, convinced that if he would stop supplying Frank, this problem would solve itself. Despite my best efforts in aiding his sobriety, Frank found alcohol or purchased more. He didn't see it as a problem. With the gym nearly ready to open, I wanted him well enough to see his good deeds brought to fruition.

"You're good people, Harry."

"Remember that next time you're in here drinking. You scare away the men, 'Nore."

"Those aren't men," I smiled. "Even boys like to dress up in their father's clothes."

He laughed. I walked across the bar to the booths hidden in the back. Sitting down next to Frank, I had our long-overdue conversation. I gave him a light pat on the cheek. When he moaned and swatted at my hand, I knew I had his attention.

"Frank," I tapped him again, "are you awake?"

He groaned.

"We need to talk. You have a problem. I think it's time you get help." The man didn't reply. His eyes fluttered open, but he didn't bother picking his head off the table. "You need help."

Frank, my father by circumstance. I couldn't think of words to adequately convey my feelings. Fear. It was the only emotion bouncing around inside my head. The best thing in my life was escorting himself to death's door, and one day, the reaper would answer. I stifled a sob.

"You saved me, Frank. I don't know what made you do it, but you got your life together for my dad. I don't know how, but you did it." I rested my head on the table so inches separated our noses. "I need you, Frank. You're the only person in my life that hasn't left. I'm not ready for another goodbye."

I couldn't save a man who didn't want to live. On the nights when he passed out on the couch, I'd sit in the chair and read to him. When I was sick, he'd read me *The Wonderful Oz*, and when the tables turned, I read him *Peter Pan*. Lately, it seemed he might be one of the lost boys. I needed him to come home.

I traced the stubble along his jaw to where it met his ear. Resting my hand over his cheek, I could feel his pulse. Minutes passed and for a time, I believe my heart beat in sync with his.

When I closed my eyes to blink, they opened to an unfamiliar room. Transported from Harry's bar, I stood in absolute blackness. I spun about, searching for Harry, but only saw glimpses of Frank. As if a spotlight shone down on the man, I watched as he punched at an unseen foe. The man swung, keeping his guard up, satisfied with the blow. In another spotlight, I watched as Frank's body hovered in the air. Struggling, he could hardly move.

I tried to scream, but found my voice deserted me. I grabbed my throat as if invisible hands kept me from speaking aloud. I tried again and managed the slightest squeak. It was then I realized I was still lying in the bar with my face touching a sticky table. Caught up in a vision of the future, I witnessed something horrific.

There were hundreds of spotlights, each with a different version of Frank. In some, I saw the man dying on the ground and in others he seemed to be holding his own. I navigated through the variations, confused about which was the right man.

"Frank," I managed a whisper.

One by one, each of the Franks ended up on the ground, writhing in pain. None remained upright. In each version, I watched my adopted father die. With my father and Benjie, I had seen a single person in the vision. Did this mean there were possibilities? Could I pick and choose? If I could, what did it matter when each of them ended with him dying before my eyes.

I blinked. I remained sitting in the dingy bar and squeezed Frank's cheek as I let the tears run down the side of my nose.

"Don't die on me, Frank." I didn't know how to convey the emotions in my chest. I resorted to begging, pleading for the man to reach from a premature grave.

Frank's fingers brushed hair behind my ear. He rested his palm on my cheek and I could see he was staring. I reached up, entwining my fingers with his. Tears rolled down his eyes. Perhaps he wasn't sent to save me, maybe we would save one another.

"I don't want to die."

It was my turn. I'd save Frank at any cost.

Chapter Thirty

1943

The music cut through the panic. The tapping of piano keys and perfectly in sync violins completed the memory. But, for a moment, I could swear I heard them as if the musicians played nearby. I looked for the source of the music, nothing visible in the pitch black. But the music was as real as if I were standing in a concert hall.

Edward.

He didn't reply, not with words. The music grew louder, a reminder of the night I stood on the roof. While I walked down the aisle in the white room, I pummeled thugs near the carousel. Edward knew I fought to keep the streets safe, and despite that, he vowed to stand by me no matter what.

The carousel had been the moment I first thought I could love the man. It only seemed fitting for it to be the backdrop in one world while he stood by me in another. It bordered on poetic. Our rough edges occasionally created friction, but most often, they were a reminder of who we wanted to be. For a time, I thought he'd broken his vows. But as the music vibrated through the water, I reconsidered.

Edward.

I called to him. The music reached a crescendo and for a moment I swore I heard him speak my name. It faded as quickly as it started. An image of Olivia's face flashed, hovering inches from mine as she held a razor coated in blood. It vanished, and I was left in the pond. For a split second, I saw through two sets of eyes. In the white room, I couldn't tell if I continued sinking or if the lack of oxygen robbed me of my sight. Meanwhile, in the physical world, I stood idly by as Olivia carved into my flesh.

I pushed away the darkness as I dissected that night on the rooftop. As he confessed his love for me, I stared into the crowd of my chosen family. Unlike before, the empty row held occupants. Poppa wore his Sunday best along with Momma in her floral church dress. Even Benjie wore the bowtie he hated.

Momma wiped away the tears with a white linen handkerchief. Poppa smiled. He gave me a slight nod of the head and mouthed a silent I love you. My baby brother didn't smile, but awarded me two-thumbs up, as close to approval as I'd receive from the little booger.

I wanted to run from the altar, to tackle my father and cover Benjie's face in kisses as he complained about cooties. I wanted to believe that even though they weren't there they took part in the ceremony. Did the appearance of Momma mean somewhere in Heaven, she kept a watchful eye on her daughter? I didn't have time to ponder the question.

My eyes opened.

Chapter Thirty-One

1943

I clutched her wrist. The blade pressed against my throat, firm enough that if she jerked back, it'd leave a nasty cut. Blood covered my fingers, fresh strips of crimson smearing along the white of her forearm.

"How?"

I replied by smashing my forehead against her nose. Blood splattered across my face, making it impossible to see out of my left eye. I lost my grip, and she pulled her hand free. She touched her face, bellowing as she caught sight of the blood on her fingers. Vanity staved off her panic as she touched her nose, inspecting the damage.

Like before, I stood on the threshold, the spot where the hallway from the locker room opened into the gym. Frank and Edward stood frozen at the corner of the boxing ring. Unlike before, neither of the men held a gun. For a moment, I wasn't sure if it was real or just another one of her tricks.

She followed my line of sight. She cursed, growling. Edward and Frank jerked forward, charging toward us. I only had a second to stop Olivia, to knock the witch backward before the two men tackled me to the ground.

I screamed as I kicked her in the stomach, launching her backward. Steadying myself, I prepared to square off against the only two men I didn't want to hurt. I barely had my fists up protecting my face when Frank leaned into his punch. My defense held, but he knocked my fists into my face hard enough I cursed.

It was real.

My body surged upward while music filled the pond. The water pulled at my clothes and hair as I sped toward the surface. My lungs no longer hurt. The water brightened as I continued the long journey toward the ice.

A speck of light emerged, the opening where Olivia thought she trapped me for eternity. I pushed my hands above my head, bracing for impact. The gloom of despair faded. Even the body of Benjie moved backward, preparing for my rally. My fists balled tightly seconds before the ice cracked and opened my way to freedom.

I picked up speed, the cracked ice growing closer and closer. I tucked my head down, waiting for the moment I smashed against the barrier.

Ice shattered.

The cold almost burned as I flew into the air. I spewed water as my lungs fought to breathe. I tumbled downward, striking the ground and rolling along the ice. The moment my lungs expanded, filling with air, I siphoned it in as if each breath might be my last.

I pushed myself up, kneeling on the ice. Much like the real world, Olivia's face held a look of disbelief. That surprise, the realization I wasn't an insignificant pawn in her game would only be surpassed when I squeezed my hands around her neck.

"You can't—"

"I can." I coughed.

She screeched. Running at me, her clothes tearing away until she wore the leather armor from our last encounter. Olivia pulled a sword from her hip and leaped into the air. Closing the space between us in a single bound, she prepared to drive the sword through my skull.

I held fast. Raising my hands, I was surprised to find a medieval shield strapped to my arm. Olivia descended, her sword smashing against the shield. She wouldn't pierce my defenses. I braced my other hand against the metal and pushed to my feet, meeting her blow.

Her sword exploded in a burst of light and screeching metal.

I shoved the shield forward, batting against her body. With a spin, I ducked low, hooking my foot behind her legs and jerked fast. She collapsed as I spun on the ice. Standing tall, I hovered over the fallen telepath.

"Let them go."

"Burn in hell."

I didn't have any intention of letting her go free. The time for mercy had long since passed. I wanted my knives, a blade I could drive between her eyes. I didn't know if killing her here would have any effect, but the satisfaction would be real. To see the blade break the skin as it sank into her brain. It'd be a start to the payback I wanted to give her for trying to gut me.

I stiffened. The fingers of my free hand elongated, merging into a single shape. The color tinted and where I should have five individual digits a blade from the sleeve of my jacket emerged. First the shield and now this, I didn't think it was possible to manipulate the white room like Edward or Olivia. I thought wrong.

I pulled back, steadying my newfound weapon. With a thrust downward, I waited to see the blood taint the pure white of the ice. Her palms clapped together, halting my momentum.

Even with my bodyweight behind the strike, she held the sword fast.

"Talented as you might be, you're still a neophyte."

With a flick of her wrist, the blade snapped clean from my arm.

Frank's belly hid years of well-honed muscle. Each jab launched at my face required both hands to deflect the force. In the ring we pulled our punches in friendly games of open-handed slapping. As his right hand came in for a finishing uppercut, I understood that with every previous bout, he never gave it his all.

I pushed his forearm wide, his fist grazing my cheek. The dozen gashes along my arms burned as I grabbed his bicep to steady myself. I kicked Edward in the hip, spinning him around and exposing his side. I could outpace both of them, but not wanting to shatter bones or crush windpipes had me at a disadvantage.

"Edward!" He was in there. He reminded me about our ceremony and the two worlds. "I need your help."

Edward, can you hear me?

The distraction cost me. Frank managed a jab to my kidney. I didn't have time to react as he barreled into me, using the force of his body to knock me off balance. I landed with a thud. There was no time to plot, just react. The toe of Frank's boot sped toward my stomach. I brought my knees to my chest, catching the impact in my shins. I was going to hurt for weeks.

"They make you weak," Olivia lectured. The only thing saving her from my hands squeezing her neck were the two men I cared for. Staying on the ground meant a brutal beating. Never would I have imagined being the victim of Frank or Edward.

I'd apologize later.

The flame had dwindled, struggling to stay lit. The anger

rolled freely, pooling in my hand like fuel. It burned bright. I gathered the fear, the reality that I was the last person to stop this tyrant. If I failed, there would be no stopping her. The weight on my shoulders transferred to my hands, and the flame tinted a vibrant blue.

It wasn't a rush of power or a feeling of omnipotence. I had fallen victim to my abilities before, letting them consume me until I acted as a vessel for the future. I tempered my emotions, present, real, and scary. The world depended on me, but I refused to let this gift take control.

It was less of a hammering against Olivia's interference. Instead of using brute force, the flame shrank and blazed brighter than before. I imagined it dancing in my palm until I closed my hands around it. There was no more flame, no symbol representing the ghosts. It was beautiful the way my skin flickered, radiating a gentle glow. No, I would not win against Olivia by smashing recklessly. She was not the only one with the ability to make surgical strikes.

I pushed past the haze and summoned the ghosts.

I screamed as pain shot up my arm. None of this is real. Despite that, my body flailed. Broken off, she threw my metallic appendage to the side. Stop panicking, focus, resist, fight back. In her realm, I couldn't be careless.

The snow along the ice swirled, a self-contained blizzard wrapping about me. Ice cracked and rocked under my feet. I thought I might fall when something caught me. I turned to see a massive wintery hand. It closed around me, trapping my arms against my side.

I kicked at its base, hoping to chip away enough to break free. With each thrust of my leg, its grip tightened until I thought it might collapse my ribcage.

"Without your ghosts, you're rather weak."

The pain transitioned to rage, my blood boiling in response. The golem's hand burned away, evaporating as quickly as it appeared. I stole a glance at my broken limb to see my forearm had returned, a slight line where she had broken it before.

"You want to talk about weak?"

Olivia had her games. If she wanted to play, I was going to reveal the great and powerful Oz to be nothing more than an insecure, wretched woman.

"Your confidence is a lie, isn't it, Olivia?" I turned around to face the telepath. Brushing off my jacket, it tore away like a crumpled sheet of paper, revealing a pristine version underneath. "The sultry telepath, beautiful and elegant, that's what you want them to see. But I've seen the woman behind the mask. You're as ugly as your heart."

Vanity hid its imperfections. Olivia had let her mask falter. The lack of taunting or cackling laughter signaled that I'd struck a nerve. I didn't care what the world saw when they looked at me, but Olivia, she needed control. She wanted them to see nothing but the polished beauty she conjured. For a moment I wondered if we all saw the same thing or if she was drawing from our individual definitions of beauty.

"I thought you wanted control. But it's not." I had to let the chuckle slip. "You want the one thing you can't have. They'll never admire you, Olivia. They won't love you."

Her mask faltered. Seconds passed where the scars of puberty showed along her cheeks. Her nose had a slight bend to it and the bold red lips were replaced for thin, barely visible strips of dark pink. Without her enhancements, she remained a rather beautiful woman. What could have destroyed her confidence to this degree? Who could spend a lifetime degrading a woman until she receded into a world of make-believe? I thought Olivia had spent...

"The Society did this to you?"

There was no room for debate, no witty words hissed in reply. Her mask returned and with it, the boom of a bomb. The air turned solid, hammering against my shield until it launched me across the lake. I had sorted through the complexity of Olivia Sincerbeaux and found the single nerve that should never be touched.

The ice roared as I landed, cracks threatening to tear apart the surface. Before I could get to my knees, Olivia was on me. Moving with supernatural speed, her fist connected with the underside of my jaw. I saw blood as I bit down on the tip of my tongue. Teeth shattered as I flipped onto my back. The ice underneath me wobbled, steadily breaking apart.

"Eleanor, you should have accepted my offer."

There was no blood, no ice, no pain. I willed myself forward, trying to bury the false beneath the real need to stop her. She picked me up by the back of the neck, as if I weighed nothing. Slamming me down onto the ice, I savored the cold. It soothed the aches and gave me something to focus on.

"You'll die here with your brother."

Before I could push off the ice, her heel drove down on my neck. Her other foot was close enough I reached out, clawing at her boots. From this angle, I couldn't grab onto anything and without momentum, I couldn't punch. Behind her, the ice had broken away and I could see the black abyss leading into the pond. It seemed fitting as she ground her heel down, proving she had emerged victorious.

I had lost.

The apology would start with the kick to Frank's knee cap. The ghost didn't wait for him to crumble to the ground before rolling away from Edward. She moved in an elegant, slow motion, getting to her feet. The ghosts diverged, and I watched as she kicked Frank, punched him, and a hundred different moves Koji had demonstrated. She blocked Edward's attempts to ensnare her in a bear hug. Hundreds of paths unfolded. A jab to the throat, a snap of the leg, or twisting his arm until it pulled from the joint.

I mapped each moment. For the ghosts, only four seconds passed. I sorted through the future, searching for the best outcome. I didn't want to hurt either of them, but if it was between broken bones and bruised egos or dying by Olivia's hand, they would understand.

Four seconds.

While the rest of the world froze, I experienced a lifetime in a series of four-second bursts. One at a time I witnessed the destination and ran backward, connecting the dots between one, two, three, and four. Here, in this in-between, I thought of all the things that could happen in that brief amount of time.

Four ticks of the clock. An inhale. A goodbye. A furious shout. A gentle kiss. The clink of celebratory glasses. A comforting hug. An orgasm. The lighting of a cigarette. A strike of lightning followed by thunder. The words, "I love you." Death. Life.

Here, in my own version of the white room, I was free of consequence. I cheated fate and defied the very existence of time. As long as I stayed here, allowing the ghosts to show me the possibilities, I need not make a choice. I didn't need to worry about the outcome. If I allowed my gifts to continue rippling, I could see the world without fear.

I was immortal. By the time I died, I would have led infinite lives. I thought of the couple shouting before making up and the farewells needing their hellos. Staying here, separate from every other soul on the planet, was unfair. I had work to do, and the world needed to continue no matter how messy it got. Dammit, that orgasm needed to happen.

Time resumed.

"You resisted, that is more than most. I'll give you the credit you're due."

She congratulated me on my false victory, salting the wound. I was running out of tricks to combat Olivia. No matter how hard I hit, she rebounded and came at me with a stronger hit than before. I summoned the army, the ghosts of my future selves. Olivia did nothing to prevent me from accessing my abilities.

"You refuse to admit defeat. I don't know if you're brave or just stupid."

In the ring, they called me both. I prided myself on my tenacity. One by one, the ghosts circled the pond. Hundreds, no, thousands of versions of myself. They watched in silence.

Olivia laughed. I wanted to punch her in the gut, to force the air from her lungs so she couldn't laugh. I wanted her to drown so she couldn't inhale enough to make that sound again. For all the things I wanted to do, I couldn't move enough to resist. Even my ghosts knew it as they lowered their head in a solemn send-off.

"Versions of what might have been," Olivia laughed, "even they refuse to come to your aid."

Unlike the ghosts in the real world, these didn't show me the future. There were no series of actions to win this fight. I had an army, but none moved in my defense. I feared my hubris against time in the gym had cost me my only allies in the white room.

"How does it feel when you can't even help yourself?"

They shuffled and parted.

"You'll die alone. I'll take my time with your father."

Their eyes lifted from the ground and turned to the gap. Olivia believed Frank was the flesh and blood that created me. He might be my father, the man who taught me to stand up for myself, but he wasn't alone. For all the horrors in my life, I had been blessed with two men who watched over me.

"Edward, I will keep for fun."

The sky turned dark, a storm unlike anything we ever saw

during the winter months. The clouds overhead bled black and spun about before thunder roared across the plains. I had seen more than my share of tornados as a child. Funnels touched down in the distance. They pulled the clouds to the ground, one stripped the roof from our house.

Poppa gave me a slight nod. Our day in the yard had ended with the skies opening and sending down a deluge of rain. He had lifted me on his shoulders, a dragon rider. He had not only protected my secret, but urged me to let my imagination run wild.

"Not alone," I whispered. It had become a theme as I waded into danger. Every night I transformed into the protector of New York City, believing I was the only person who could keep the city safe.

Poppa mouthed, "I love you, Ellie."

Olivia kneeled down, sure to keep her weight pressing on my neck. She dipped low enough I could hear her whispers. "What is that? Not alone? Eleanor Valentine, once you're gone, I'll destroy everything you've ever loved."

"I've never been alone," I muttered.

Olivia shrieked. She pulled the weight from my neck as she tried kicking something behind her. As she flipped over, struggling, I caught sight of two blue-tinted hands reaching from a break in the ice.

"Leave Ellie alone." I didn't need to see the face to know the owner. Benjie's voice was just as I remembered it, high pitch and whiny, a sound I never thought I'd miss.

He pulled at Olivia, firmly tugging on one of her boots. She tried to grab me but I rolled away. Fingernails broke as she scratched at the ice. With a strength far beyond his years, Benjie dragged Olivia screaming into the water below.

I rolled onto my back and let the tears flow. It was one thing to see Poppa in my corner, rallying me for another round. But for Benjie to defend his sister, after what happened, it was a sigh of relief. Tears froze along my cheeks that quickly turned to sobbing. With Benjie literally reaching from beyond the grave to protect his big sister, I finally forgave myself.

In the gym, I kicked Frank's knee. The bone shattered, and I followed in the footsteps of my ghost. I rolled away from Edward and got to my feet. Frank didn't howl from the wound. Like the Barren, he remained focused on his goal to kill me. I kicked him in the hip and retracted before he could catch my foot. Falling onto his back, I had a moment to focus on Edward.

I need you to wake up.

My call fell on deaf ears. Unlike Frank, Edward didn't have any aptitude for fighting. He threw a punch, and I ducked, followed by a jab to his side. Like the Barren, he didn't let the pain deter him. His other fist struck me across the jaw. My head hurt from Olivia's efforts, but now the bone and muscle ached to match. I tasted copper.

He tried to snatch me in a bear hug. I grabbed his hand and stepped around him and up behind. I raised the arm high enough that it popped. One-armed Edward was hardly a threat. Using the arm, I shoved hard, knocking him into the brick wall.

I didn't waste time, hand on the gun, I spun about, prepared to end this once and for all. The first shot came nowhere near Olivia, but it was enough to make her jump. At this distance, I would be lucky to hit anything.

I steadied myself, staring down the sight. I only need to hit her once, and then I'd take my time making sure I put a bullet between her eyes.

The second shot hit the floor as Frank tackled me. The gun spun along the gym floor, between me and Olivia. I didn't take her for a gun person, but she ran for it while Frank tried to climb on top of my legs.

Kicking him in the shoulder, I pulled my other leg free. There was no point in crawling for the gun. I shot up onto my knees and pulled the knife from its sheath at my back. With a quick flip, I hurled it. Olivia squealed as the blade struck the meat of her upper arm. It wasn't the killing blow I wanted.

She slowed as she inspected the wound. It was the only delay I'd get. Frank couldn't walk, and Edward was staggering from a knock to the head. I made a mad dash. My feet slipped at first, nearly falling. I was close. It might be the only opportunity I'd have. I could end it right now.

I just needed to get my hands around her neck.

The clouds continued to swirl and darken. The entire landscape broke away, as if the funnels were destroying reality. I watched as a long dark shape snaked its way through the clouds. If I wasn't thrust back into the gym, it meant it wasn't over, not yet.

I glanced at the shoreline where my ghosts watched Poppa carry a smaller version of myself on his shoulders. Her arms were out wide as she pretended to fly. When I was an innocent child, I wanted to be a writer, to change the world with my words. I had achieved that. Not in the way I expected, but my words could very well end the war. Even sobbing, I smiled. He'd be proud.

A flurry of red fabric broke free of the hole in the ice. Olivia soared into the air just as I had. All around her, red robes flapped in the wind, looking almost like wings as she landed. She looked like every evil step-mother in every fairytale my father read.

Like the ghosts on the shore, Olivia reminded me of a reflection of myself. Through a series of choices I could be her. I stepped dangerously close to the line that would transform me from the heroine into the wretched step-sister.

"It's over," she growled.

From within the folds of the robe, she drew out a magnificent sword. Nearly as long as she was tall, she held the hilt with both hands. She moved closer until she stood at my feet. I made no move to conjure a shield or try to battle her one last time.

"I have won."

"You haven't."

That laugh, I hated that laugh. "It appears other—"

The dark shape from the sky descended downward. It appeared as if another funnel might touch down, but then I saw the wings flapping. The beast landed behind Olivia.

Olivia turned and raised the sword to do battle. With a roar that shook the ground, its maw came downward. Its foot-long teeth bit into Olivia's waist. It swallowed her upper half. With a ferocious shake of the head, the lower half of her body tore free and flew into the nothingness of a fractured white room. Blood sprayed across the snow and ice, peppering the white with tiny drops of crimson.

"Meet Eleanor," I said.

Stop her.

I had never been so happy to hear Edward's voice. Leaning forward, I dipped my shoulder. Olivia tore the knife free as I crashed into her. I held her arms tight to her side, hoping she couldn't stab me in the back as we barreled downward.

The blood from her nose dripped down the side of my face. We struck the wood. I had already felt the sting of Olivia with a knife once; I didn't need a matching scar on the other side.

My blood-slick hand made it impossible to grab her arm. The knife tip dug into my shoulder, not deep enough to be fatal. As the tip struck the bone I screamed. I drew back my fist and punched her in the nose. It wasn't a powerful blow, but striking broken bone caused a shriek.

I'm coming.

I pulled back for another blow when she turned the knife, tearing the fabric of the jacket and the flesh underneath. Pushing back, I pulled away from her. Both Olivia and I scrambled to our feet.

Blood poured down her face. With a red stripe cascading along her chin and into her blouse, she reminded me of the Devil. I was exhausted, my right arm barely able to make a fist without creating waves of nausea. My head continued to throb, and I feared the next blow would be the knockout.

Almost there.

I raised my left fist, ready to fight until one of us hit the mats. She wailed like a banshee as she raised the knife over her head. For a second I swore I saw double, no triple, of the vile woman. She ran forward, prepared to sink the knife somewhere in my face. At least with Edward and Frank free, they'd be able to finish her. I wouldn't be here to see the victory, but knowing they'd stop her made me smile. My part was done.

I've got her.

Edward jumped between us, prepared to save me from Olivia.

Bang.

Chapter Thirty-Two

1943

The end of the gun smoked. Frank let the weapon slip from his fingertips. Two thuds followed. The sound of the gun forced me to wince. The tension in my body softened, and I eased opened my eyes. I looked to the source of the gunfire to see Frank on one knee, holding his revolver between two hands. Frank's face had frozen in horror, his mouth slack as he tried to process what happened.

"I... I..."

I followed his eyes to the gore. Olivia's body twitched, her hands gripping her throat. Blood pulsed, creating a gurgling noise. Her eyes remained fixated on me as her life spilled onto the wooden planks of the floor.

Kill... die... no.

Her thoughts grew quiet. Even while she died, she lamented about my death. The growing puddle of blood mingled with the red of her blouse. Her body convulsed and then her hands slipped away. Through the blood, I could see the massive hole caused by a bullet. Two of them, an entry and an exit...

"Edward."

Eleanor, my love.

Working my way down Olivia's body, her legs intertwined with another pair. Edward lay on his stomach, unmoving. Flashes of my vision passed before my eyes. I froze, too scared to go to him. The hatred in my heart, the part of me that feared the moment we came face-to-face melted away. Now, the messy hair only reminded me of the devilish man I first met.

I collapsed, falling to my hands and knees. I took the first step forward, to a future I didn't want to be true. When I reached him, my hand hovered over his back, waiting for the rise and fall of his chest. There was no movement, only a still body.

"No, no, no." Forcing myself to touch his back, there was nothing. I reached for his shoulder, pulling at his body. Tears blurred my vision and dripped onto the back of his vest.

Frank spoke, but I couldn't hear his words past my own sobbing. I pulled at Edward, rolling him over onto his back. I scooted closer so his head rested in my lap. The vision had come true, almost exactly as I had foreseen.

"No, you can't be dead." I cried. "It was me she wanted."

I'm sorry, I was stubborn.

His eyes fluttered and came to a rest, his eyes glassy and staring into the void. In the center of his chest, the red continued to spread through his vest. I reached for his hand, holding it tightly. Where there should have been a ring, only an empty indent remained.

I love you, Eleanor Valentine.

His words trailed off, soft and barely audible. That thread that connected Edward and me, the invisible line established from invading one another's minds—snapped. He didn't simply drift out of my thoughts, he vanished. Edward died with my name on his lips.

I pushed through the tightness in my throat and screamed. At the end of the breath, I inhaled and repeated the action.

"No." Try as I might, death claimed another soul.

I bent over, hugging the man, coating my arm in the warmth of his blood. Rocking back and forth, something slipped from his neck, brushing against my hand. A gold chain I had never seen before. Sliding my hand along the course metal, feeling the warmth of his neck, I found the end.

The ring. The metal chain wove through the metallic band. He might not have worn it on his finger like a typical husband, but nothing about us had been mundane. He had taken it from his finger and wore it around his neck.

Pain struck my chest. Each thump of my heart pushed against the surface, forcing a whimper. The grifter, the man I loved, I couldn't imagine a world without him. All the questions, the anger I felt toward him streamed down my cheeks.

I already missed the arguments, the heated way we debated over the responsibility of our powers. The lovemaking. The way he stimulated my mind in the white space while doing the same to my body. Each memory flashed in my head, the good and the bad. I recounted every decision at once, trying to sort out how I could have done this differently.

"Eleanor," Frank's voice was barely more than a whisper. I wanted to scream at the man, to blame him for killing Edward. His bullet. His trigger. His finger. Without knowing Edward had saved us, he had killed him, my husband. "I'm sorry."

I thought I outwitted fate and mastered death. My arrogance brought us here. Frank may have pulled the trigger, but it had been my inability to see the future that created this very moment. I killed Edward. It was like watching the pond for a third time.

I turned my head, looking up at a sullen Frank. Over the years I had seen a wide range of emotions from him, but never this. The military trained him to be a soldier, to kill, but he never knew the names of those on the receiving end of his rifle. The weight of responsibility pulled at his face, leaving him struck with grief.

"I did this." I allowed the walls in my head to surge upright from the ground. Bit by bit, I locked away my emotions. Childhood prepared me for the crushing blow. As I shoved my feelings inside the tiny rooms, the crying stopped. I leaned down, kissing Edward on the forehead.

"Goodbye, my love." He died a hero.

I ran my fingers over his eyes, closing them. The boy in my lap wasn't the man with questionable ambitions. His soft features looked at peace, as if all his struggles had been righted. I guess in a sense, they were.

Edward Valentine would always be my first love.

Laying Edward's head on the floor of the gym, I forced myself to my feet. I pushed the hair out of my eyes, the stickiness of my fingers coating my face. Frank crawled closer on his hands and knee, hesitating if he should come closer. He's the only man left who understood what it means to be Eleanor Bouvier. No, what it once meant to be her.

Eleanor Valentine.

New York was safe for the moment. But there would always be more, a new threat, somebody wanting to oppress those weaker than them. There would be more like Olivia, and I would stand in their way. I'd crush anybody who threatened my home.

In my head, I planned what the new Society would become. Theodore might stand at my side and help recreate the organization, but we will no longer remain in the shadows. The Society would be a driving force to protect mankind. I would make sure of it.

"I can do better."

Epilogue 1

1943

The heat bordered on oppressive. While summers in New York could ruin even the best-kept hair, in Georgia, the air was as moist as the ocean. It was only April and I couldn't imagine being outside during the height of summer. I treasured the benefits of being a Northerner. We endured the cold while the south endured the heat. I'd take my layers any day.

"Tea?"

Her hair was short. With the heat, I understood why. Her neck held only one strand of her iconic pearls. I wondered if she reserved the rest for appearances in the newspaper?

I gave a slight nod. "That would be lovely." Susan Lee would be proud of my civilized demeanor. It was rare for me to be so ladylike, but between the powder blue skirt, matching jacket, and white gloves, I believe I played the part quite well.

I expected her to bring a teapot and small cups. Instead, the tray held tall glasses with brown liquid and a wedge of lemon hanging on the rim. The subtle differences between us were many, but as I sipped the concoction, I could very well become a convert.

I sat the glass on the tray. "It's delicious, Mrs.—"

"Eleanor, please." She sat down on the couch opposite Theodore and me. The woman was the epitome of grace and class. Nearly three times my age, her composure was flawless. Straightening my back, I tried to mimic the woman's demeanor.

"Eleanor," I said with a soft smile. I had never met another Eleanor prior to this.

"He shouldn't be long," her hands rested on her lap, one hand perfectly posed over the other. I couldn't wait to indulge Susan Lee's curiosities and just how right she had been. The woman across from us was perhaps the most influential woman alive, and here we sat sipping her tea as if nothing were out of the ordinary.

"Your home is lovely," I said.

"There's no need for false pleasantries. It's a modest place for us to escape the hubbub of the world."

Theodore held his glass, spinning it about in his hands. I hadn't taken him for an easily intimidated man. If I didn't know better, I'd say she made him nervous.

"Do you know why we are here?" I asked.

Theodore couldn't hide his disbelief. While we were here by request, talking about it openly made him uncomfortable. More than that, I began the conversation with the lady of the house and not her husband, the man who demanded to speak with us.

She gave a slight nod.

"Pardon Theodore," I rested my hand on his leg to stop it from bouncing up and down. "He doesn't quite understand that great men are made by great women."

I couldn't tell if she agreed, or if she found the comment childish. Eleanor's poker face was far more advanced than I expected. I cheated and glimpsed into the future to see her ghost's cocked smile. Knowing her state of mind put me at ease.

"Your husband is a great man, it's an honor to sit here."

Without twitching a muscle, she replied. "Let us skip the

pomp and circumstance. Those conversations are best left in Washington."

"Perfect. Why are we here?"

"He has questions," she leaned forward, her eyes threatening to burrow a hole through my face. "As do I."

"There is speculation about how I know what I know? You want answers?"

"Yes." A single word, but it carried a great weight. The woman sitting across from us wasn't sure what to make of Theodore and me. Perhaps we were spies sent by the Germans, or perhaps we had spies of our own. I did the most unpredictable thing possible, I told the truth.

"I can see the future."

"You expect me to—"

"You will call for the man standing in the rear of the building. When he enters, you'll ask him to select a number."

"And what will he say?" The woman held herself, composed.

The ghosts whispered, but making out words remained just beyond my abilities. Thankfully, the man's ghost held up three fingers.

"Three."

I waited for her to call the man, but she relaxed in the seat. Now that I could see versions of the future, I struggled to pick the most likely path. For most of my life, I wanted the ability to influence fate. Now that I had it, I could no longer rely on certainties, making it frustrating when I chose the wrong version of the future.

"You're not going to call him?" Theodore remained nervous. His leg continued to bounce despite me squeezing his thigh.

"By not calling him, do I ruin your prediction?"

Eleanor was a sharp woman. The average person would not have thought about the non-linear nature of time. "You ruin one prediction. But the future is infinite. There is a future where he stands there, another where he selects a different number."

"Then how did you—"

She stopped short, standing as her husband entered the room. Even in a white button-down shirt, he wore an American flag pinned to his chest. Despite the casual clothes, he remained a dignified man. I didn't know how to appropriately greet him, so I stood. He was far taller than he appeared on television.

"Mr.—I mean, President Roosevelt," I stammered. I gave him a slight curtsey, but he waved his hand. Reaching out, I took his hand, mammoth compared to my own. With a single shake, he took a seat next to his wife. He rested a hand on hers, a slight sign of affection. It warmed my heart that even in his last days, she would remain by his side, the diligent wife.

"I'll be honest, I'm not entirely sure how to begin this conversation." He was an honest and transparent man. But more than that, he was a good man. "I guess I should begin with, thank you?"

I waved away the thanks. "My presence makes people nervous. I would be shocked if I didn't. You're not worried that I'm a spy. Your men have been doing research on me for the past two months. They had difficulty tracing my origin. That is why I reached out to them directly. I have no secrets, President Roosevelt. It is not entirely pretty, but such is life."

"Mrs. Valentine, how is it you knew? How did you know that Eva could help end the greatest war in history?"

"I saw the future. I see the future. Since I was a child, I have always been able to see the future. It has evolved to where I can see possibilities and with a simple interjection, change fate. That is why I sent Mayor La Guardia to speak with you."

"To what ends? Money? Fame?"

"I suppose a war would make me suspicious as well. But no, I have no desire for any attention. My goals are entirely altruistic. I have done more than my part to protect New York City. But rolling bandages and working at soup kitchens only mend the wounds."

"Are there," he leaned forward, his eyes threatening to burrow a hole through my own, "more of you?"

"Not like me, but there are more of my kind out there."

His mind raced through the possibilities. He assessed the threats and the potential outcomes. While this great man wouldn't survive to see next month, our secret was officially out in the wild. It would nearly die with him. But with her, with Eleanor, the Society would begin a relationship with the outside world.

"I mean no offense, but are they dangerous?"

"Very."

He wiped his face with both hands. The news of people in the world capable of performing acts beyond normal humans was both amazing and terrifying. Had I been Olivia, this meeting would be less than pleasant. Given time, I firmly believe she would have extended her reach into the White House itself.

"How many?"

I shrug. "Enough. I've encountered at least a dozen."

"Are you building an army?"

It was a tricky question because, in our own way, we were building an army. But not one with any ambition of challenging the powers in place. "Our society has upheld a simple idea. There must always be four."

"What about the others? Are you not recruiting them?"

"If they wish to reach out, then we welcome their participation. But our organization relies on four mentalists."

"And your abilities?" The question turned to Theodore. The bouncing leg suddenly stopped, and he nearly dropped the glass of tea.

"None, I'm afraid. I am a researcher. I study the things in the world science can not explain. Our organization strayed from its path for a time. But we have returned to our original mission."

"Which is?"

"Discovery. We want to watch mankind flourish. If we can help with our unique resources, then so be it."

President Roosevelt leaned back on the couch. He folded his hands in his lap, digesting the conversation. I could sense there were a million questions crossing his mind. We had no plans this evening other than breaking down the wall of secrecy that allowed the Society to become a danger to mankind.

"He won't be so crass. But I am not a politician," Eleanor said. —I found her a breath of fresh air each time she spoke.— "Eleanor, Theodore, what is it you want?"

It was the million-dollar question. Theodore had been tentative about this meeting, fearing that we'd be locked up and considered traitors. But at some point, we needed to take a leap of faith.

"Today, this very conversation," I couldn't hide the smile, "we step out of the shadows and begin building relationships."

"You must know the outcome."

I liked her more with every statement. "I do."

President Roosevelt eyed his wife. The sideways glance gave away how much he trusted her judgment. His cabinet, men who questioned every statement for their own gain, could surround us. But Eleanor Roosevelt, she saw potential in this partnership. All knew her altruistic nature, and I couldn't think of a better woman to join us in this endeavor.

"What does the future hold for us, Eleanor?"

"I see a world of possibilities."

"As do I," she smiled.

"I knew you'd say that."

Epilogue 2

1943

He dodged through the streets of Savannah with a comfortable familiarity.

The sun had settled, but the streets turned lively as the night's air cooled. Music filled the air, pouring onto the verandas wrapping about the front of the street-facing homes. Under different circumstances, it would have been rather lovely. But the air remained oppressive, and the thought of running made me cringe.

"Want me to follow?"

Walter's dark skin faded into the black of night. He was a kind man, quick to say his please and thank you's and mind his manners. For a year he accompanied me on these fact-finding missions. I had grown quite fond of the gusto in which he volunteered. The world would do well having a few more Walters spread around.

"Follow, I'll be waiting."

"Yes, ma'am." He'd stopped calling me Mrs. Valentine, but he'd never stop calling me ma'am. I didn't need psychic abilities to know that some habits were impossible to break.

"He's just a child." On my other side, Maxene tried to hold her composure. Her gloved hands fidgeted as she crossed her arms this way and that. Unlike Walter, she had only been with me for the past month.

"Age makes no difference. You must have been younger when you discovered your gifts?"

I hadn't needed to chase Maxene. Susan Lee discovered her while doing rotations in the hospital. I never asked to see her hands, but I assumed they were like the bit of skin that revealed itself around the collar of her blouse. The deep grooves and waxy smoothness were telltale signs of a vicious burn. I might inquire someday when we had more than a working relationship.

"Much younger," she admitted.

"When I was that age, I needed a mentor," I said. "So we make him an offer."

"And if he refuses?" Maxene remained skeptical, fully aware of the legacy Olivia sought to leave behind.

"We make sure he knows the offer will always be good should he change his mind."

Maxene remained nervous. As our most recent inductee, we did our best to give every member our story, the *entire* story. We refused to bury Olivia's mutiny and determination to wretch control of New York City as misbegotten altruism. I demanded we act with transparency, even if it meant taking longer to gain the trust of our newest recruits.

Walter hadn't moved a muscle. His body had a slight sway, as if the wind itself were keeping him upright. If I stared into his eyes, they'd be distant, staring at something I couldn't see with my own. His body might be standing next to me, but Walter's mind had darted after the man.

While he exercised his abilities, I did the same. Ghosts stepped out of my body. There were dozens running in different directions. I glimpsed Walter's mind touching a human before leaping into the next available body. His particular brand of telepathy could only be akin to possession. Thankfully, he brandished it with the utmost care for the bodies he inhabited.

Seeing through my ghosts' eyes should have been a sensory overload. Instead, it was like reading an overly descriptive book. The information filtered through my brain and by all accounts, I lived the life of every ghost I created. In a fraction of a second, I saw the beginning and end of each choice I could make.

Only one ghost led me to our target.

"Watch Walter, I'm going to speak with this young man."

This was her first time recruiting. I couldn't tell if she condoned our methods or if she believed we terrorized the young man. I brought her with us, but I didn't want her engaging. While she might not entirely trust us, I wasn't sure I could trust *her*, or at least her abilities. The last thing we needed was Savannah burning to the ground.

The mills were massive. They reminded me of Boston and its persistence in using red brick for every exterior wall. I ran down the street, parallel to a building that overlooked the water. Walter silently tailed the boy, trying to track him so we could extend our offer. But having the man speak through the mouths of his bodies was jarring to even the most knowledgeable individual.

The factory had an arch, a walkway that spanned over a street into the next building. I turned down the street, heading closer to the water on the other side. Had this been a recreational trip, I might have hired a guide to learn more about the architecture. New York City had its charm and it would always be home, but I found the more I learned of the outside world, the more I wanted to explore.

Savannah blended the industrial necessity of the mills with sprawling green areas. For every block of plantation houses, it seemed there was another block of green. New York City could do with more greenery.

The lights from the city vanished as I walked underneath the archway wide enough for two cars to fit side-by-side. The arch itself was all windows, providing a spectacular view of a green square. Somehow, my ghost had made it up there. Fussy as always, they showed me a destination and decided not to make it clear how I reached it.

I found a door. With some convincing from my shoulder, it pushed open. It was almost impossible to see inside the mill. Only a faint light illuminated the stairs. I had to hold on to the rail to make my way up. Had it been daytime, I'd be able to see the grandeur of the mill. Did they make fabrics? Or were these lumber mills? I knew so little about the city, I just assumed it was lumber like the northeast.

Feeling along the wall, stacks of boxes hid a door to the arch. It seemed as if this hadn't been in use in quite some time. I wonder if the people working in the factory knew they had a squatter living in one of the most beautiful parts of the building?

"Why can't it ever be easy?"

I pushed at the boxes until I could pull the door open and squeeze my way inside. The arch remained empty. I summoned the ghosts, and it appeared I arrived before him.

He was young, only a child. His ghost levitated through a broken window, and his feet never touched the ground. With his hand stretched out, he held my future self off the ground. It wasn't the first time somebody with telekinesis pulled this trick. The last time I had killed the woman. I hoped it didn't come to that.

There was little more than a blanket and pillow on the floor. A few piles of clothes littered the space and I could make out a lamp on a makeshift table. He had built a wall around the light to keep it from giving away his location. I struck a match and lit the lantern. It surprised me how much the mess reminded me of Benjie's chaos in our room.

Children's books littered the floor next to the lamp. I picked one up, surprised that a teenager would read something meant for children. Poppa insisted on reading me fantastical tales far beyond my years. I inspected the floor, looking for signs of another person hiding in this makeshift home.

The direction of the air changed. I set the book down and waited for the familiar pressure to surround my body. Before I turned, the weight on my feet grew lighter and I hovered in the air. The boy had practiced with his abilities. Based on the way he gently lifted me, he could easily be more gifted than Catherine.

"I could kill you." His voice quivered. He had considered the possibility, but I recognized a voice still virgin enough to not have drawn blood.

"But you won't," I said. I turned slowly, letting my body go limp. There was no point in fighting his hold. I applauded his fine motor control and ability to divide his attention while keeping his gestures precise.

"You don't know that."

"But I do." There was no point in being coy. "Like you, I have gifts."

He faltered, nearly dropping me. He landed, walking toward me with a raised eyebrow. "Does that man work for you?"

"Walter? No, we are working together to find people with gifts."

"I don't believe you." I couldn't blame him. Granted, we didn't send serial killers ahead, but I recalled the first time I met Olivia. The boy was smart to be suspicious.

"Walter can occupy the minds of humans. Maxene, she can conjure fire."

"You? What can you do?" There it was, the need. I remembered the ball in which I first discovered Edward. That moment forever changed my life. Not only did I meet a dashing young man, but I learned I wasn't alone.

"I can see the future."

"Like one of those gypsy women?"

I had never met one before, but I had to assume many of them were charlatans. "Not quite. I see the ghosts of the future. They show me what will happen before it does."

"Then you know I could throw you through the window. Stop following me. I don't need you. I've never needed anybody."

It was a lie. I scared the boy. Not too long ago, I stood in his place. But where Olivia used threats to try and bend me to her will, I wanted to make him a simple offer. I imagined he had been on the streets for a long time and with his gifts, he wouldn't need to rely on anybody. I wondered how long had it been since…

"*The Wonderful World of Oz.*"

"What?"

"My favorite book, *The Wonderful World of Oz.*"

"I don't—"

"You're teaching yourself to read." I tried to gesture to the books, but couldn't do more than move my eyes in their direction. "My abilities started when I was a kid. I know what it means. You've been alone for most of your life."

He wiped the tears from his face. His emotions got the best of him, and his grip on my body retreated and I dropped to my feet. I made no move to reach out.

"We're an organization trying to help people like us. Nobody should be alone."

He sniffed, steadying himself. "Who are you? Why… why me?"

"My name is Eleanor Valentine. I'm here to offer answers, that is, if you want them."

He didn't answer aloud, instead nodded. I remembered the moment Edward first spoke in my head. It had been a weight lifted from my shoulders. I could only imagine this was similar, or at least I hoped so.

"Are there more like us?"

"Many."

He mulled over the possibilities. I watched his face as he contemplated a new reality. If he came with us, he would no longer sleep cold and alone. Through Theodore's tireless efforts, we had resources to make him more than comfortable.

"Let me grab your books," I said as reached for the stack of books, "I'll make sure you get the education you've missed."

"What if I don't want—"

"I can see the future, remember? I knew how this ended before we started speaking." He didn't need to know I hadn't seen that far. But if he needed a swift kick in the butt to help motivate him, I'd gladly do so.

"Christopher," he almost whispered the word.

"Nice to meet you, Christopher. I look forward to learning about what brought you here."

In no time, he'd be whisked away to his own version of Oz.

One of the books slipped from my grip and it hung suspended in the air. He cautiously walked toward me and then grabbed it out of the air. If I had my way, I'd have interceded when he first discovered his gifts. There would be no more isolation for our kind.

I offered a slight smile and gestured to the lamp. The light snuffed out, and we headed toward the door.

"For our kind, this is the genesis of a new era."

- The End -

**Visit RemyFlagg.com
for More Children of Nostradamus**

About the Author

Jeremy Flagg is the creator of the dystopian superhero universe, CHILDREN OF NOSTRADAMUS. Taking his love of pop culture and comic books, he focuses on fast paced, action packed novels with complex characters and contemporary themes. He continues developing the universe with the Journal of Madison Walker, an ongoing serial set two hundred years in the future.

Jeremy spends most of his time at his desk writing snarky books. When he gets a moment away from writing, he binges too much Netflix and Hulu and reads too many comic books. Jeremy, a Maine native, resides in Charlotte, North Carolina and can be found in local coffee shops pounding away at the keyboard.